Dannelle Barnes is the author of *The Merged*. Born in Atlanta, Georgia, he now resides with his wife, Nancy, and two cocker spaniels, Belle and Pepper, in the Appalachian foothills of Northeast GA. He enjoys the outdoors, playing guitar, and reading all genres of literature.

For Sherrie, who showed me as a child that a good story could be
the greatest escape.

Dannelle Barnes

# THE MERGED

AUSTIN MACAULEY PUBLISHERS™

LONDON * CAMBRIDGE * NEW YORK * SHARJAH

**Ordering Information**
Quantity sales: Special discounts are available on quantity purchases by corporations, associations, and others. For details, contact the publisher at the address below.

**Publisher's Cataloging-in-Publication data**
Barnes, Dannelle
The Merged

ISBN 9781647501648 (Paperback)
ISBN 9781647501655 (ePub e-book)

Library of Congress Control Number: 2023917239

www.austinmacauley.com/us

First Published 2024
Austin Macauley Publishers LLC
40 Wall Street, 33rd Floor, Suite 3302
New York, NY 10005
USA

mail-usa@austinmacauley.com
+1 (646) 5125767

20240220

A special thank you to Nancy. Your unyielding support, passion for the artistry of language, and downright maddening attention to detail helped make this book possible.

# Table of Contents

# 1. Small Things

**Alaska**

"I'm going to kick your ass," Adi threatened, clearing a pack of Skittles from her workspace. "These samples are almost ready for analysis, and the last thing I need is your junk messing up three days' work."

Jake Myers had a knack for finding the one thing that drove you absolutely furious. Adi's 'thing' just happened to be other people touching her stuff. Especially when her stuff pertained to a highly classified bioengineered medical marvel of science.

Jake passively looked from his microscope down to a scatter of notes and said, "Calm down, Adi. I'm certain you have about a thousand hidden other samples somewhere in this place."

"That's not the point and you know it." Adi began fiddling with a dropper propped in a nearby petri dish. "We only have 24 hours to get our heads right before Dr. Hersey arrives with more Federal Brass than a marching band," she chastised.

Adi had been working on a potential wonder drug for the past few months and was close to testing the new batch for the first time.

"The Doc just wants to look good for the president, and he needs us to make that happen," Jake said.

"Well, while that may be, without Hersey, we have no funding, and without funding you won't have a place to leave your trash lying around," Adi said as she stealthily placed seven drops of staphylococcus into the Skittles bag, one for each remaining candy.

Jake peered up from his microscope and grumbled, "I can't believe how bad you want to impress him."

Jake had never had a reason to humor the doctor, especially not for money. Even if he had, it would have mattered little as Dr. Hersey was indifferent toward Jake.

Adi replied, "No, it's an intentional charade that mutually benefits both of us. He needs our microbes, we need his money." At this, Adi gently tossed the Skittles bag back onto the table Jake was working on.

Jake responded, "Right, that's why he gets all the credit while we do all the work."

"Someone has to keep this place going, and I need to know that I can count on you, Jake."

Jake conceded, "Okay, I'll have the final results from batch 23 as soon as the cultures are ready."

"I need to grab yesterday's lab charts from my office. We can go over the new batches when I get back," Adi said.

Jake reached for the Skittles, not knowing the cruel but necessary prank. She had known Jake for some time now but had not quite figured out how to deal with his sophomoric behavior. Adi found that the best course of action from time to time was to give him a good scare. Fear can be quite a motivator, and Dr. Adilene Roth had an assortment of nightmarish substances within the lab that could do just the trick. Jake played with the Skittles bag the way you would a fidget toy. Then he pushed out an orange one, rolling it in between his thumb and forefinger. Just before popping it in his mouth, he heard Dr. Roth call out from across the lab.

"By the way, you might not want to eat those unless you're planning on beginning a study on the effects of pathogen-coated candy in which you are the test subject." With this, she pressed the door release button.

Jake peered over to Adi's workstation and scanned the materials set about. Jake eyed the petri dish labeled staph, and it finally registered what Adi had been doing during their discourse. The lab door slowly came to, as Adi headed down the hallway to her office.

"How do you argue with that?" Jake mumbled to himself.

This was why Adi was the boss and why no one, not even Hersey, wanted to visit her bad side, not really, not for too long. Adi always got her point across.

The sparsely decorated office reminded her of home. There were photos from her days at Vanderbilt University and numerous other institutions, tokens of appreciation from former patients, and an old beat-up Fender Stratocaster Adi's dad had given her on her tenth birthday. However, of all the accolades and 'stuff', it was no secret that her most prized possession was an old photograph of her parents that she kept at a perfect forty-five-degree angle…right corner always.

Her father, Dean Roth, was quite the outdoorsman and would often take Adi along for fishing trips and hunting expeditions in the North Georgia mountains. Mr. Roth, a game warden, had recently retired after putting in thirty years of superb service. He was a large, strong man who loved his family. Most people in the Roth's hometown referred to her father as one interesting character. Adi's father trusted animals and nature more than people, and the folks around town knew that. Being a game warden allowed for total immersion in his element, and he never felt he had worked a day in his life.

Adi's mother, Ethel, was a part-time nurse in Atlanta's Northside, a more affluent part of the city. However, sickness and disease were and had always been non-discriminant for the rich or poor, so work was always busy and hectic. Although a skeptic of people's good intentions, she loved her work and embraced helping people with a passion few would ever know. Adi resembled her mother, and their baby pictures proved too hard for almost anyone to decipher which was who.

For some time now, Adi observed illnesses becoming more rampant across the country. Over the course of years and years of habitual use of antibiotics and pain medication, bacteria and infectious diseases had gained immunity from almost every form of medication. Americans were growing tired of losing the ability to feel safe. President Frank Richards had launched a campaign to battle the growing outcry. New medicines were studied and created to combat the sicknesses. Doctors and scientists across the country were in competition to create the next miracle compound hoping to restore confidence in modern medicine. Adi's current employment could be credited to this as well.

Adi's mother would say to her during car rides through Atlanta, "The human body is a living miracle and given the chance, it knows how to take care of itself."

Ethel believed relying on pills and shots to cure every ailment had caused people to lose their ability to fight against illnesses themselves. Ethel Roth would tell anyone willing to listen, and sometimes those who didn't care to hear, about how crazy people were to put all of their trust and confidence in serums and compounds created by magicians of medicine, further advocated by money hungry politicians. Adi would often recall one of the most horrifying statements her mother ever told her.

"You see that building with the blue dome?" Ethel asked.

"Yes," a young Adi responded.

Adi's mom continued, "That is the most dangerous place on earth. The stuff contained there could kill every person on the planet a thousand times over."

The little blue domed building Adi's mother was referring to was the Atlanta Centers for Disease Control and Prevention (CDC) headquarters. Countless vile bacteria, viruses, and poisons were locked deep underground there. With this memory, Adi couldn't help but look out the third-floor office window and gaze at the beauty of the Alaskan wilderness. The moon illuminated and reflected off snow-capped mountains sweeping down to tall evergreens. The valley in the distance showcased a true depiction of the last frontier. The beauty was captivating and mysterious, yet calming. Adi loved her office view, it provided mental clarity.

"So clean and pure," she whispered.

Adi gathered the previous day's notes and began skimming over the SAP batch nine sample analysis. Synthetic Antimicrobial Proliferation (SAP) put Adi on Dr. Hersey's radar. Adi believed that she was close to creating a substance that would eradicate all microbial infections forever.

However, trials had not been going as planned. In its current state, SAP was nothing more than a very efficient and interesting way to kill rats.

"Sorry, Mom, but I have to try," Adi said while closing the office door. Ethel was staunchly against creating more man-made medicine to solve problems created by other synthetics. Adi, however, was not keen on being told what she could or could not do. Ethel Roth could have well blamed herself for her daughter's current path in life. Adi hated being told no. She knew it was a major character flaw, but humility wasn't her strong suit either. Her personality was indomitable. The higher the wall, the further Dr. Roth was willing to climb.

She headed back down to the lab, passing by numerous military guards and through several bio-retinal scanners. Private Jones guarded the last stretch of the hallway from the elevator to the lab.

Jake was still switching pensively between his microscope and a small mouse test subject.

"I gave Moucious Clay (AKA test subject 628) a ten-ml dosage from batch 23," Jake said while turning toward Adi.

"Moucious Clay…what…why," Adi replied.

SAP trials had not graduated from animal tests yet. The number of mice brought into the compound was staggering, even for larger labs. The goals of the next few tests were to finally break through and prepare for human administration.

"This little guy's a fighter. He took the shot like a champ…not even a squeak," said Jake.

"Okay then, any luck?" Adi replied.

"Nothing yet, I modified the ribosomes to allow more protein synthesis. This should produce a more rapid reaction to the infection."

Injections into the previous 627 mice test subjects had not panned out so well. Each and every injection of different SAP batches produced promising effects that were then followed by a horrifying demise of each test subject. Some of the mice would fall asleep peacefully and never wake up, while others would literally hemorrhage out of every orifice of their bodies. To say SAP was behaving randomly and unpredictably would have been a gross understatement.

Adi was not accustomed to failing, and her recent hypothesis with SAP serums was putting her genius to the test.

"Dr. Hersey is going to have a hard time selling a military grade pharmaceutical that has a 100% recipient death rate, " she said.

"Yeah, but there isn't a single evasive microbe that has lasted more than a second when coming in contact with SAP," Jake said proudly.

Leave it to Jake to find the good in everything. For all his quirks and impulsive behavior, Jake Myers was brilliant, as brilliant as they came. Meyers was a leading thinker in molecular biology and had proved his worth time after time. His greatest strength was his ability to never lose patience or become discouraged. The man never lost heart in what he was trying to accomplish.

Tomorrow, Dr. Hersey along with numerous heavy hitters from the US government, specifically the Pentagon, would be pouring into this facility for what they each hoped would be a promising exhibition. It was Adi's chance to put herself on the map with a major medical breakthrough, and she was banking on the SAP formula. Despite the pressure, Adi appeared flawlessly strong and steadfast on the exterior, but internally she was tense. This endeavor was proving to be impossibly challenging. Her insides were rigid with resilience. She refused to surrender to defeat.

*We are so close. We have to be*, Adi half thought, half prayed to herself.

While the two waited for batch 23 to work its magic, Adi began going over her notes pertaining to SAP-9. Batch 9 up to this point, had shown the most promising results. It was the only solution that would not cause the demise of the host at least not because of the initial injection. The problem with SAP-9 was how it interacted with a test subject's white blood cells. SAP-9 attacked white blood cells even more effectively than it did the bacteria. Jake was producing great improvements with batch 9 but was still no closer to showing any definitive results. As of now, the user of SAP-9 would have to weigh the decision of either dying of the infection or the medicine. The first was quicker, the latter more inhumane.

"I'm sure Dr. Hersey would love the fact that after one dose of SAP-9, the patient would forever rely on an even newer unfound creation to stay alive. Imagine something simple like an ingrown toenail causing death due to your body not having the ability to defend itself," Jake said.

Adi angrily threw her notes down and turned away from Jake. Our determined young doctor could just hear her mother now.

"Congratulations, dear. You have stamped your place in the little blue-domed building as its most horrifying contributor."

Adi's dream was to create a substance that could both destroy bacteria cells and regenerate human cells destroyed by the bacterial infection, hence the proliferation aspect of her serum. Her train of thought immediately took her back to when she was eight years old near Blood Mountain, Georgia. The longtime favorite animal of Adi was the native blue-tailed skink lizard which was known for having the ability to regenerate its tail after a predatory attack. She spent countless hours of her childhood near camping spots on the Appalachian Trail catching as many of the lizards as her specimen containers could hold. "Funny little boogers 'eh, Adi? The trick to their survival is giving the attacker what they want, a good target," her father would say.

The blue skink's colorful tail was basically a bullseye for would-be attackers. The creature would lose a limb while retaining its life. This creature cure survival adaptation was a perfect example of the remedy that Ethel Roth prescribed instead of man-made pharmaceuticals; the marvel of nature healing itself.

"How does it do that?" Adi asked her father.

"Don't really know, to tell you the truth." Adi's father paused and scratched his chin, "It just does."

One evening Adi and her father passed by a young couple headed north. "Where y'all headin'?" Dean asked the young couple.

"North, toward Tate City," the man answered.

"Tate, no way you get there by dark," Dean said. As out of town tourists often did with advice from locals, the hikers disregarded Dean's warning. Adi, Dean, and the hikers continued on in their own directions, as most people do when they meet on a trail. Adi was examining her latest captured specimen. She glanced up for a moment and noticed the lady hiker was missing her left arm up to the elbow. Adi looked down at the lizard missing its tail and immediately looked back at the young woman's arm. She wondered if it could grow back too. Most people can't tell you the particular moment in their life when they felt destiny's call. Adi's moment came while meeting that young lady. Her goals were lofty, to say the least, but she possessed a scientist's most crucial element, an inquisitive mind.

"Whoa…check it out Adi," Jake said while standing up. The mouse began squeaking and pacing the cage frantically.

Adi came back to reality from her daydream, "Check the temperature. Any fever?"

"Nothing, he's just super hyper… seems to be experiencing an adrenaline rush," responded Jake.

The squeaks from the mouse started slowly, then accelerated only to slow down again. The two scientists watched for over twenty minutes as the mouse paced back and forth inside the cage.

"Do you think the mouse is consciously making those sounds or are they involuntary?" Adi asked.

"Who cares? The main thing is that he is still kicking," Jake said.

After weeks of tests and countless trials with numerous subjects, this was the longest a mouse in the lab had been able to stay alive. Adi's eyes were fixated on the small rodent. She couldn't even blink. It was as if time itself had stopped. Eventually, Adi turned to Jake and asked, "Are there any signs of the Tuberculosis effects? What about damaged kidney cells?"

"Let me check," Jake said.

As Adi and Jake continued to problem-solve, the mouse paced and squeaked around inside the cage. "Wait, shut up, Jake. What do you suppose it is thinking?" Adi asked.

"No idea, I don't speak rat."

Adilene Roth and Jake Myers were two of the brightest scientific minds in the entire world, and they were both glued to what the little this mouse was about to do next.

"Guess my man really had to go," Jake said.

*Really, Mouse, I'm waiting for a wonder of science and all you can do is urinate all over my cage and lab*, Adi thought.

"Wait…he's urinating, Jake!" Adi exclaimed.

"Yes, he certainly is. And how the little guy can hold that much liquid should be our next experiment." Jake was beginning to laugh and imagining an article in the next scientific journal explaining the ability of mice to expand their bladders.

"Look, it's clear, Jake. There's not a trace of blood. It's crystal clear. Subject 628 had previously been infected with tuberculosis and was suffering severe kidney deterioration. For many days, the mouse had excreted blood every time it peed and wasn't expected to last the week."

"How long since SAP-23 was injected?" Adi asked.

"Fifty-three minutes. Told ya' he was a fighter," Jake replied.

"I want an MRI of the subject's kidneys. Correction, make that every cell by the time I get back," Adi demanded.

"No problem, where are you going?" Jake asked, taking the cage over to a large machine.

"I need a minute." Adi exited the lab once more and let out an enormous sigh of relief. As she breathed back in, it was not just oxygen, nitrogen, carbon dioxide, water vapor, and other trace gasses that entered her body but hope.

"You okay, Ms. Roth?" Private Jones asked.

"Yes, perfectly fine, Sam. I just needed to clear my head for a moment."

"Seems like you and Dr. Meyers were having one hell of a conversation in there. These doors are soundproofed, but I know hoopla when I see it," Jones said.

"Oh, you know how it is Private, boring lab stuff that's all," Adi tolerated Dr. Hersey's men at best, but Jones seemed like a decent person. He never dove too deep into questions about the work of her and Jake, so Adi wasn't too upset over his comments. Most of the time, Adi would say as little as possible to anyone at the compound other than Meyers.

"Heard Hersey is coming tomorrow with an entire entourage. The whole base is buzzing. We don't get many high-profile visitors here at Camelot you know."

At that very moment, as if the devil himself was eavesdropping, Adi's cell phone rang. She stepped into the next room and hesitantly answered.

"Ms. Roth, how is the research going, my dear?" asked Dr. Hersey.

"Dr. Hersey…what a surprise, I wasn't expecting to hear from you until tomorrow," Adi said in a tense tone, turning away from Private Jones in the window. Under no circumstances was Roth going to let Private Jones hear this conversation.

"Since the last time we spoke, it seems your work has experienced fresh success. Perhaps you have actually begun to earn us back just a bit of the prodigious investment that I made in you." Dr. Hersey's words stung.

He continued, "I received a message from Dr. Meyers stating you have successfully tested a solution that has shown great promise. SAP-9 if I'm not mistaken."

"Yes, but did he also tell you that SAP-9 is basically a more potent man-made AIDS," Adi quipped back, her tongue equally sharp as Hersey's. She immediately regretted speaking in such a manner to her senior and dropped silent. She knew this was not the way to interact with him, but the pressure of producing a successful product for Hersey was only further compounded by his questions.

"Sir, when you chose me to lead this lab, you told me to go out and change the world. I'm close…very close to doing just that," Adi answered in a much more civil tone this time.

"Look, my dear, joining me tomorrow are some of the most powerful people in the United States government, and they are not coming to watch you *try* and change the world. They are coming to witness you *do* just that," Hersey snapped back.

"I understand." Adi was once again staring out at the Alaskan horizon. Clouds were rolling in from the Bering Strait which normally meant inclement weather would be following soon.

"I should think that after tomorrow either one of two things is going to occur. One, you renew faith in my ability to provide a reason for your being chosen over hundreds of other qualified candidates, or two, you take your high-school science projects back to Georgia and work the graveyard shift at one of those drive-through clinics," Hersey said sternly.

"I haven't failed you yet, have I?" asked Adi.

"Yet… Ms. Roth, like time, 'yets' are finite, and yours will soon run out." Hersey was starting to cross the line and even he knew it. "How about we meet for an early dinner before your exhibition begins tomorrow. I know things can become hectic when the pressure mounts."

Dr. Hersey's attempt to establish a common ground was to no avail as Adi was at the tipping point of telling him to go to hell. However, as much as Adi hated conceding to him or for that matter any person, she knew the pecking order and currently was in no place to call her own shots.

"That will be fine, sir."

"Ms. Roth, one more thing, make sure you do all of the talking tomorrow. I don't want another debacle like we had the last time Mr. Meyers opened his mouth in front of my guests."

Jake Meyers had begun the last exhibition with an ode to the late Rodney Dangerfield by going through a couple of quips from his extensive comedic catalog. The president of Harvard University was none too happy with the joke about a doctor and mother during her baby's delivery. Meyers' attempt to break the ice had broken a lot more.

"Right, I'll be sure to do all of the speaking, sir. You have my word," Adi reassured.

"I don't want your word, Ms. Roth. I want a modern miracle." Dr. Hersey was not much for small talk, and Adi still had not quite figured out how to tell when he was angry, excited, or joking. The three all came across the same. She normally defaulted to anger and this had served her well up to this point.

As Adi reentered the lab, she overheard Jake talking to mouse 628.

"You did it champ! I've got an entire pack of peanut butter crackers with your name on it," Jake cheered while printing the results.

"Geez! Adi, you look like you've seen a ghost. I thought you would be happier. We just made a serious breakthrough tonight, right?" The look on her face was cause for concern. Jake had seen it time and time before, and usually, she had good reason for being mad.

Adi walked slowly toward Jake, narrowing her eyes as she went.

"Did you send Hersey a message about SAP-9?"

"Wah…well…" Jake stammered and began walking backward away from Adi.

"It's a question of the rhetorical variety, you juvenile…moronic… imbecile! I can't believe you would go behind my back to Hersey! You know how he gets when he feels I'm not performing up to his expectations." Adi was flailing her arms at him now. It was one of the worst blow-ups he'd seen since coming to join her at the compound.

"Look, I know how hard the last few weeks have been, and I wanted to give the doc some good news before the next time you two spoke. He just needs to lighten up a little, that's all." Jake ran out of space for backing up and considered himself surrendered to whatever was coming next.

"Good news? You failed to mention that subjects have to live inside a literal bubble the rest of their lives to avoid death, Jake." Adi was referring to the white blood cell issue discovered upon testing SAP-9.

"Yeah, I may have left that part out," Jake said, turning his head and slightly coughing.

"Whatever! We'll finish this conversation later before I figure out what other foods you like, so I can poison them too. Give me the results."

For all her proper charm and quiet charisma, Adi was still no pushover. Years of being told to remain calm and refined during altercations by her mother had long been thrown out the window. Adi admired Dean Roth's more direct approach to conflict.

"All vitals appear to be normal. There's not a trace of tissue damage or even any signs of molecular stress," Jake told Adi, as they circled the cage.

"What about any excrement, still normal?"

"Crystal," Jake replied.

The little mouse continued gnawing the crackers only pausing long enough to let out one long squeak every few minutes or so. Its eyes were becoming slightly darker but nothing else appeared to be wrong or abnormal.

"So, all signs of bacteria are eliminated, all damaged tissue has been repaired and seems to be normal, and the mouse is eating and acting as expected." Adi was thinking out loud as she liked to do when serious analysis took place within her mind. It was her way of reorganizing the synapse for maximum power.

Jake slowly approached Adi, stuck both arms out and smiled.

"What are you doing?" Adi asked. Jake was now the fly in the room. A few seconds ago, he was trying his best to avoid her, now he wouldn't leave Adi alone to think.

"Don't really know. If there was ever a time a hug would be appropriate, I assume this would be it," Jake said.

"We've cured one mouse, Jake, and we have no idea how SAP-23 would react to a human test subject. Furthermore, we don't even know what is going to happen to 628 either. We've been down this road so many times before."

"So, what about tomorrow? We both know Hersey is not coming all the way from Washington to hear that we cured one rodent and need more time," Jake pointed out.

Not that Adi needed reminding of this. He was annoying, but he wasn't wrong.

Adi bravely pushed forward. "You just leave Hersey and his bureaucratic brutes to me, Jake. Tomorrow, I need you to keep your mouth shut."

He tried to play down the situation, but Jake knew exactly why Adi was worried about him speaking.

"Still on verbal lockdown from last time, huh? Yeah, looking back on it, that probably wasn't a good idea."

"I mean it, Meyers. Not one single syllable."

Jake shrugged his shoulders like a toddler after being told they couldn't have ice cream before bed.

"Well, I'm tapping out anyway. I've got a hot date tonight with the associate professor of applied physics from the University of Anchorage." Jake was almost five years younger than Adi, and at times, she thought he was still holding on to his college years.

Jake stopped abruptly before leaving the lab to salute mouse 628, "Can't believe we actually did it."

As Adi powered down the equipment and prepared to leave for the night, she stopped at the lab door, turned slowly toward the mouse, and said, "You better still be alive tomorrow. Please, stay alive." Adi was well aware of the caliber of guests that would be in attendance. The countless hours of studying and experimenting, the successes and failures she had experienced were all culminating into one single show of ability tomorrow. Everything rode on this-funding for the lab, her career, her reputation, her legacy. Though Adi worried about all of these things, there was something far worse looming. Something no one could have ever imagined.

# 2. Brass Tacks

**Jekyll**

5:15 a.m., without fail, the alarm would sound. A closet containing pressed tailored suits awaited Dr. William Joseph Hersey each morning. Each one handcrafted with perfection in mind. The scenery outside his Virginia gothic-inspired mansion was spectacular, to say the least. Hundreds of soft rolling hills surrounded by amazing examples of maples and red oak trees guarded the perimeter of the estate. 'The Refuge', as deemed by Dr. Hersey, featured one of the finest antique firearm collections in the world. Over the years, he had procured a vast collection of rare automobiles. Though he had not driven, nor sat in them, in over fifteen years. There were countless attendants for all trivial matters that may arise. Details of extremely armed and highly trained guards watched over the estate day and night. Hersey had acquired a disdain for unwanted guests and properly so, as he held little regard for the totality of human physiology. Hersey cared more about the individual cell than the entire body of work.

No, there was not much Hersey had to provide for himself except his next metaphorical mountain to conquer. He was leagues ahead in intellect compared to the majority of the population and had only acquired a taste for life's finer luxuries as they provided comfort for his ambition. At first, like most young scientists, Hersey simply wanted to make a difference, but after his first breakthrough as a geneticist, notoriety arrived and with it a newly found ego and ambition for more than he was accustomed to.

Dr. Hersey currently served as Chief Operating Officer of the CDC and more importantly, Chief Medical Advisor to the president as well as the president's personal physician. Hersey had to be all in or not at all. That was his mindset. He had no wife, no children, and no pets. His own mind was his only true companion.

At 6:15 a.m., Hersey's room intercom chimed, "Sir, the president has arrived and will meet you on the second-floor balcony." This balcony had become the premier meeting place for Hersey's most honored and important guests. It featured artisan chairs from the best woodworkers in Asia and overlooked a vast floral garden with each display of flowers from a different country. Hersey believed in charming his guests into submission, the view from the balcony helped his cause.

"Excellent, Henry, I will be right down," Hersey said.

The president made monthly trips to 'The Refuge' for updates on possible pandemics, growing international health concerns, and new scientific discoveries that could be used for leverage on the upcoming re-election campaign. Hersey, who never had much interest before, was beginning to set his sights on politics as his next mount to conquer.

One aspect of meeting with the most powerful human on the planet that still infuriated Hersey was having to be checked out by secret service agents in his own home each time before meetings could ensue.

"Mr. President," Dr. Hersey said, with a half-cocked smirk.

"Still upsets you I see, eh, Bill," the president chuckled.

"With all due respect, sir, very much so."

"Alright, stop patronizing me, you old hound. Tell me you have something I can use for my next speech, Bill. The media is killing me out here. We've got to find a way to get these protestors off my back. It's either the damned eco-extremists, foreign affairs committee, or lately, big pharmacy. People are hurting out there. Americans are hurting, Bill," the president said.

President Frank Richard's first term had gone better than expected. President Richards was of the old-guard mindset, and his patriotism was infectious. However, one black cloud continued to loom over, not just President Richards', but several previous administrations. America, as well as the world at large, was experiencing a period of increased suffering due to the rampant health crisis. Contracted infectious disease rates had increased steadily over the last decade due to weakened antibiotics and therapeutics. Medicine simply was not working the way it had fifty, even twenty years prior.

"You have another miracle stashed away somewhere like the one that saved Sarah's life, Bill? That would be more than a literal lifesaver at this point," Richards said.

After Harvard, Hersey continued his research of human DNA molecular structure, mainly organ tissue. Up to this point, people in need of organ transplants were placed on long waiting lists in hopes of finding a suitable donor. Countless lives were lost as many could not weather the storm of waiting. One of the first people to receive the enzyme inoculation that would allow universal transplants was Sarah Richards or better known at that time as Senator Frank Richards' only sister.

"I assumed the protests would be the focal point of our meeting today, sir. I can also tell you that I may have just what you are looking for but won't know for sure until I return from Alaska," Hersey said.

Hersey had been granted certain rare privileges by the president. Most agencies had to account for every dime spent and were audited yearly for fiscal transparency. However, Dr. Hersey was allowed a portion of CDC federal funding for 'special studies' and was given full control of the reins in deciding on how to allocate those monies. For the past six months, millions of dollars had been poured into a remote installation near Elmendorf Air Force Base. The moniker Camelot was given to the hidden base by Hersey as he believed it would usher in a new era of a medical revolution. Only unlike the Arthurian Camelot, there was no round table…only a throne and everyone knew who sat upon it. Currently, the proverbial keys to the castle had been given to an up-and-coming scientist, Dr. Adilene Roth.

"Must be important if you are flying all the way out there, Bill. I spoke with Secretary Renner last night, and she is looking forward to finally getting a tour of your baby." The president continued, "Well, touch base as soon as you have something for me. I have to get moving, daily briefings at the White House in forty-five minutes."

"Frank," Hersey said.

"Yeah, Bill?"

Hersey hesitated then asked, "Have you made a decision about our last conversation?"

"You get me my miracle, Bill, and I might just be meeting monthly with Vice-President William Hersey this time next year," Richards said.

Despite his narcissism and disdain for playful banter, Dr. Hersey did respect his friend and knew that Frank Richards, as gullible as he may be at times, was a strong leader and knew how to dominate a situation when the events called for it.

Hersey finished his breakfast on the second-floor balcony and then motioned for Henry who was a loyal trusted friend and estate overseer. "Have the car ready in ten; my flight is scheduled to leave in one hour and you know how I despise tardiness."

"Yes, sir, right away. Shall I prepare 'The Refuge' for guests upon your return?" Henry asked. There were never guests aside from President Richards, and even he never stayed long.

"Not hardly. I see your sense of humor has not escaped you today, Henry," Hersey concluded.

"Not hardly," Henry mumbled to himself as he phoned the escort detail.

As Hersey boarded his private jet, he was handed a bright red folder labeled Jekyll. This was Hersey's code name given by his personal security detail. Dr. Hersey was not very fond of the name but gave it little concern as he thought of soldiers as necessary tools, nothing more.

"Morning, sir, here are the reports you requested," a man dressed in all black said as Hersey took his seat.

"And our guests?" Hersey asked.

"We have confirmed arrival in Anchorage of the following: Surgeon General Dr. Dan Roberts, Major General Harold Reuben, Madam Secretary Maggie Renner, Secretary of Defense General Theodore McMillan, and the Head Joint Chiefs of Staff."

"Excellent, make contact with their people and inform them I am en route," Hersey said. Hersey dismissed his security and began scouring the lab charts and analyses Jake Meyers had previously provided, especially those pertaining to SAP-9.

"Interesting," Hersey murmured to himself as he took a sip of cranberry juice, "The cellular fusion is amazing, no capabilities for microbial synthesis. Hmm… now to solve this autoimmune necrosis issue."

Hersey looked up and glared out the window. Even now, after all he had accomplished the scientist in him still took hold from time to time. Politically charged ambitions or not, Dr. Hersey still reveled in a good molecular hypothesis to solve. However, his reversion to a purist only went so far. William Joseph Hersey was no hero. Indeed, he would do *whatever it took* to further his ambitions.

SAP-9 itself was nothing short of miraculous and did provide promise for finally solving the harmful bacteria question. However, every living creature also relied on helpful probiotics to function properly. SAP-9 was non-discriminate as it destroyed all forms of microbes and had an even more adverse property of attacking white blood cells. Without white blood cells, any sickness however minuscule would lead to death.

Hersey sat back into his plush seat and began brainstorming out loud pausing after each statement, "This may be even better. I would have little problem procuring pharmaceutical company interest in a drug that required lifetime dependency. Immoral? Yes, but the sheer practicality outweighs any adverse effects. I already have the scientific research communities for autoimmune and oncological diseases in my back pocket. I'll have little trouble managing any concerns that surface. Next steps are to continue serum synthesis and move into human trials. I have been provided a gift of just the person for the task. It seems, in more ways than one, you are the dark horse, Mr. Meyers."

Jake Meyers was discovered by Adi Roth at a scientific exhibit just outside of Nashville. Meyers had devoted his life to finding a cure for autoimmune diseases and Roth and he soon became friends after viewing each other's presentations. Meyers was introduced by Adi to Dr. Hersey eleven months prior to the development of SAP-9 and was granted a position at Camelot only under the stewardship of Adi.

Hersey stood to stretch after the sixth hour of a seven-hour flight. He was in strikingly good physical shape for a man of his age. His build was tall, thin but not gangly. He combed his hair in the old pompadour fashion popular during the 1980s as if he were still fresh out of Harvard. His blue eyes however were like icy daggers. They could see through any lie and discern within moments a person's aptitude. Hersey was indisputably handsome, an intellectual elite, and was brutally ambitious. William Joseph Hersey was power embodied and dangerously so as his moral compass contained a few additional directions not yet possessed by ordinary people. Weird science itself could not have constructed a more perfect storm of human manipulation, and in less than two hours, Hersey knew he would have dinner with a younger manifestation of himself. At least, he hoped that sentiment to be true.

Adilene Roth was Hersey's favorite protégée, if there could ever be such a thing. There was no denying it. No matter how hard he tried to show impartiality, the cold hard fact was that Dr. Hersey admired Dr. Roth. While everyone knew it, none would ever exhibit the audacity to speak on the matter.

Hersey had to remind himself each time before he and Adi would meet in person, "Too much respect and you'll never gain the upper hand, too little and you lose control." This personal philosophy had served Hersey well throughout his life. An ego without manners becomes volatile and more times than not, leads to self-destruction.

"Higgins, a word if you please." Major Tom Higgins was head of Hersey's personal security detail. He along with most of his current team had spent the last five years as part of Task Force 11 a joint military force charged with executing various off-the-books missions around the globe for the US Army.

Like Dr. Hersey, Higgins was ruthless in a visceral way. He held no regard for anything except the mission. Higgins took the 'tip of the spear' metaphor literally, and he only answered to Hersey.

"Sir," Higgins said as he entered Hersey's personal sector of the plane.

"Make sure the base is secured and only those that are on the agenda are allowed access to the research wings of the facility." Hersey continued, "I'm not going to take any chances with Elmendorf's 'regulars' keeping out unwanted guests. Dismiss them if necessary. Those soldiers may work for the US government, but that lab is under my command, and they shall do as directed. Understood?"

"I'll personally see to it, sir," Higgins said.

"One more thing, Major. Once we've landed, I want you to keep an eye on our guests until they return to Washington."

"Sir," Higgins said, closing the door and exiting Hersey's personal cabin.

Hersey had hand-selected each member on the guest list, Secretary of State Maggie Renner being the only exception. The Pentagon believed all research conducted at Camelot would first be utilized by the military to gain an advantage over international threats. It was only after military appropriation that the science would be provided to the private sector for civilian adaptation. The State Department thought of Hersey's lab as rendering of debts from the past paid in full by the president and essentially was exactly the case.

Secretary Renner in particular was requested and given special permission to attend by President Richards. It was no secret Renner wasn't a fan of Hersey, and was one of few people that would refer to Dr. Hersey as Jekyll to his face. How that information was leaked Hersey will never know, but the fact that Renner knew this, only solidified Hersey's paranoia about not being able to trust anyone.

Hersey, on the other hand, had ulterior motives. He wanted to create a reason President Richards could not proceed with his administration without Hersey by his side. He needed to create new leverage for himself. If the SAP program produced the desired results of helping with the current medical climate of America, Hersey would have an open door to anyone, anything, at any time… forever.

Hersey's plane landed at Elmendorf AFB at 3:00 p.m. As Hersey exited, he summoned Higgins, "Have your team remind our guests that the exhibition begins at 6:00 p.m., Higgins."

Higgins asked, "On it. Should we prepare for an overnight stay, sir?"

"Let's see how this evening goes. First, I have a scheduled dinner with Ms. Roth. I will meet everyone at the east entrance at 6:00 p.m. promptly. From this moment, not a soul enters or leaves this compound for any reason until they leave for Camelot."

Hersey was offered an escort provided by the USAF, but he declined it. He had his own personal security stationed at the base. Major Higgins instructed two men from Hersey's personal security to escort him. They made their way toward Camelot which was located about forty-five minutes east of the base. The facility did look out of place when compared to military structures in proximity.

Hersey found the contact labeled Roth in his cell phone. After two short rings, Adilene Roth answered, "Sir, welcome back. Thank y–"

Hersey interrupted, "I'll expect you in the administrative conference room within the hour, Ms. Roth."

He ended the call and, for a brief moment, found solace in taking in the landscape. As staunchly unsentimental as William Joseph Hersey could be at times, he knew beauty when he saw it. Alaska was, if nothing else, breathtakingly beautiful, and if not for the possibility of Camelot becoming a failure, would have embodied natural perfection.

# 3. Show and Chase

## New Tornado Alley

"Barometric pressure is falling fast. This is it, Barry! I can feel it," Jeremiah Wilson exclaimed as he entered the van.

"How far outside the city do you reckon?" Barry asked.

"Barry, really? Dude, just drive toward the dark clouds."

Just as the two were about to pull out of the Huntsville National Weather Forecast Office, Jeremiah's supervisor burst through the loading dock doors and began screaming, "You are not going out there again, Wilson! Not in that van!"

"Jack, this could be a cat 4 or better! I need to get close enough to get footage. Aren't you always the one telling me to be more assertive!" Jeremiah shouted back, as Barry accelerated through the parking lot and out the gate.

"Damn it!" Jack Crowder slammed the door as he went back inside to monitor the fast-approaching storm.

Jeremiah Jamal Wilson, or 'JJ' to almost everyone on Northern Alabama local TV, was a meteorologist for the Huntsville National Weather Service. JJ was also an adrenaline junkie, and it seems that the only reason for him becoming a legitimate weather scientist was due to storm chasing offering little in the stable career category. JJ's wingman for the past two years was local investigative reporter Barry Winters. Barry didn't have much interest in weather matters but realized that interesting situations seemed to find JJ. As much as JJ loved a good storm, Winters never turned down an interesting story. Tornado season had been well underway for over a month now and, so far, was not disappointing.

There had been twenty-two tornados recorded so far, in what recently had become known as 'New Tornado Alley', which included most of the Tennessee Valley including northern Alabama. Coincidently, there had been the same number of elevated solar flares reported by NASA. Thus, the conspiracy concocted by Wilson that a major astrological event was imminent.

"I'm telling you, Barry, these solar flares are causing environmental anomalies. This is the tenth super cell system in the last forty-eight hours," Jeremiah touted as he readied the camera.

"Well, I'm no scientist, but solar flares have been going on for thousands of years, JJ. I think you need to stay off of the internet for a while," Barry said.

"You do know there are more than just funny cat videos on the internet, right?" JJ replied.

Barry stopped the van near a clearing between two fields while JJ checked the radar. The pasture provided a long line of sight, and the wind began to whip ferociously. The rain intensified as the sky continued to grow darker.

"There better not be a single scratch on my van Wilson...do y..." Jack Crowder crackled through the radio communicator.

Jeremiah noticed that the van's radio was flickering and the camera was stuttering viscously.

"Barry. Barry...are you seeing this too?" JJ asked.

"Yeah, I can't start the van, and none of our battery-powered equipment is working either."

In what seemed like a microsecond, hail the size of golf balls poured down, and the sky turned an eerie yellow. The wind seemed to be blowing straight down while thunder and lightning abounded.

"We've got to get the hell out of here, this is it," JJ screamed, "Start it, start it."

"I can't. It's... it's shorting out or something," Barry said.

Out of nowhere, the two spotted an enormous twister no further than a quarter mile away. The tornado, destroying everything in its path, was headed straight for Jeremiah Wilson and Barry Winters.

As the two frantically continued trying to start the weather van, but to no avail, they watched the tornado devour three crop silos, each over one hundred feet tall. In an instant, all traces of the structures had vanished and debris began smacking against the front of the van. The tornado was less than two hundred yards from inhaling JJ, Barry, and everything else in the vicinity.

"Should have listened to Crowder," JJ could be heard mumbling to himself. Just then the van puttered then roared to life along with every electronic device.

"Go, go, go!" JJ shouted, and had just enough time to swing the camera around and caught about twenty seconds of the monstrous natural disaster as they peeled away.

Fifteen minutes later, the van pulled into a parking garage. JJ and Barry sat silently together for about ten minutes. JJ slowly turned to Barry and said in a low voice, "Find me someone at NASA I can talk to."

## Dinner for Two

Camelot had been constructed with functionality and covertness in mind. The top of Camelot was painted a dull green with the sides an even duller brown. Engineers had incorporated special stealth masking properties which accounted for the lack of any satellite or radar presence. Nature played the largest role in keeping the compound unknown as large Alaskan evergreens helped in aiding the concealment of the installation. Consideration of covertness was given even down to the fencing structure of the compound which was designed to mimic rows of short interlocking boulders and trees.

The layout of the building consisted of three levels. The first floor was where the cafeteria and guard barracks were located. Floor two contained east and west laboratory wings. The east for animals and the other for human trials. The top floor contained a large conference room along with a dozen offices including those of Adi Roth and Jake Meyers.

Both Adi and Jake were allowed by Hersey to find quarters off-base as long as they were in close proximity to the labs. Jake rented a loft apartment in downtown Anchorage as he favored the nightlife and crowds of the city. Adi purchased and remodeled an old rustic cabin on twenty acres just north of Camelot. Dr. Hersey allowed Adi to hand pick the equipment and any staff (personally screened by Adi) she felt were needed to further test and make advancements with SAP.

Camelot was guarded by no fewer than ten soldiers at any given time. Most guards were concentrated on the ground floor, with two to three positioned on the research level. Unless guests were on site, the top floor was normally unguarded. Adi would not have prying eyes on her when in her office. Any emergency or breach of the compound would trigger air and ground reinforcements from Elmendorf AFB.

"I want every ground-level door checked again," Dr. Hersey said to the base guards as he made his way toward the private elevator.

One member of Hersey's private security detail would remain near the ground floor elevator entrance and the other would wait beside the third. Caterers had been flown in from Japan and had preceded Hersey and his team in order to prepare for the dinner with Adi. Even though the meal was basically a formality, Hersey had no issue with spending thousands of dollars for fresh, authentic Japanese cuisine. If Hersey was going to take the time to eat, he wasn't going to settle for the local catch of the day.

Adi grabbed her lab coat and keys to a blue '94 Jeep Wrangler Safari. The Jeep had been a gift Dean Roth had provided after graduating high school. Adi cared little about fancy cars or the newest fashions but was a sucker for sentimental items. Although archaic in design, Adi relished every moment of driving the old machine and personally drove it from Georgia to Alaska after accepting the new position under Dr. Hersey.

The cabin at one time belonged to an Atlanta attorney who considered himself a fly-fishing enthusiast. However, after ten years of owning the property, the only time he ever stood foot inside the cabin was the day he bought it. Adi purchased the cabin about eight months ago and made several subtle changes to make it feel a little cozier. Back home, the Roth family had a small cabin of their own near Tallulah Gorge. Tallulah Gorge State Park was a common tourist destination in northeast Georgia. The gorge exhibited breathtaking views of the mountainsides with an enormous waterfall at the bottom emptying out in a clear greenish hue basin. It was one of Adi's favorite places in the world. Dean would use the cabin as a base of operations when work pulled him away from the city for longer periods of time, deer poaching normally being the main reason.

Adi passed through the gate and headed toward Camelot for what she hoped to be a productive dinner with Hersey. Her mind kept going back to mouse 628 and how surprisingly helpless it made her feel for her future to rely on such a small creature. SAP was her life's work. For the last twelve years, she had poured every ounce of her mental and physical abilities into it. Once again Adi could hear her mother, "Don't put all your eggs in one basket." One thing about growing up in the South is that there seemed to be an expression for every circumstance.

"Well, this is the only basket I've got, and SAP is one doozy of an egg," Adi said out loud as if her mother was listening.

It was just before three o'clock when Adi entered Camelot. As she made her way toward the elevator, Private Jones passed by, nodded, and continued back to his post near the front entrance. Adi took one final deep breath and exited the elevator onto the third floor. She entered the conference room and was caught off-guard by the amount of food present.

"I hope you like sushi," Hersey remarked, motioning for Adi to sit. "I took the liberty of orchestrating our selection for this afternoon."

*Yeah, in more ways than one*, Adi thought, as she couldn't help but think about the people that would be in attendance later on. Adi was not fond of politicians and was indifferent to military leaders as she had little use for either. Hersey on the other hand was unlike anyone she had ever dealt with.

"Yes, sushi is fine." Adi took a seat directly opposite Hersey.

In front of Adi was a plate of lightly seared Bluefin tuna rolled with rice and seaweed. There were many other small dishes spread out on the long table, but Adi had no clue what they were. She did recognize one of the bottles labeled Sapporo as Jake had mentioned the beverage to her before. Jake even tried to explain how people would travel around the world just to try it. Adi did not drink alcohol, regardless of how special any beverage was, so his enthusiasm was lost on her.

Adi and Hersey began to eat and each could feel the tension in the room. It was as if their eyes began jousting one another and so far, the match was a stalemate. Hersey decided to break the ice and said, "I noticed you are still driving that old contraption." If this was Hersey's idea of breaking the ice, he knew he would have to do better.

"Yes, it still gets me around after all these years," Adi said while pausing to get a better grip on her chopsticks.

"I hope you understand the reason for this exhibition, Ms. Roth. I have long put full confidence in your abilities, and I am sure you will not disappoint me in front of our guests," he said. "I met, just this morning, with the President and even he has high hopes for your work."

"President Richards knows my name?" Adi's eyes lit up as she responded.

"I never said that, Ms. Roth, but your work here at Camelot has gained interest from various sectors of our government."

"So, funding, not running out soon?" Adi asked.

"My dear, you need to focus on the greater idea of human advancement, don't concern yourself with fiscal matters. Think about what must happen for your legacy to be cemented in history and time," Hersey said while leaning toward Adi.

Adi thought to herself, *That's easy for you to say. You control all my fiscal matters and have nothing but time to remind me.*

"Later this evening, when you unveil your new synthetic antimicrobial proliferation to the world, please remember that opportunities like the one presented before you do not come along very often, and I expect success." Hersey trapped Adi's eyes with his own as he spoke these words. His gaze was clear, cold and endlessly intelligent. Looking into his eyes always reminded Adi of looking into a well where you couldn't see the bottom but surely it must have been there.

Coming back to the moment, Adi said, "Sir, Dr. Meyers and I feel confident that we may have found a cure…"

"I do not want to hear about your findings Ms. Roth. Seeing is believing, and I will spare any dignity you have left with me by not allowing you a chance to open your mouth and remove all doubt of my conclusions." Hersey arose and partially bowed to Adi, then exited.

At that particular moment in time, Adi felt as if a metaphorical line had been drawn before her eyes by Hersey. No longer would she have to decipher cute threats by Dr. Hersey. Adi felt genuine discomfort.

Adi's mind was instantly transported back to her interview with Hersey at the CDC in Atlanta twelve months ago. The vivid memory replayed in her mind.

"Good morning, Ms. Roth, please sit down. I want you to know that I have read and analyzed your research on cell regeneration and am quite impressed."

Adi's SAP-1 solution was first designed toward repairing the cells of severely burned victims. The compound produced amazing results in regenerating the cellular structure of the damaged cells. This in itself would have been enough for Adi to stake her legacy, but there was an unattended hidden gem with the original SAP-1 solution. SAP-1, at random, would sometimes destroy any bacteria infecting the patient while at the same time showing increased cellular recovery for the destroyed tissue. For burn victims, this was a godsend because open wounds were notoriously difficult to keep clean and infection free.

"Thank you, sir, I am honored to be here. Your breakthrough with universal organ transplants is beyond remarkable. One of my neighbors received inoculation last week for a kidney transplant. It saved her life. I am sure of it," Adi said.

"I am glad you find my work interesting and useful. But it is you and your research that I find even more intriguing."

This came as a shock to Adi.

He continued, "You are aware that it is no secret that current medical trends show a decline in antibiotic proficiency?"

"Yes, sir. I believe microbial adaptation is to blame along with the overuse of certain medical treatments."

"Well then, see to it that we have a way to remedy those issues, Ms. Roth. You will report tomorrow to cellular research as lead scientist. If anyone has a problem with that, have them contact me. Understood?"

"Does this mean I have the position, Dr.?" Adi asked.

"Ms. Roth, we would not be in the same room if I didn't already have plans for you."

Adi made her initial base of operations in the CDC headquarters but was soon relocated to Camelot as it reached final construction. Adi had spent every moment since trying to improve on SAP-1, and now variant 23 was ready for an unofficial unveiling. Hersey stopped in front of Adi's office on the way back to the elevator and noticed the picture of her parents and honey blond guitar. He smiled and then entered the elevator.

"Take me to the research level. I always hated being late to a show. You can never find a good seat." Dr. Hersey was not worried about seating. He just wanted to see how each guest looked at him as they entered the room. Hersey's intensity combined with his intellect allowed for quick analysis of weakness in people. The mental manipulation never stopped with him.

Adi regained her thoughts and was just about to stand up when she heard Jake busting through the conference door.

"Hey, Adi, you ready to rock? Sushi, no way," he said, grabbing a couple of sushi rolls and stuffing them in his mouth.

Adi replied, not without annoyance in her voice, "I need you to go now and make sure everything is ready. I'll be down shortly."

"Yeah, I saw our 'guests' pulling in right after I did. How'd it go with Hersey?"

"Just go, Jake. Prepare 629, and remember to keep your mouth *shut* tonight."

Jake could be heard as he left the room, "Alright…alright… I'm going. Save me a Sapporo!"

Adi entered her office and grabbed her notes from the previous night. Specimen 628 had survived the night and was showing no signs of degeneration. The only difference in behavior since the shot was the erratic squeaking that came and went at random. The pattern remained the same, two short squeaks followed by one long. Adi was feeling confident that everything would go as planned and even took a minute to strum a few chords on her guitar. She looked down at her watch and the time was 5:30 p.m.

"Thirty minutes," she mumbled to herself as she picked up the picture on her desk and took a long gaze at it.

Dean Roth would say at times like this, "Don't worry about what you can't control. Focus on what you can."

Adi threw her lab coat on and walked confidently toward the elevator, "I'll show him. I'll show them all."


**Showtime**

General Rueben, General McMillan, and Dr. Roberts came into the observation room together. They could be heard speaking on certain mundane military and national security matters. They really were not expecting too much from the exhibition but were always up for a chance to see potential aids for military and governmental use. The main reason the men agreed to come along was to view Camelot in person.

"Gentlemen, please sit here by me," Hersey said.

"Quite the place you have created here, Hersey. I need one of these for myself," General McMillan said. Dan Roberts and Harold Reuben both laughed.

Hersey replied, "Yes, well if everything goes as planned, I'll have one of your grunts construct a replica out of those Lego toys to put on your desk in the Pentagon."

"That's why we like you, Hersey. You never back down," Dr. Roberts said. Hersey said under his breath, "Not hardly."

Secretary Renner could be heard arguing with someone at the entrance to the observation room. The argument carried over into the room as the door opened.

"Look, jackass, I don't give a damn who you are. You're not getting my purse."

"Major, it's quite alright. I don't think Madam Renner is concealing anything more lethal than that which is present within this installation."

Higgins dropped the matter and went back to securing the entrance. The other three men in attendance chuckled at each other but did not dare look at Secretary Renner. "Madam Secretary," each man said, including Hersey, as she found her seat.

The observation room contained one seat for each person in attendance with a double-sided mirror that provided clear visuals into the lab work area where the demonstration would be conducted. There were intercom capabilities between the lab and the room, but they had never been tested as this was set to be the first exhibition conducted with observers. Private Jones had been correct with his earlier statement to Adi that Camelot did not receive many, if any visitors at all.

Jake Meyers entered the lab, waved at the glass, and began preparing the equipment and materials for Adi. Hersey prefaced his audience with a quick synopsis of why they were brought to Camelot by saying, "Guests, I wanted you to see firsthand the future of American scientific prowess. My scientists have potentially discovered a way to end the infectious disease epidemic plaguing humankind for thousands of years." This was a vast oversimplification of what Hersey actually knew to be true, but it seemed to suffice the crowd.

Both generals could be heard saying, "Imagine an army with no sickness."

"Imagine no more national security threats due to hazardous outbreaks," Dr. Roberts added.

Even Secretary Renner was taken aback by the sheer enormity of the proposal, that her interest in the matter grew exponentially. Whatever interest Renner had gained in anticipation was soon equalized by her lack of trust for Dr. Hersey. *Sounds like some Jekyll and Hyde stuff to me*, Renner thought. She turned to Hersey and whispered, "I only came here as a favor for the President you know. If this little science fair project blows up in your face, I'll personally see that this place is turned into a hazardous waste dump."

Hersey replied, "I enjoy your conviction, Madam Secretary. It shows you care."

Renner rolled her eyes and stared down the three men, who at this point, were more focused on Adi Roth as she entered the lab.

Adilene Roth was tall with an athletic build, yet she played no sports. Years of hiking and being outdoors had made her surprisingly strong. Her dark green eyes were deep and full of emotion at all times. Her brunette hair was straight and kept around shoulder length. She had a fair complexion and exuded a simple, yet elegant beauty. Adi was by no means an unattractive woman, but she did not care to see herself as an object of anyone's affection.

Adilene walked toward the table where Jake prepared the solution for administration to the new test subject, mouse 629. Jake gave her a quick wink and nodded as she turned to face the glass. Adi began, "Welcome to all in attendance. Today, you will witness the first official exhibition of Synthetic Antimicrobial Proliferation variant 23."

General Rueben looked at Hersey and asked, "What the hell is synthetic antimicrobial proliferation?"

Hersey just smiled and motioned toward the glass.

Adi continued, "Please focus your attention on test subject 629. Twelve hours ago, specimen 629 was injected with highly concentrated dosages of *Bacillus anthracis,* better known as anthrax, *Clostridium botulinum* or botulism, and *Salmonella bongori.*"

Several eyebrows in the audience raised.

"Normally, it would take a few days for symptoms to overcome the host and cause death to this particular species. However, due to the greatly increased dosage administered, the effects of the harmful bacteria should already be visible to all in attendance."

The mouse was exhibiting signs of illness and a screen showing the rodent's vitals read a temperature of 42 degrees Celsius which was well in the deadly range for mice.

General McMillan asked Hersey, "The rat looks like it's going to explode. We are safe here, right?"

"Quite safe. Please, sir, focus."

Jake presented Adi with a small aluminum tray with a single syringe. The needle contained ten ml of bluish serum.

"SAP-23, if successful, should eradicate, within minutes, all traces of the injected bacteria while simultaneously repairing all tissue damaged during the test. Test subject 629's vitals and behavior should quickly return to normal after the solution is injected," Adi said.

The mouse began to convulse violently inside its cage. Blood could be seen seeping from open sores on its back as well as from its ears and nose. Adi approached 629, took the syringe from the tray as Jake secured the animal with a pair of rubber forceps, and injected SAP-23 into the subject.

Even Dr. Hersey at this point in the show, was on the edge of his seat. His sharp eyes exuded laser-like focus toward the rodent. The scientist in him had become pure again, only caring about the results of the test. For a brief moment, William Joseph Hersey was not raging with ambition but relished the feeling of an exciting experiment. The rest of the observing panel gripped the arms of their seats and held their breath for what seemed like an eternity but was merely seconds. Adi stepped back from 629, and Jake came and stood beside her facing away from the glass and said quietly, "It's going to work, Adi, don't worry."

Adi closed her eyes and flashed back to the first lizard she ever caught, but before the memory could play out in her mind she was startled by mouse 628, who began to squeak loudly.

Jake walked over to 628 and shrugged his shoulders. The mouse seemed fine but was definitely agitated for some reason.

"Squeak!" 629 rolled over onto its side and then jumped to life, running around the cage frantically.

Secretary Renner turned to Hersey, "Congratulations, Hersey, on your new breed of professional racing rats."

Adi stood in military fashion with her hands clasped behind her back doing her best to not reveal her nerves.

Hersey did not respond nor look at Renner. He remained hyper-focused on the test subject.

"Time?" Jake asked.

"Eighteen minutes twenty-three seconds. Please, please, c'mon, little guy," Adi silently begged, gripping her own fingers tightly.

After another few minutes of running in circles, 629 came to an abrupt stop, looked straight into Adi's eyes, and collapsed. Adi's heart dropped to the floor.

Failure.

Jake approached to cover the cage. Just before he placed the cloth over the top, the mouse let out one long squeak and then stood. The bleeding ceased to seep from its nose and ears and the sores had completely vanished. Test subject

629 went straight to the water dispenser and began to drink while Adi and Jake stood motionless.

Hersey stood and said proudly, "Brilliant, my dear. Brilliant."

# 4. Homecoming

**Exit Plan**

Jake stayed in the lab and continued to monitor mouse 629 while Adi stepped into the hall and met with Hersey and the guests. 629 was eating and behaving normally as if the bacteria had never entered its body. SAP-23 had performed wonderfully.

The two generals were the first to approach Adi, "Can you make more of that? How well does it react with people?"

Renner interrupted before Adi could answer, "What are the long-term effects of your SAP-23, Ms. Roth? What problems or side effects have you noticed?"

"Yes, are there any complications to worry about?" Dr. Roberts asked.

"Guests, please give Dr. Roth some space. What you all just witnessed was nothing short of miraculous," Hersey said. "My dear, you did well. We are all in awe of your amazing display this evening. Higgins, please escort our guests back to the motorcade. Ms. Roth, walk with me."

Renner could be heard as the two walked away, "This conversation isn't over, Hersey." Maggie Renner was one of the few people who did not like, nor trust, anything associated with Hersey. That would never change, and she would pay a heavy price for her personal vendetta. Hersey reminded the panel that they were under a strict nondisclosure agreement as the work in the lab was classified Top Secret. After this, he paid them no further mind.

Hersey and Adi exited Camelot's main entrance and found seating near and outside. He began, "Ms. Roth, I want you back in Atlanta in three days. I have to say that I had my doubts, but I have never been so pleasantly surprised in all my time."

"Sir, it was only one mouse. We still have no idea how SAP-23 will react with people," Adi said.

Hersey didn't hesitate.

"That is precisely why I need you to return to the CDC headquarters and prepare human trials at once."

"I don't understand. Shouldn't I stay here to prepare for human tests?" Adi asked.

"You will have the full support of all my resources. Use them. I'm giving you seven days to complete trials and prepare your serum for mass production, Ms. Roth. Consider it a challenge."

Adi was in an incredibly difficult position. No matter how many scientists or tools Hersey gave her, she knew a week was not enough time to prepare for human trials. Adi also felt guilty as the moral implications of conducting experiments on people so soon were not first on her mind after hearing Hersey's words. Adi was more worried about failing.

"Sir, what about Dr. Meyers?" Adi asked.

Hersey stood and motioned toward Higgins, "Dr. Meyers will remain here at Camelot. Meyers may offer assistance remotely." Hersey's last statement to Adi was a lie. Meyers was going to be directed for something much more. Adi went back into the lab as Jake was cleaning up and shutting down the equipment preparing to leave for the night.

"I'm going back to Atlanta on Friday, Jake," Adi said.

"Nice, I've always wanted to see firsthand the little blue dome you're always blabbing about," Jake said.

"No, I'm going back to Atlanta. You're staying here," Adi said.

"By myself, and just what am I supposed to do here while you're gone? Is this your idea of a joke, Adi?"

"It's not a joke, Jake. Hersey wants you here for some reason. You'll have to take that up with him."

"I will." Jake stormed out of the lab and headed down to try and catch Hersey before he left the compound.

Higgins was waiting for Jake as he stepped out of the elevator, "Dr. Hersey wants a word with you before he leaves." A black Mercedes SUV stopped beside Higgins and Meyers. They both entered and headed toward Hersey's private jet.

Adi gathered her belongings and left for her cabin, still trying to work through the events of the evening. It had all happened so fast. The last few hours had vanished into a few seconds of reflection. SAP-23 worked to perfection and everything Adi had ever wanted was coming to fruition. She forgot about Hersey and the panel of guests. She lost the ability to recall exactly how the mouse had responded to SAP-23, yet knew that it had worked.

"No biggie, Adi," she said to herself while driving. "You just have to condense ten years of work into seven days, without killing anyone. That's all. No pressure."

The crunch of snow and ice beneath her tires ceased as she clutched the Jeep into park just outside her cabin. Adi slammed the driver's door. Walking toward the cabin door, she slipped on a patch of ice. She reached out to grab the torso high trash can to steady herself. This lid gave way and instead she and the trash can fell to the frozen, unforgiving ground.

"Bear resistant...with tightly secured lid...yeah, okay!" Adi fumed sarcastically as she fumbled in the dark picking up the trash that had poured out onto the ground.

"Today, right now this has to happen!? My day has been plenty already! Ugh...gross," split through the otherwise silent evening as her fingers closed around a particularly slimy piece of trash.

Adi's rational mind understood why things like this occur at seemingly the worst times. When you're mentally fatigued, you make careless mistakes, but understanding did not make it any less frustrating.

Finally, Adi stepped across the threshold of her cabin, shut and locked the door behind her, and breathed a great sigh of relief that today was over. There was no dog to pet or fish to feed. Adi lived entirely alone. Her career was the consuming element in her life.

Entirely drained, Adi headed straight for the shower. The warm water always helped relax her tense muscles and melt away stress. What was usually a ten-minute shower, turned into thirty tonight. She kept spacing out, mid loofah. Her mind kept running away from her, churning over possible solutions to the situation she had just been plunged into.

Suddenly, the growling bleat of a dall sheep grazing just outside her bathroom window shook her from her thoughts. These big horns ventured near her cabin at night drawn by the lure of grass in the yard. She turned off the water and stepped out of the shower only to realize she'd completely forgotten to wash her hair. Too tired to care, Adi headed for the bedroom. She thoughtlessly drew a single finger across the strings of her acoustic guitar propped in its stand as she passed by. She dropped her towel and left it where it fell, slipped into her pajamas, and was asleep before she even hit the sheets.

As she slumbered, the howls of a black wolf pack drew ever closer brought in by the dall sheep grazing around the cabin, contentedly filling their bellies.

## Ulterior Motives

"I've got to get one of those," Jake said.

Hersey looked at him, swirling a cocktail, "Mr. Meyers, I will be blunt to spare both our time. I want you to continue working on SAP-9 and have human test results by the end of next week, understand?"

"SAP-9 human tests in a week? Impossible. Are you crazy? Does Roth know about this? Why wouldn't she…? So, this is why am I not going with her," Jake frenetically analyzing the situation.

He figured Roth was purposefully creating a scenario for failure, so Hersey would dismiss him from Camelot. *She doesn't have the guts to tell me herself,* Jake thought. However, there was no way for Jake to prove this concocted theory.

For the most part, he and Adi had worked alongside each other well and it wasn't usually in Jake's nature to so swiftly see treachery in someone he'd previously allied with. However, Hersey had a way of finding, maybe even creating, darkness in people and exploiting it. Even those lusts you didn't consciously realize existed he saw clearly and commanded for his own gain without qualm. What's even more baffling is the certainty he gave you about what you were doing.

Hersey placed his drink on a nearby table and folded his hands in his lap, "Ms. Roth has her assignment. Now you have yours. Is there a problem, Dr. Meyers?"

Jake was silent, not sure how to respond. With his head cocked slightly to one side he evaluated his circumstance feeling as one does when about to try a new food for the first time. With skepticism and hesitation tumbling over each other only to be overstepped by the desire to discover new delectability.

Hersey glided on, "Ms. Roth was not the one who called me about SAP-23; you were. Marcus Aurelius said, 'A man's worth is no greater than his ambitions.' I see your enthusiasm and avidity and choose to reward it. Shall I withdraw my munificent offer?"

Now Jake was beginning to understand, or so he thought. He relaxed his shoulders, inhaled, and straightened his head.

"Not at all. Yet, tell me, what about SAP-9 interests you? SAP-23 just proved itself as a potential miracle with no negative side effects," Jake prodded.

Hersey's eyes pierced through Jake and for a moment Jake Meyers understood why Adi feared Dr. Hersey. This time, he came across differently. Jake was not afraid of being reprimanded or experiencing setbacks in his career but was genuinely feeling apprehension for his well-being.

"You let me worry about the details, Dr. Meyers. One week," Hersey commanded.

Hersey had accomplished what he always had before, established dominance. Jake conceded. Without asking any further questions, he agreed to continue working on SAP-9.

"And Dr. Meyers, not a word to Ms. Roth about our little discussion," Hersey concluded. Both men stood and shook hands.

"I'm looking forward to great things from you, Mr. Meyers," Hersey goaded.

Jake nodded and was escorted off the plane and back to Camelot.

For the first time, William Joseph Hersey and Jacob Meyers knew exactly where each stood in relation to the other.

Moments later, Hersey was just finishing a swift transaction on his phone when one of the pilots chimed over the speaker. "Sir, we're going to have to delay take-off for about fifteen minutes. Some of the instruments are malfunctioning. We need to run diagnostics."

Hersey replied with disgust, "What do you mean malfunctioning! This plane was over one hundred fifty million dollars."

"Not sure yet, sir. We probably just experienced a minor glitch of some kind. Wait, systems are returning to normal. We should be good in ten, sir."

Hersey summoned Major Higgins and the two could be heard discussing various other security matters as the jet lifted off headed back to 'The Refuge'.


## The Footage

JJ Wilson walked past a large group of television screens with various readings of weather information. Jack Crowder marched up to JJ and began giving him down the road about the van again. Jack chewed JJ out over that van with an impressive level of enthusiasm. The kind that should be saved for sermons and sports. "Shut up, Crowder, not now."

"Whew…That was a close one, JJ," Barry said while falling into a chair beside the main screen of the command center. Barry pulled a little green notebook out of his jacket pocket and began strumming through the pages. He had acquired numerous contacts throughout his years as a chief investigative reporter but wasn't certain he had ever spoken with anyone that knew much about anything having to do with NASA before.

Jack Crowder wasn't going to be ignored.

"What happened out there, JJ? All phone communications went out and every device in this place went haywire. I've never seen anything like that. My guess is the storm knocked out all the power substations, right?"

"Geomagnetic storm… just a little one." JJ continued mumbling to himself while inserting the camera memory card into a laptop.

Crowder was puzzled by JJ's words.

"What? Yes, a storm, JJ. There was a big storm…a tornado. Tell me about it."

The laptop came to life with the footage. The camera showed the massive tornado then began to flicker in and out until freezing completely.

"Holy–," Jack said after witnessing the sheer size and presence of the tornado in relation to everything in the landscape around it. "That is the biggest tornado I've ever seen."

JJ came out from his hyper-focused trance of the footage and responded to Crowder. "Category 5, Jack. It was terrible. I hope everyone had enough time to get to safety, and as for the power, I think I know what is going on."

JJ continued to replay the short clip over and over again. He looked for signs of malfunctioning as the storm intensified but couldn't really find anything that would account for the instruments behaving as they had. Wilson was just about to give up on his theory when he noticed a strange light above the tornado. The light was faint but spread in every direction out into the storm clouds.

"It's an aurora," JJ said while zooming in on the screen. "Aurora borealis! I knew it. Barry, it's an aurora borealis. I was right!"

"No way, kiddo, there has to be something wrong with your camera. Never heard of anyone seeing 'northern lights' in Alabama," Barry said.

"Never mind that, Barry. You found me a contact yet?"

Jack Crowder turned to JJ and Barry, shaking his head, and said, "Do you two really expect me to believe that an aurora borealis caused a category 5 tornado in Huntsville, Alabama? That's it. I'm having you drug tested Wilson."

"Jack, geomagnetic storms are not that uncommon, and records have shown auroras being seen as far south as Texas. As for the tornado, it's that time of the year."

JJ was right about one thing, 'northern lights' had been recorded in Texas. The storm he was referring to happened in the late 1800s but had never happened again since.

"Tim Shirley," Barry called out as he circled a name on page 30 of his green book.

"Who?" JJ asked.

"Tim Shirley's nephew works at the Houston Aquarium. He was contracted by NASA a couple of years back to build the dunk tanks astronauts practice spacewalking in. I'll give him a call and see if his nephew can get us a name," Barry declared and stepped outside to call.

"Look, JJ, I know today was hectic, but please get it together and get your mind right," Jack said, then returned to his office.

JJ continued poring over the footage. After a few minutes, he shifted his gaze to the radar screens depicting the next wave of storms in the forecast.


## Prodigal Daughter Returns

Dr. Meyers met Adi at the base airstrip. Adi said to Jake while loading up her luggage onto a C130 cargo plane, "Thanks, Meyers." She preferred to ride as luggage for the military, rather than face the crowds of public flights out of Alaska. Jake made no mention of his last conversation with Dr. Hersey but did feel guilty about concealing the matter from Adi.

"Take care of the place while I'm gone," Adi said. As the plane roared to life, Adi had one final message for Jake, "I'll be in touch soon, and keep your hands off my stuff."

Jake could be heard as the door of the plane closed. "No promises."

The pilot came over the intercom, "We should reach Dobbins AFB in eight hours, Ms. Roth, try to get some rest."

Adi enjoyed being on the plane alone as it gave her plenty of time to think about starting human trials with SAP-23. In theory, it should be very simple. Find people willing to join an experimental study, and make sure they have bacterial infections at the time of testing. *Simple, what could go wrong*, Adi thought.

She exited the plane and made her way to the base front entrance. There waiting for her, was an old forest green F-250 driven by Dean Roth with Ethel riding shotgun. Dean had purchased his old Department of Natural Resources service vehicle. After years of relying on it, he'd grown quite fond of the truck. He simply had to have it.

Adi could see on their faces that they were happy she was home.

"So, where to first?"

"I was thinking that Brazilian place where they bring the meat out on a stick," Dean said.

"Sounds good to me," Adi replied as she closed the door.

"One of these days, I'm coming up there. I heard the fishing is out of this world. Not too keen on grizzly bears or wolves though. But I'm sure there's plenty of other stuff I can get into," Dean continued as they pulled away from Dobbins AFB.

"More than you can imagine, Dad," Adi said while leaning forward to see her mother. "I brought you something. It's an Inuit wind chime."

"Supposed to ward off evil spirits or something?" Ethel asked.

"No, it's supposed to make soothing sounds when the wind blows, Mom, nothing more."

"Been almost a month since I've heard from you. We were starting to think one of your experiments blew you up or something," Ethel said as she fidgeted with the moose antler wind chime.

Adi deflected her mother's comment and took in the scenery as they approached Atlanta. Atlanta, despite its normal big city problems, had a certain charm about it. The city had many great places for food and Adi would make her way to Underground Atlanta for blues and rock festivals whenever she had the time.

As they entered the restaurant, Ethel nudged Dean as she asked Adi, "How long are you staying this time? You coming home?"

"Let's just enjoy this meal, and we can talk more about it tonight. Let's eat," Adi ended the conversation there, and they all took their seats.

**Pay the Piper**

"Okay, Hersey wants SAP-9 tested on human patients. I guess Hersey expects my test subjects to fall from the sky," Jake said to himself out loud, while entering the lab. This was the first time Jake had been all by himself at Camelot and was having a hard time not hearing music coming from Adi's office or in the lab. "Guess I get to play my own mix." Jake connected his phone to the speaker and began preparing vials of SAP-9 for testing.

Jake answered the lab phone, "Hey there. Jones. What's up?"

"Wait, what? My subjects are here?"

"I didn't order any subjects. Who are they? Where'd they come from?" Meyers went down to the lobby. Four patients on hospital beds were being wielded into elevators. Each patient had one nurse assigned as their caretaker. "What is this?" Meyers asked.

"Sir, this note and folder were also delivered for you," Private Jones added as he handed Jake a small envelope on top of a red folder.

The note read:


*Dr. Meyers,*

*I organized your first set of test subjects. If SAP-9 is successful with these patients, I may have to reconstruct your contract and duties. They are all yours. Impress me.*


"Advanced spinal meningitis. This is bullshit," Jake said as he read through the folder. SAP-9 had cured many rats containing different bacteria, but no one, not even Roth nor Meyers, had a clue how the formula would react with human patients. Jake was not comfortable with the situation but knew he had no other choice but to proceed.

After placing the patients in the east wing holding area, Jake addressed the four attendants, "Who can tell me where these people came from? I have no names, only current symptoms and conditions."

The nurses in unison all shook their heads no and returned to tending to the patients. "Great, this place is turning into a madhouse," Jake said while wielding patient one into the main lab.

Patient one was a young man, most likely in his early twenties, and according to the chart, was suffering from bacterial spinal meningitis for what looked like a few days at this point. He continued to examine the man, who had clearly been sedated before entering Camelot, and noticed severe stiffness of the neck and signs of a previous seizure. After connecting the patient to the necessary monitoring and recording devices, Jake wasted no time as he prepared a vial of SAP-9 for injection. The patient's nurse waited by the lab door, never speaking, just watching.

Jake administered the shot and waited. Just like with the mice test subjects, nothing happened at first. The problem this time was that the patient was non-responsive. All of the mice had been alert when the injection occurred. Jake circled the bed only pausing every few seconds to check the monitoring screens. More than ten minutes passed without any change. "Nothing, not even an increased heart rate or change in core temperature. It doesn't make sense," Jake said. "Something should have happened by now…something." As if on command, the patient's eyes burst open, and he began grabbing at his restraints. His eyes were intense. He made no audible sounds except for his breathing which was heavily labored. Jake moved closer to the man.

"Sir, can you hear me? Nod your head if you can hear me."

The man began shaking his head left to right violently.

"Oh no, another seizure…wha…" Before Jake could finish his thoughts, the man went still. His breathing returned to normal, and his eyes slowly closed. Jake was perplexed. It was as if the procedure never occurred. "Okay, first nothing, then my man goes insane, then nothing again." Jake continued to pace the room for another hour or so before noticing a change in the man's vitals. Jake took blood samples and quickly began analyzing for signs of bacteria. There were none. The patient continued to remain unresponsive, but his complexion seemed to change before Jake's eyes. He looked at peace. "Unreal," Meyers said out loud toward the nurse.

Even the nurse in the room placed her hand over her mouth and asked Jake, "Is he dead?"

"Not dead. Just resting," Jake replied. Meyers grabbed a stool and placed it beside the nurse.

Jake needed to find out who these people were. "Who is he?"

The nurse replied, "Sir, Dr. Hersey gave explicit instructions not to talk about the patients."

"Okay, who are you?"

"We were all contracted by Dr. Hersey. He told us that we would work in a lab for around a week, then he would send us to the AFB." Jake could tell by the woman's accent that she had to be from the southeastern portion of America.

"The Refuge. Does that mean anything to you?" Jake asked.

The nurse's eyes shot up to meet him, but she did not say anything. At that moment, Jake lost his harsh tone, stood, and approached the test patient. Jake was certain SAP-9 had worked but wasn't going to risk further disaster by injecting the next three subjects until he had more time to evaluate the first young man. That would be all for tonight.

By the next morning, Jake returned to find the young man having breakfast and reading a book.

He was completely coherent and seemed to be in perfect health. The nurses all smiled and said good morning to Jake, which really freaked him out. The young man placed his drink on a nearby table, closed the book, looked straight into Jake's eyes, and said, "Thank you." Jake left the room for his office just down the hall. He sat at his desk and stared at the phone. "Who should I call first?"

## Before the Big Dance

Adi placed her bags on the old antique bed and reached for her high school diploma on a nearby table. She thought about how uneasy she used to feel the night before a big exam, a science fair, or a homecoming dance. Tomorrow, she would begin testing SAP-23 on actual people, and the sheer weight of the situation was terrifying.

The door cracked open. "You need anything, Adilene?" Ethel asked while placing two towels on a chair.

"I'm good. Thanks."

"Your father and I know you're back to work downtown, and we just want you to be careful and stay safe. Okay?"

Adi knew that her parents would support her no matter the situation, but Adi had spared most of the details of why she had been brought back to the CDC. Dean and Ethel knew Adi was working on medicines to help people but were ignorant of SAP-23 and Dr. Hersey. Adi wanted to keep it that way.

"Good night," Ethel said as she closed the door. Adi turned to the window and looked out at the city horizon. Twenty-four hours earlier majestic mountains had filled her window. They were now replaced by tall buildings and an array of orange glowing street lights. The landscape wasn't the only thing changing, and Adi knew it.

# 5. Mutualism

**Health for Everyone**

Hersey made it down to the second-floor balcony where, so many times before, he and President Richards had conducted their meetings. The balcony provided one of 'The Refuge's' most stunning views consisting of a large rock fountain surrounded by various flowers (mainly tulips imported from Holland) and marble sculptures.

Henry, Hersey's personal butler, showed Frank Richards to the balcony where Hersey waited with an assortment of refreshments. At the balcony entrance, President Richards excused four secret service men and thanked Henry for escorting his team to the meeting, "Henry, I appreciate it, as always."

"Pleasure is all mine, sir," Henry responded while closing the doors behind him.

The President sat and, for a moment, no one spoke. Hersey knew that the next words out of his mouth needed to be concise and perfectly orchestrated. His latest ambition was set to become reality.

Hersey spoke, "Mr. President, I have good news to report. It seems that the miracle you asked for has been granted."

"Go on, Bill, I'm listening," Richards said while reaching for a small danish.

"My recent trip to Alaska has provided a means to an end for infectious diseases, which you can understand, has been plaguing many citizens of this great nation for quite some time."

"We will soon no longer have to worry about Americans losing loved ones over underperforming antibiotic medicines," Hersey said.

"You mean no more infections, Bill?"

"Is that what you're saying…as in done, forever?" President Richards said.

"Yes, no more, ever."

President Richards sat back in his chair and stared out at the fountain with disbelief.

"And it's safe, Bill?"

"Quite safe, sir. My scientists performed a flawless exhibition with no adverse effects on the patient," Hersey said. The lie had been performed to perfection. President Richards had no knowledge of the previous *patient* being a mouse or that SAP-23 had only been tested twice in its short existence.

"With your permission, sir, I would like to begin a program to inoculate citizens with serious infections or those who show tolerance to antimicrobial medicines."

"Are you sure it is safe, Bill? I can't put my name on something if it has a chance of backfiring on me."

"Sir, you trusted me with your own flesh and blood once, at a time when we had never met. Please allow me the opportunity to make a withdrawal from that trust once again," Hersey said.

The President took a long time to respond. He did not like the fact that he knew so little about how this would all work but the pressure he was under to improve his reputation and restore faith in his administration was undeniable. He sifted through the circumstances like a miner panning for gold.

*If the options were a gamble on Hersey or on some unforeseen source emerging just in time to give the boost in the polls he desperately needed, well, Hersey was definitely the safer bet… especially, given their history. I mean this is the guy who stepped up to save Sarah's life when no one else could. Yes. Why was he even hesitating? Another homerun from Hersey was just what was needed to get ahead in the poles. The country needs another four years with my leadership. No one else knows what this nation is going through with the health crisis. With Hersey at my side, with his skills in my arsenal, we'll be stronger than ever. Yes, this is it.*

Leaders must have the strength to move forward confidently with a decision. He pushed doubt aside and took the next step.

"Okay, you have my blessing, Bill. Make it happen," the President said while standing and facing Hersey. "I'm a man of my word. If it works as well as you say, I'll announce you as my new running mate during next month's campaign address."

"Thank you, sir. There is one concern. Secretary Renner, she seems skeptical of the possibilities I spoke of."

"I'm meeting with Renner in a few days. I'll tell her to cool it, so you can focus on work," Richards assured.

"Thank you, Frank. I won't let America down."

Frank Richards paused by the balcony door and gave a reassuring nod then left for Washington.

Hersey sat back in his seat and called for Higgins, "I need you to dispatch a team to Atlanta to make sure Ms. Roth remains *safe*." Higgins knew what this meant. Adilene Roth was soon to be under the *protection* of Dr. Hersey at all times at the Atlanta CDC, whether she liked it or not.

"It's time for the world to be introduced to SAP-23," Hersey concluded as he entered back into the manor.


**The Test**

Adi reached the Atlanta CDC early the next morning and made her way through several checkpoints.

Adi parked at the bottom of a secure, closed garage labeled basement level one.

The deputy director of the CDC met Adi at the door, "Ms. Roth, it's a pleasure. I received the equipment lists that you requested upon your arrival. You have been granted the entire infectious disease sector for your work."

The deputy director had almost finished speaking with Adi, when a voice chimed in over the intercom, "Sir, Ms. Roth's security detail has arrived. They will meet you at basement level 3."

As if on cue, Adi and the director turned toward each other with perplexed looks on their faces, "Security detail?"

"Is this standard procedure?" Adi asked.

"No, this is new to me. I was unaware of any added security other than what we have currently present."

*Hersey*, Adi thought to herself as they made their way to basement level three.

Major Higgins had done as Dr. Hersey instructed and called in a favor to his old commanding officer from Afghanistan, Commander General Gerald Baskin, who was now the base commander in Fort Benning, GA. The major specifically asked for John Fortner to lead the security detail. General Baskin was told not to inform Fortner that it was Hersey that requested his services.

General Baskin knew Higgins and Fortner had a history together but was not about to cross Dr. Hersey. The major secretly hoped to one day settle an old score from a mission the two men were a part of in the war in the Middle East.

"Ma'am, this is Echo Team, and we have been assigned as your personal security for the duration of your time here in Atlanta," Fortner said.

Adi heard about half of what was said as she couldn't help but notice the sheer immensity of the captain. "That is one big handso... hugely... unnecessary... pain in my ass."

Adi broke from her moment of blankness and responded, "Captain, I did not ask for, nor need added security. This facility is safe enough as it stands."

Fortner ignored Adi, "Where would you like us to set up a base of operations, sir?"

"You can have the main ward of the infectious disease level," the deputy director said.

"No, he cannot. I do not need nor do I want soldiers interfering with my work, and I don't care who sent you here."

Fortner looked at Adi, "Ma'am, I do not take orders from you but will protect and assist you with any emergency that may arise."

Adi was furious. She felt like a little child being told who she had to play with at the park. "I don't take orders from you, ma'am…ma'am, just who the hell does he think he is?!" Mocking that moronic mammoth of a man, Adi fumed, mainly to the director, but purposefully loudly enough to be heard by everyone in the area.

The director would normally never let any unscreened personnel of any kind into the facility not approved by himself, but this was a unique situation. Dr. Hersey was still in charge of all CDC operations and had the authority to place whomever he wished at any location.

Fortner's men placed all of their equipment in an office adjacent to the lab where Adi would start conducting her work. There were three other men on Fortner's team: Gunn, Mabrey, and Sims. Corporal Gunn was new to the team but came highly regarded. Lieutenant Mabrey had worked with John the longest. Sergeant Sims was recommended by Fortner's base commander, General Baskin. None of the men, including John, had a clue who Adilene Roth really was, or what work she was producing for Hersey. And none, especially Fortner, knew the extent of Higgins' involvement.

Lt. Mabrey said, saluting Fortner, "Captain, everything is ready. Corporal Gunn is running surveillance, and Sergeant Sims and I will patrol the level perimeter."

Adi returned to the lab with the deputy director and inquired about the test patients that were willing to participate in a paid medical test study. Two patients had volunteered and were prepped for analysis.

"Your test subjects are sisters suffering from advanced necrotizing fasciitis," the deputy director told Adi while handing her the patient's medical charts. "Unless you have any further questions, Dr. Roth, I must return to my office and see to the operations of this facility. Good luck."

Adi watched the director shake hands with John Fortner before exiting down the hallway. *Ma'am*, Adi thought. Adi had never been keen on being called ma'am. That title to her was for little old ladies getting their groceries bagged at the market.

The patients were twin sisters, around eighteen years of age, who contracted the flesh-eating bacteria by swimming in a contaminated portion of the Chattahoochee River just outside Atlanta. The oldest sister deemed Subject #1, was showing severe necrosis of their right leg. The younger sister, Subject #2, was in a much more serious condition as the bacteria had entered through her nasal cavity into the brain. Neither was responding to antibiotic treatment and jumped on the chance to try a 'new innovative' procedure, as they had been told by doctors, for a cure. They were brought into the lab in a medically induced coma.

Adi took biopsy samples from both sisters and began preparing vials for the blood and tissue to be combined with SAP-23.

Adi spoke to an attendant standing nearby. She administered SAP-23 and began to wait, "Should take about forty-five minutes to see if the solution neutralizes the bacteria and if any cell regeneration occurs."

Adi noticed John Fortner looking through the lab door window as if he was understanding what was happening, "He has blue eyes, interesting." Adi had never paid much attention to the blond-haired, blue-eyed campus superstar type, but there was no denying that John Fortner was a handsome man.

She approached the tubes labeled 'SAP-23/1 and SAP-23/2' extracted one drop of each and positioned them one on top of another under the microscope. There was a screen on the wall that projected the slides for the attendant to view while Adi worked through her observations.

"Cell structures were clearly still damaged but no signs of bacteria. I'll give it a few more minutes," Adi said.

SAP-23 had performed as it did with the mice and destroyed all traces of harmful bacteria but was not showing signs of cell regeneration, at least not yet.

Adi told the attendant as she made her way to the door, "Get me if anything changes in the next few minutes. I need a minute."

Fortner stood tall as Adi came into the hallway, "Everything alright, ma'am?"

"Look, if you must be here, please refer to me as Dr. Roth," Adi demanded.

"Roth, understood," John said, paused for about two seconds, then said, "...ma'am."

Adi rolled her eyes and shook her head with disgust as she removed herself to a nearby restroom to regroup. Her situation was stressful enough without this mountainous man getting in the way. Jake had not called or messaged yet, Hersey was being abnormally quiet and distant and she had only gotten to see her parents for a short while. She usually enjoyed being able to focus on her work. She just needed to clear her mind of everything, mountainous or otherwise, and get back to it.

*That guy probably sleeps with his pet bald eagle every night.*

Adi's mind ran away thinking about the absolute absurdity of a grown man coddling a bald eagle.

*I'm really losing it.*

She wet a paper towel, wiped it across the back of her neck, looked at herself straight on in the mirror, took a few deep breaths, then returned to the lab and immediately went back to observing the slides. She did notice that the attendant was no longer in the room but paid it little mind. She entered the lab and continued her analysis, "Okay, bacteria are still gone, and cells, wait, there are too many." SAP-23 for both specimen samples from the sisters had caused rapid exponential cellular mitosis. The new cells were flawless in appearance and were all functioning as expected. Adi pushed herself away from the table and jumped to her feet, "There are more cells than before. No signs of abnormality." Once again John Fortner peered into the lab intently. He was intrigued by what was taking place in the lab at the moment.

Adi phoned the deputy director, and he dispatched attendants to retrieve the sedated sisters for the night. She also informed him that tests would resume tomorrow morning. As she prepared to leave the lab, the fact that Jake had not made contact yet kept annoying her. This was very unusual for Jake.

As Roth left for the night Fortner asked, "When and what time can we expect you to return, ma'am?"

Adi snapped, "Look, Captain America, you can call me Dr. Roth, Ms. Roth, or even, crazy science lady, but if you call me ma'am one more damn time, I'm going to expose your whole team to a deadly biologic so powerful your eyes will explode out of your fat heads."

John Fortner was caught off-guard by the tone and violent delivery of Adi's threat. He was impressed, "Have a good evening, Ms. Roth," Captain Fortner said, stepping back from the car.


**Collect Call**

"Hello, Mr. Shirley," JJ asked as the call connected.

"Yeah, who is this?"

"Mr. Shirley, my name is Jeremiah Wilson of the National Weather Service, and I received your number from Barry Winters. Sir, I'm calling about your nephew."

"Stevie? What the hell does the weather channel need Stevie for? He didn't make a fool of himself talking on TV about all these damn tornados, did he?"

JJ was already losing his patience even though he had no reason to. People from the South had always taken a long time to ask the simplest questions.

"No, sir, I just need a number for Stevie. I need to talk to him about some work he completed for NASA. I want to talk about the tanks he built for the astronauts," JJ said.

"Yeah, he did build some of those I reckon."

JJ threw his hands up in the air and was just about to give up when Barry entered the conversation.

"Hey, Tim, it's Barry."

Barry ended the call and handed JJ a small piece of paper with a name and number on it. Winters had a way of making people feel comfortable and that had served him well in getting facts for his stories over the years. He was approaching his sixties and had been retired for almost five years but was having a hard time with life after work.

"Dr. Julie Reiser, NASA astrophysicist," JJ read aloud.

**Great Deception**

Dr. Hersey spent the rest of the morning making phone calls to multiple CDC offices in the eastern United States. The directors were informed that the new medication, SAP-23, had received rapid approval from the FDA and that President Richards was ready for distribution to hospitals and local health departments. This was all a fabrication by Hersey to release SAP-23. Thus, helping complete his promise of a lie to President Richards. Hersey was hoping that SAP-23 performed as seen with the mouse, but even if it failed, Adi would bear the blame.

Hersey told numerous health department directors, "Yes, hundreds of doses are en route. That's right, the injections only work with bacterial infections, no viruses."

"Higgins, make sure that our 'little helper' at the CDC is heavily compensated and be certain to report back to me any information from your Atlanta security team."

"Sir." Major Higgins left the room.

Before the SAP-23 tests, Adi's 'attendant' was contacted by Higgins prior to Roth's arrival at the CDC. She was promised ten thousand dollars for every vial of SAP-23 successfully extracted from the lab. The lady could not pass up the offer. She stole four hundred vials of SAP-23 (twenty individual doses in each vial) while Adi briefly stepped out of the lab. SAP-23 was currently en route to locations from Miami all the way to Boston. In less than three days, thousands of infected patients would receive injections. Hersey had kept his promise to the president but to what cost was unknown.

"Now, we wait," Hersey said out loud as he began switching through several news channels on multiple screens in his office of 'The Refuge'. Each covering headlines about President Richards and large storms battering the southeast.

He mulled maniacally over Adilene Roth, Jake Meyers, and President Richards. Hersey was a deeply reflective man. His mind was his personal hard drive of useful information he used for the next calculated move. He not only had perfect recall, but he could also visualize people, events, conversations, motives, and triggers as though pieces on a chessboard moving back and forth in order to achieve his desired outcome.

Hersey continued thinking aloud while powering off the screens, "If this works my dear, I'm not going to know what to do with you."

# 6. Emotional Decisions

## SAP-9

Jake returned to the patients the next day for further observations. Additional blood and tissue tests were needed in order to analyze how SAP-9 was interacting with the patients. All three patients were now talking amongst themselves and showed no signs of sickness. But unlike SAP-23, any major damage done to the organs or cells was not corrected. SAP-9 had saved the lives of the test subjects, but they still had a long road to full recovery.

"Okay, I guess I'm ready to make this call," Jake said.

"Mr. Meyers, tell me you have good news," Hersey answered.

"SAP-9 works sir, the patients you delivered to Camelot are all doing well. I feel that with a few more weeks of testing, I can provide better data for you to analyze," Jake said.

"I will send a plane for you soon, Mr. Meyers."

"What? I can't leave. I'm just getting started. Isn't this the reason you left me here?"

"You performed well, and now I need your expertise here," Hersey answered sharply.

"Virginia?"

Jake almost dropped the phone. He had never heard of anyone from Camelot, not even Adi, getting an invitation to Hersey's home.

"I want you in Elmendorf in two days' time. Bring every vial of SAP-9," Hersey commanded.

Jake sunk into his chair after the call, and it was at this very moment he knew something more was in play. He was worried about more people than just himself.

"Adi," he said aloud while picking up her guitar. "She has to know."


## Crashing the Party

JJ dialed the number for Dr. Reiser's office and was informed that she would not return until next week. Reiser was chosen as this year's commencement guest speaker at her alma mater University of Alabama Birmingham (UAB). Dr. Reiser was a renowned astrophysicist at Johnson Space Center located in Houston, Texas. Her work spanned the better of twenty years.

JJ turned to Barry Winters after speaking with Dr. Reiser's office, "We have to go there. I have to talk to her."

"Go where? Houston? That's all you kiddo."

"No, Birmingham," JJ said while emptying out an old backpack on his desk. "Graduation is tonight, and if we leave now, we can make it to Birmingham before she leaves."

"Graduation, Birmingham…JJ, NASA doesn't even have an office in Birmingham," Barry said.

"Dr. Reiser is in Birmingham at the UAB commencement Bar-ry!" JJ retorted saying Barry's name like squashing a bug. Hitting the first syllable hard and the second syllable even harder. JJ began stuffing old clothes and toiletries from his office into the pack, looking over at Barry every few seconds, waiting for Barry to start preparing his own bag.

"Look, JJ, I agree that some strange things are going on right now, but you really need to think hard before you crash a college graduation to hound some scientist. Are you absolutely sure this is what you want to do?"

"I just almost died trying to get footage of a tornado that just so happened to have aurora lights shooting out the top of it. So, yes. I'm doing this with or without you."

Barry stood, stretched his old back, and started out the office door. JJ zipped up his pack and followed. "I guess I'll see you when I get back," JJ ceded.

"Hold your horse, kiddo. I'm not letting you go to Birmingham and make a fool out of yourself. But first, we need a ride."

Barry walked into Jack Crowder's office and closed the door. After five minutes or so, Barry emerged with a set of keys. The two went to the garage and Barry clicked the remote to unlock a new weather chaser vehicle. The truck contained state-of-the-art storm tracking instruments and provided more safety features than the old van from before.

"How?" JJ asked.

"I appealed to Crowder's humanitarian side," Barry responded.

"What humanitarian side? That man is wound up tighter than a banjo string, and he hates me right now!" JJ scoffed.

"All I did was ask nicely," Barry said.

As the truck roared to life, JJ climbed in. Wearing his best-worst poker face, Barry put the storm chaser in reverse and began their hour and a half trip south.

"You know you are a terrible liar, right?" JJ said about two miles down the road.

Barry smirked and finally told JJ what he had really said to Jack Crowder. "Look kiddo, I told him that if he let us borrow another chaser, then you would pay for the van repairs with retro pay for all the other times you broke it."

"What! You dirty backstabbing…" JJ shook his head and turned away, cutting his eyes to the side rear view mirror just in time to catch a glimpse of the 363-foot-tall Saturn V moon rocket replica standing outside the U.S. Space and Rocket Center. He seethed angrily to himself, *I'd like to put Barry on that thing right now and shoot him to the moon!*

Then he thought of the German scientist's unadulterated focus on science in the midst of the world going to hell. These solar flares held so many possible detrimental ramifications for the planet. So, in one sigh, JJ released his anger and, in Van Braun fashion, decided to get on side with those who provided what he needed to chase the science. JJ laid his head back and shut his eyes.

The storm chaser entered UAB the campus at around two o'clock. Every parking lot was littered with newly crowned graduates and their families. Barry parked the truck near the stadium where graduation took place, and JJ ran through the open gates and onto the field. He quickly scanned for Dr. Reiser. Dr. Reiser was tall with dark curly hair and wore glasses. JJ noticed about a hundred women that fit that description, so he switched to a different method.

"Okay, Winters, let's look for the brightest peacock." Near the stage was a lady wearing a black robe with more tassels and different colored stripes than anyone else. "That has to be her." JJ ran to the stage and with barely any breath left, "Dr. Reiser from NASA, Julie Reiser?" JJ paused to catch his breath.

The woman looked oddly at JJ, "Yes, I'm Dr. Reiser. Who are you?"

The other school officials began to come toward JJ. "I work for the National Weather Service, and I need to talk to you about the solar flares. You and I both know something weird is going on, and I think it's just the tip of the iceberg." JJ paused again for another breath. "Something big is about to happen. Please, ten minutes."

"Ten minutes, Mr.?"

"Sorry, Jeremiah Wilson from the Huntsville National Weather Service, and this is my partner Barry Winters."

"Nice to meet you." A polite response edged in suspicion.

Barry was standing outside the van inspecting more of the vehicle's features and equipment.

JJ motioned toward the storm chaser. "Please, I'd like to show you something."

"Wait, I'm not getting into that truck with you guys. I've heard about this before."

JJ pleaded, "No, it's not like that. I swear. Just please watch one short video clip, and I swear you won't question our motives then."

JJ opened the rear door and began pulling up the most recent tornado footage.

"Okay, show me the clip, but you two, step back," Dr. Reiser agreed. The astrophysicist watched the clip, then watched it again, then paused it for a few seconds, and watched it once more. "It seems you have captured evidence of a solar event gentlemen," Dr. Reiser said finally.

"What about now, mister I've never seen an aurora borealis in Alabama?" JJ looked at Barry and smirked while nodding his head in agreement with Dr. Reiser clearly feeling vindicated.

Barry the investigator started to take over. He began rifling Dr. Reiser with questions. "Doctor, what could have caused this? Do you expect there will be more?"

"My office has noticed an uptick of solar events since the beginning of spring. As for how many more there will be, who can tell?" Reiser continued, "I personally believe that an extreme coronal mass ejection is likely to occur soon."

"EMP possibility?" JJ asked.

"Sure, if the event is large enough, say…the Carrington Event."

JJ stopped Barry before he could even ask the question, "Remember the Texas thing I told you about? That was the Carrington Event. It fried all the telegraph lines and electrocuted a lot of people." Barry made a funny face while nodding sarcastically.

"We track solar winds and flares from my office every day, and normally we have plenty of time to determine if they will cause disturbances in the electromagnetic field of Earth," Reiser informed them. "However, an event as large as the Carrington storm would be absolutely devastating if it occurred today."

"Millions without power, public water and hospital infrastructures disabled, flight interferences. Not to mention the chaos it would reign on the financial sector. Anything that requires electricity to function would be crippled if not destroyed." Reiser paused thoughtfully then instructed JJ, "I would continue tracking large storm formations and follow them. Especially those containing large quantities of lightning as massive bolts can interact with Earth's magnetic field."

Instinctively, JJ's eyes sought out the radar monitors projecting inside the storm chaser. Even as Dr. Reiser had been speaking, he'd noticed a large group of storms beginning to form over the Gulf of Mexico. "Dr. Reiser, how much time of warning could you give if an event that had EMP capabilities was imminent?" JJ asked.

"In most cases, around eight minutes. Why?"

JJ closed the truck door. "I'm going to give you my number, and if the big one hits, you call me."

Reiser nodded her agreement.

"Thank you for your time and insight, Dr. Resiner, and especially for showing my friend here that I'm not crazy." JJ shot Barry a look.

As they climbed into the truck, Dr. Reiser approached JJ's door, "Listen, you're not wrong. You're on to more than you or even I understand right now. The sun has been behaving strangely of late. Be ready."

JJ reached his arm out of the window and shook Dr. Reiser's hand, "Thank you."

Dr. Reiser phoned her office about the footage from JJ before making her way back into the stadium.

"That was fast! We're heading back to the office already! She was willing to talk to us kiddo, as long as we wanted," Barry beamed.

"Not the office, I-20 east," JJ corrected, "We're going to Atlanta."

The astrophysicist struggled to focus on the commencement ceremony. What future were these graduates really walking into? What would this campus be in the face of such a solar storm? Forget the campus, what of the country?

Indeed, what would the impact of such an electromagnetic field disturbance have on the human body? Just as she began to really spiral, the sound of bagpipes reverberating off of the arena walls, a UAB tradition, brought her back to the moment. She smiled, clapped, and pretended for the next few hours that the world wasn't on the brink of chaos.

## Merging Effects

Adi left her parent's home early the next morning and headed for the CDC center. And just like the previous morning, John Fortner met Adi near the basement entrance and escorted her to the lab.

"Coffee, Ms. Roth?"

Adi said while entering the lab, "No, Captain, I have much to do this morning." There wasn't an attendant today, but the twin sister test subjects were still present and sedated. "Now let's check those samples again." Adi approached the additional blood and tissue samples she'd taken the previous day. All were the same. Success. There were no infections, and cellular growth was beyond what Adi had hoped for. Adi thought while staring at the subjects, *I can't. It's too soon.* As much as Adi wanted to conduct more tests, she also was curious about the results if she were to administer SAP-23 to the young women. Curious but not confident. Not yet. *One day,* she thought, *I just can't.*

Adi went to the door and asked John Fortner if he had noticed anyone go into or leave the lab before she arrived this morning. "Negative, Ms. Roth, you are the only person that has entered the lab," Fortner replied.

*Interesting*, Adi thought. She felt that something was off but could not place a finger on what it may be. Adi spent the next few hours analyzing the samples and observing the subjects. She thought about Hersey and the mice at Camelot, but mostly she wondered what Jake was up to.

"Ms. Roth, phone for you, says his name is Dr. Jake Meyers," Fortner said.

Adi took the call from her office beside the lab, "Jake, are you okay? Is everything okay?"

Jake took a few seconds to respond, "I think so, Hersey has had me working on…on stuff here, then I got a call that he's bringing me to 'The Refuge'."

"Hersey's Refuge?"

"Yeah, I know it's crazy, right?" Jake said.

Adi became enraged, "You mean, I've been here worrying about you being alone in Alaska, and now you are going to meet Hersey at his house!"

"Going behind my back again I see. Old habits must be hard to break, huh, Meyers?"

"No, that's not it at all." He understood why Adi was mad, and that upset him even more than what Hersey had made him do. Jake genuinely wanted to tell Adi about the SAP-9 tests and how Hersey threatened him to stay quiet, but instead a lukewarm warning left his mouth, "Look, just be careful, okay? Don't trust Hersey."

Adi erupted, "Oh! Now you have the audacity to tell me who I can trust?" Adi's loudness and words caused enough concern for John Fortner to enter the office. "I hope Hersey keeps you at 'The Refuge' because I don't want to see your face when I get back." Adi slammed the phone onto the desk and hadn't even noticed Fortner had entered the room. "Great, now you," she scoffed. "I swear if you say something stupid to me right now…"

"No, I heard the commotion, and I came to check on you, Ms. Roth."

"And this Meyers, boyfriend?" Fortner asked.

Adi rolled her eyes as she pushed past Fortner and back into the lab. Jake's words pushed Adi over the edge. Unlike any time before, Adi let her personal emotions elicit a physical response that overruled her ethical rationale. "Fine, I'll show you working on stuff," Adi said while preparing two syringes of SAP-23. She was so angry that she overlooked the missing samples the attendant had stolen the day before. Adi injected the sisters and immediately regretted her decision. "Oh no, what have I done?" Adi stormed out of the lab and into the parking garage. John Fortner and Echo Team was hot on her heels.

"Ms. Roth, what is the threat? How can we assist you?" Fortner asked. John motioned his hands to the team, and they dispersed in what seemed like all directions. Adi was completely broken. She crumpled to the parking deck and began sobbing profusely.

"That's it. I'm returning you home, Ms. Roth," John said.

Adi pleaded, "You can't. I have to go back!"

"Inform the deputy director to send someone to monitor the patients," Fortner said.

Lt. Mabrey came close to the window and John said, "Stay alert, I think there may be more going on here than we know."

"Make sure to keep eyes on anyone who goes in or out of this level," John concluded.

"Sir," Lt. Mabrey said proudly, and Echo Team reentered the lab.

The car pulled into the Roth's driveway a few minutes later. John escorted a crying Adi into the home and placed her on the nearest couch. Dean and Ethel came running into the living room where Adi was. "What happened, Adilene?" Dean asked.

"Who are you?" Ethel asked, walking toward John, "What happened to my daughter?"

"Ma'am, sir, my name is Captain John Fortner, Army Ranger. I have been assigned to watch over Ms. Roth as she conducts her work at the CDC," John said.

Adi stopped sobbing, stood, and left for the restroom to compose herself. "I knew her work was killing her inside," Ethel said to Dean, "That place is nothing but evil."

"Now, we don't even know what's going on yet, Ethel," said Dean. He motioned for John to sit. "Do you know what Adi was so upset about because I've never seen her like this before?"

"Mr. Roth, all I know is that she received a phone call from a Dr. Meyers, mentioned something about 'The Refuge', and then became irate," John replied.

"Hersey," Adi said, startling the others. "Dr. Hersey has Jake up to something. I can feel it." Ethel stood and went to the kitchen for water as she began coughing profusely.

"Mom," Adi said to Dean, "Is she alright?"

Dean stood and followed Ethel turning to say, "Doctor says she's developing pneumonia. Doctors caught it early though, so no need to worry." While Dean and Ethel were in the kitchen, Adi sat across from John and thanked him, "I appreciate what you did for me back there. I've never lost control like that before." Adi was alluding to the SAP-23 injections, but John thought she was talking about her collapsing.

"It's alright, Ms. Roth, emotions are powerful and can overwhelm you if you let them."

"Thank you for stating the obvious, Captain," Adi shot back, shaking her head. "What planet are you from? Do you even know how to talk to an intelligent woman?"

John's face turned red, "Please forgive me. I'm used to helping soldiers refocus for battle, not usually female scientists dealing in experimental medicine."

Adi noticed the slight and was secretly pleased with herself for getting to him a little.

"Are you married? Any little Captain Americas?"

Now John was really turning red, from embarrassment, "No ma'…Ms. Roth."

Adi smiled and, for a moment, sensed some underlying charm inside John Fortner. He really was helping Adi remain calm.

Dean and Ethel returned to the living room with water for Adi and Fortner. "So, what now?" Dean asked. "Are you done or done, done at that place now?" "Are you okay, Mom?" Adi asked, completely ignoring her dad. Then Dean's words struck Adi, "That place…oh no, the sisters." Adi jumped to her feet, "We have to go back right now."

"Ms. Roth, I'm not sure…"

"Now Fortner, and I'm not asking," Adi commanded.

Dean and Ethel both looked at each other with blank faces. John stood and thanked the Roths.

As Fortner and Adi went for the front door, Adi stopped and told her mom to go to the doctor and make sure to take care of herself.


John Fortner took one hand off of the wheel to answer his phone.

"Sir, you need to get back here now! There's a lot of commotion in the lab," Lt. Mabrey exclaimed.

John whipped into the parking garage and, before the car had completely stopped, Adi jumped out and ran for the lab. The deputy director was there with a handful of attendants. The sisters were wide awake and thrashing about in their beds. They would pause every so often to speak. Sister #1 kept saying, "Cold," while sister #2 kept repeating, "Hurts."

Adi was thrilled that the sisters had come to and were still alive. However, she was terrified by their words and the way they were speaking. "What is happening to them?" the director asked.

Adi paused and told the attendants to conduct a full body scan for signs of infection. Adi moved quickly to #1 and pulled the sheets back to expose her infected leg. The infection was gone. The leg looked normal. "Scan #2 first,"

Adi said, turning toward the director. "I don't know yet," Adi confessed while drawing blood samples from #1.

"Where were you, Dr. Roth?" the director asked. "This is a completely unacceptable practice. I will not have unattended test subjects left in my lab."

John Fortner interrupted, "Sir, you need to exit and let Ms. Roth conduct her business."

"You don't tell me what to do, Captain! These are my labs, and I'll ask any question I wish!"

"Sir, I'm going to ask you once more to exit the lab before I remove you myself," John said.

"Dr. Hersey will hear of this. You better believe it, Ms. Roth!" The director turned toward Fortner before leaving the lab, "And as for you, the sooner you and your boy scouts are gone, the better."

Fortner looked at Adi and grinned. Adi returned his with a quick smile of his own and then turned back to sister #1. Fortner escorted the director out of the lab.

"Absolutely remarkable," said one of the new attendants, going over the printout of results for #2.

"Let me guess. No bacteria found in the brain?" Adi asked. "Is the brain showing signs of regenerative mitosis?"

The attendant asked, stepping back from the table, "How did you know?"

"SAP-23, that's what it does or what I had hoped it would do," Adi said, taking the results. The two sisters were mildly sedated again and remained in the lab for a few more minutes, so Adi could observe their physical behavior. She began what she would often do at times like this, reflect.

"Okay, SAP-23 worked flawlessly. Sisters showed sporadic behavior just as 628 and 629 did. They spoke in a weird pattern and then returned to normal." Adi switched her focus from the sisters to the housing container for SAP-23 as she continued reflecting, "Bacteria have been eliminated and cellular regenerative properties are exponential like with the tissue samples."

Adi concluded, "It works. We're going to need a lot more." Adi approached to check her supply of SAP-23. She had brought close to one thousand vials of the solution with her when she had left Camelot.

Her equipment and formulas needed to prepare new batches were left in Alaska. She opened the door and saw the empty spaces where the four vials were used on the sisters, then looked on the bottom row and saw the empty spaces for vials 600-1000. Adi's face went ghost white and she began to panic. "They're gone…gone."

Fortner entered the lab again. "Ms. Roth…wha—"

Adi interrupted Fortner, "The vials, they're missing. I don't see them."

Fortner was becoming irritated as he did not know the situation or what the problem was. Fortner turned to Lt. Mabrey, "Get Sergeant Sims on the comms. I want to know everything that has happened in this lab since we arrived."

"Sir, did you see those girls?" Mabrey asked. "Whatever that was, it wasn't normal."

"I don't know, Lt., but I'm going to find out," Fortner said. Fortner reentered the lab to find Adi frantically recounting the remaining vials of SAP-23. John came beside her and slowly closed the door to the container. Adi almost snapped again, but she stopped herself and looked deep into Fortner's eyes before speaking.

"Thank you for helping me, Captain," Adi said.

"Ms. Roth, my team is going over all of the camera recordings now. We should know soon if anyone took the vials. Are you sure you brought 1000 vials?" John paused then bluntly asked, "What exactly are you missing vials of? I know important intel when I see it, and you are mixed up in something more than you are letting on."

Adi took a deep breath and let it all out, "Synthetic Antimicrobial Proliferation variant 23. It's a chemical compound I developed along with Dr. Jacob Meyers at a secret compound called Camelot near Anchorage, Alaska. It destroys infectious diseases and causes the damaged cells to regenerate. You getting all of this so far, Captain?"

John Fortner had never been so astonished as he was at that moment in his life. He felt insignificant compared to what Adi explained to him. He was understanding but was having a hard time believing.

Adi continued, "Dr. William Hersey, or the boss of your guy Higgins, hired me here at the Atlanta CDC years ago. He later built the installation in Alaska, and I've been there ever since. Then out of nowhere, I'm giving a presentation on SAP-23 to Generals, NSA personnel, and the Secretary of State. I cured a mouse and Hersey sent me here for human trials."

"So, let me guess, this Dr. Hersey guy is giving you little choice in the matter," John said, crossing his large arms.

"I have not had a say in the matter in a long time, Captain, and I'm very tired of it."

Fortner asked Adi, "And Dr. Meyers, you don't trust him anymore?"

"No, I do. It's just, well, he can be impulsive and sometimes only thinks about himself. I know he would never hurt me, but I also think he's in more danger than he knows."

John sat quietly taking in and processing all the information. His mind worked like an old but reliable mechanical computer. This mindset had served him well in combat and when dealing with difficult individuals. He was careful at the onset, but once he made his mind up on something, John Fortner was an unstoppable force. The matter would be done.

"Sir, we got something," Lt. Mabrey called over the comms.

John and Adi rushed into the surveillance room. "Show me," John said. Sergeant Sims turned a laptop toward everyone in the room and played a short clip of surveillance footage. Adi saw herself leave the lab with Captain Fortner following close behind. The attendant during Adi's first day at CDC was seen opening the lab door carrying a briefcase. Minutes later, she came back out of the lab still carrying the briefcase. The lady was caught on camera looking back and forth down the hallway before exiting toward the garage elevator. She never returned.

Adi angrily turned to Fortner. "If you hadn't followed me to the bathroom, I'd still have my vials," she snapped. The other men, including Fortner, turned to her and stared. Adi was way out of line.

"Look… sorry... but I need to find out where that woman took my vials."

"Clip number two for your viewing pleasure," Sergeant Sims said as he pressed play.

A black SUV like the one Adi had seen at Camelot approached the woman just outside the garage. The woman entered the vehicle and disappeared.

"Stop right there," Adi said, pointing at the screen. "I saw this man with Dr. Hersey two days ago in Alaska."

"You saw that man two days ago?" John asked.

"Yes, I'm sure of it," Adi replied while starting to shake.

John Fortner quickly stood knocking his chair back. "They work for Higgins."

Adi's eyes became large, and she could barely speak, "Hersey, what have you done?"

# 7. Harbinger

**Wildfire**

William Hersey awakened from a terrible nightmare just before dawn. He grabbed a nearby glass of water and drank profusely. Hersey was not easily troubled by mental fabrications, but this dream had shaken him to the core. He replayed the images once again.

*In his dream, he saw a raging fire consuming all that came in contact with the flames. The heat was intense and the scope of the fire spread as far as Hersey could see. In the shadows of the flames, he saw silhouettes of people, but could not see their faces nor could he hear them. Above the fire, a dark void, and below, a mirror presenting Hersey's downcast head. The reflecting Hersey slowly raised his head exposing black, hollow eyes.*

The doctor came to his feet out of the bed and began pacing the room trying to rationalize what he had dreamed. The sun was beginning to rise on, what should be, the most important day of Hersey's life. President Richards would be nominating Hersey as his vice presidential running mate during a speech at his campaign headquarters near Washington. Hersey went to the nearest window and took many deep breaths while also examining the perimeter of 'The Refuge'. He worked to organize his thoughts and compose himself. "The absurdity," he said aloud to himself. "Dreams are for the weak-minded." He paused then continued, "To think I should become enthralled in such phantasms." Hersey finally rationalized the dream as his subconscious figuratively portraying ambition. The wildfire was his undeniable thirst for advancement, while the people needed Hersey's leadership. His reflection was a test to see if he thought himself ready for the next phase.

Health departments and hospitals had already begun administering SAP-23 to severely infected patients all along the eastern United States with tremendous results. Patients were healing within minutes of the inoculations. SAP-23, although medical professionals knew the solution as Antimicrobial Designation 1, was deemed a wonder treatment, a modern miracle of science. Hersey renamed the drug AD1 as a patronizing tribute to its creator.

The President was getting reports that AD1 was performing beyond anything the professional community had ever seen. Richards was beyond pleased to see that the morning news reports were showing an uptick in his approval ratings.

Richards had met with Hersey the night before his dream and told him to prepare his estate for a vice-presidential campaign. "I don't know how you did this, Bill, but I'm glad you did."

"You better get ready for a wild ride because politics aren't won over in a lab," Richards said as he chuckled.

Hersey could not help but see the irony of that statement as this had been precisely the case. "Thank you, sir, I will do my best."

"I know you will. Just be ready tomorrow night."

"Of course, Tim will take it as a hit, but he's getting on up there in age and doesn't really need the stress of the vice presidency anymore," Richards said standing to his feet. Tim Harding was the president's current VP but was not tagged by Richards as his choice for running mate. The President had caved to party pressure and went along as it gave him the best chance of winning the party nomination. Tim Harding up to this point had been a lame-duck VP, and everyone, including Richards, knew it.

"I know you're not a man of many words Bill, but I'd have a speech ready. Also, people are going to have a thousand questions for you, so you better be ready for that too," Richards concluded.


**Houseguest**

Jake boarded the plane with a much different feel than he had when meeting with Hersey before. The prestige of flying like a millionaire on a private jet had lost some of its appeal. Jake carried Adi's guitar and placed it in the seat next to him and sat back into the plush leather seat. "Not a scratch, I swear," Jake said, taking a brief moment to eye the old Strat. Jake never was into music much until he met Adi. He would listen to her play old blues and country when time allowed for it at Camelot. Jake was more of a 'TOOL' man himself, but he tried to respect different types of music.

One of Higgins' men entered the cabin where Jake was located. "We loaded all the crates you designated. Are you sure this is everything Dr. Hersey asked for?"

"Yes, that's everything."

Thousands of vials of SAP-9 were being loaded onto the plane. Jake thought about leaving samples behind but decided against that as he did not want to take the chance of any SAP-9 vials falling into the wrong hands. Jake figured, as long as I'm with the vials, I can keep them safe and secure.

"How long until we leave? No chance I could get my phone back either eh?" Jake asked. As soon as Higgins' men arrived with Jake, they took his cell and all other electronic devices. Jake would be in the technological dark until arriving at 'The Refuge'.

Once the plane lifted off, Jake began to anticipate what lay in store for him at Hersey's compound. He wasn't exactly sure how concerned he should be for his own wellbeing but was definitely disturbed by what Hersey planned to do with SAP-9. The human trials at Camelot had produced the desired results. The patients all recovered but still needed time for analysis. Jake did not have enough time to test for the negative effects experienced with animals. Jake and Hersey both knew that it was a matter of time before the solution began attacking the white blood cells of the test subjects. How long until that may be, he had no way to tell without staying and monitoring the subjects.

Jake had a couple of theories about Hersey's plans. His first theory was that Hersey intended to compare the effects of SAP-9 with SAP-23 to determine which of the two variants he could profit from the most. This would make sense as Hersey was clearly accustomed to having plenty of money. He could further his professional reputation by finding a new powerful drug for mass production.

*There has to be more than just money at play here this time though*, Jake thought. The second theory, and most plausible, was to keep Adi and Jake separated but busy enough to take concerned eyes away from Dr. Hersey. *Hersey is doing something that he doesn't want either Adi or myself to be around to see. What can it be and why wouldn't he just leave me in Alaska? I mean, that would put me way out of the picture from everybody. Unless–* Jake's mind suddenly illuminated with an extraordinarily evil epiphany. He felt confident he had deciphered Hersey's plot. "I know what you want, sneaky weasel."

Hersey was going to conduct a mass implementation of SAP-9 and cure it with Adi's SAP-23 as the latter would regenerate white blood cells. Adi would have never tried SAP-9 on people under any circumstance. By sending her to Atlanta and making an appeal to Jake, Hersey had created a way to have his cake and eat it too. Even though Hersey was playing a diabolical hand, Jake knew he still had time to throw a wrench into the distribution of SAP-9. *All I have to do is make sure every vial is destroyed and Hersey has no plan,* Jake thought to himself while trying the cabin door.

*Unlocked. Sweet, now I just have to find where these goons are holding my serum.*

Jake entered the next compartment of the plane. There were containers of food, various drinks, and many seats, but no one was present. He went to the bathroom and checked the door. "Empty," he observed aloud.

*Okay, it's going to be in the very back of the plane*, Jake thought. He came to another cabin, but the door was locked. *Great… I could use some James Bond right about now. The best I am is a bootlegged version without the gadgets… or the moves,* Jake thought eying the door.

He decided. *Well, let's try the last thing Higgins' men would expect.* Jake began knocking on the door. No answer. He knocked louder but still no response.

*Well, if I'm going to be stupid then I might as well go for the gold.* Jake approached the door once more and raised his right leg reading to kick it open. He threw all his might forward as he lowered his leg. Just before making contact, he felt a sharp cold blow to the back of his head. Jake collapsed to the floor unconscious. One of Higgins' men barked the orders, "Tie his hands and feet then put him back in his cabin. We only have a couple hours left until we reach Virginia. Jekyll can deal with him then."


## Contingency Plan

Adi began dialing the only number she had for Dr. Hersey. Echo Team connected her phone through a recorder so that every word of every detail could be saved as evidence.

"Ms. Roth, you still have almost a week left on our deal. Don't tell me you are abandoning your research so soon," Hersey said.

"What did you do with my serum, Hersey?"

"My dear I've done nothing. However, you have done so much since returning to the CDC, haven't you?"

Fortner began pacing behind Adi clenching his fist and his jaws sounded like grinding cement. "The deputy director told me you left two patients all alone in the lab with no supervision, which means you left all of that untested, unrefined biological solution unattended, correct?" Hersey continued, "Just imagine the implications if a volatile biologic made its way into the civilian population, Ms. Roth. It would be catastrophic."

Hersey was playing a heavy card by using Adi's obedience to her job and sense of responsibility as leverage. Hersey was not worried about SAP-23 getting out into public circulation, as he had already achieved that plan. He was using Adi against herself, and it was working to perfection.

Adi could feel the scale tipping in Hersey's favor and even with so much damning evidence, Dr. Hersey was a step ahead.

"I don't care what you have to say, you sick son of a b– ," Adi seethed.

"I know you stole my vials of SAP-23, and you're going to tell me where they are, now!" Adi began shaking again like before in the parking garage. John Fortner took the phone from Adi and said, "This is Captain John Fortner. I don't know the history of you two, but if you have taken CDC property from this building, you will be held accountable."

"Ah yes, the security. Captain, I believe you also work for me so do your job and secure Ms. Roth for transport," Hersey commanded.

"Transport? She's not going anywhere, and neither am I," John snapped back feeling his blood rise. "We know your informant stole the vials. We have her on camera, and we also have known associates working with Major Tom Higgins driving her away with the evidence."

"Captain, I am ordering you to apprehend Ms. Roth and bring her to Dobbins AFB at once. I will make sure she makes it safely back to her home in Alaska," Hersey said, trying to lighten the tone.

"I work for the United States Army and was directed to this assignment by my base commander. I work for no one else," Fortner snapped back.

"Who do you think told the commander to send you there?" Hersey asked, as a sardonic laugh left his lips. One couldn't help but be entertained by the irony of their situation. The chess master was enjoying himself.

John suddenly thought about Higgins and the assignment that came out of the blue. He had no idea all of them were connected. John had not spoken with

Higgins in years but had little trust for the Major and his men. As for Hersey, Fortner had no clue who this man even was until meeting Adi. John had been fooled into an assignment simply for Higgins' enjoyment of having control over him.

"Now that you understand the lay of the field, Captain, I'm ordering you to hand Dr. Roth over immediately," Hersey said, hashing his tone once again.

The tension between the doctor and John Fortner reached a fever pitch as John responded one final time, "Dr. Roth is staying with me until I feel she is safe. As for you, I'll see that *you* answer for *all* of this."

Hersey answered, "Fine, have it your way, Captain, kidnapping and holding a hostage against their will is a serious offense last time I checked."

John Fortner looked at Sergeant Sims, "Did you get all of that, Sergeant?" Lt. Mabrey interrupted before Sims could answer, "Sir, there isn't anything on that tape that we can use against Dr. Hersey." John reluctantly knew the Lt. was right about not having any evidence that could be traced back directly to Hersey.

While Echo Team continued to brainstorm the next course of action, Adi was still sitting with a helpless look on her face. Dr. Hersey had literally stolen her life's work. Adi did not know what to do. She could not stay at the CDC as she knew Hersey would send Higgins for her, and she also knew Alaska was now off limits now, too.

Then Adi thought about her parents and hesitated. *My parents. He wouldn't, would he?* She was afraid to even think it. Dr. Hersey had never threatened hostility toward Adi or anyone she could remember, but he had become different ever since the presentation at Camelot.

Even before Camelot, Hersey was particular and calculating, but this was different. "I can only imagine what he'll do when he finds me," she said to Fortner.

"You don't have to worry about that, Ms. Roth. Okay, this is what we're going to do. Echo Team, pack everything up for evac in ten." John turned to Adi, "Ms. Roth, I hate to ask this of you and your family, but we need to regroup at your parent's house until I can make contact with my commander at Fort Benning." Adi was secretly relieved as this gave her parents extra security as well.

"Ten minutes, people," Fortner said, as he opened the office door.

Adi returned to the lab and began packing the remaining vials of SAP-23. The twin sisters had been taken to another lab for observation, but Adi could not help but want to find them and check on them one last time. After packing the last of the SAP-23 vials, she went to the elevator and told John, "I need five minutes, just five minutes."

"You have three," John said while carrying two enormous bags over to the exit door.


**The Rookie**

Dr. Hersey opened the door to the armoire and ran his hand across several jackets before stopping midway, pulling a dark blue peak lapel suit and laying it on the bed. In a matter of a few short hours, Dr. William Joseph Hersey would be standing alongside President Richards as his official running mate. The matter with Adi would have to wait until the morning. *Once I have Jake Meyers on site, she will come too.*

Higgins knocked on the door. "Enter," Hersey commanded. "Shouldn't Dr. Meyers be here by now, Major?"

"More storms, sir, like the one in Alaska. My team has encountered turbulence over Wyoming but should be here safely in a few hours. Sir, I have reports that Dr. Meyers was caught wandering the plane and had to be *reseated*."

Hersey paused, tilted his head, and peered over at Higgins. "He will be cognizant and able to communicate upon arrival, Major? Is this your definition of arriving safely?"

Higgins did not get Hersey's sarcasm and replied, "Uh, yes, sir, he should be fine, maybe a slight headache."

Normally Hersey showed great patience with Major Higgins, but this act of sheer barbarism had irritated the doctor and Higgins knew Jekyll was not pleased. "How about you instructing your men about not striking a scientist with a vastly superior brain when compared to theirs…yours…in the head," Hersey said, while placing Italian leather shoes beside the suit.

"Sorry sir, it won't happen again. I'll personally deliver Dr. Meyers to your quarters once they have arrived."

"No, I have other business in need of your attention," Hersey explained. "Unfortunately, Ms. Roth has discovered the missing vials your team brought to me and has video evidence of the getaway vehicle." Hersey gave Higgins a look of disdain that shook the Major to his core. Higgins after many years of service, saw himself as Dr. Hersey's adopted father figure of sorts and hated failing assignments directed by Hersey.

"It seems that the very man you sent to keep Ms. Roth has taken the job literally. He says he will not hand her over," Hersey goaded.

Higgins immediately responded, "Are you in danger, sir?"

Hersey turned and faced Higgins with a look of confusion. "In less than three hours, I will be with the most powerful man on Earth. I have no one to fear. But you may very well be, as those were your men driving away with CDC biological property." Higgins' face went white, for he too was now on the chopping block for Hersey. Hersey was threatening the Major, and once again, just like with Adi, he was a step ahead.

"How do we fix this sir? What should we do?"

Hersey laughed loudly, "We. There's no we, Major." Major Higgins was a fly with a string tied around its hind legs. There was nothing for him to do but hope Dr. Hersey had already planned the next course of action. Which, of course, he had. "Major, I want you to find and bring Adilene Roth to me." Hersey continued, "Make sure you bring the remaining vials of SAP-23, I mean AD1, to me as well."

Higgins nodded before asking one more question, "What about Captain Fortner and his team?"

"That is for you to decide Major. You chose him, so I'll let you deal with him. Now leave me. The Secret Service will be here shortly," Hersey concluded, closing the door in Higgins' face.

Henry came to Dr. Hersey's door at six o'clock and informed him that Secret Service members were waiting outside. Hersey felt kingly as he headed down a long spiral staircase and into the unmarked SUVs waiting outside. "Evening sir, the President will meet you behind the stage once we've arrived."

"Excellent, gentlemen. Thank you," Hersey replied. Hersey enjoyed every moment of the forty-five-minute drive. He was ready to further his legacy beyond that of a person of science and medicine. He wanted more. The ride through Washington D.C. only strengthened his resolve of belonging as he passed by the Jefferson and Lincoln Memorials. Those were great men. They believed in *rising above any challenge*, Hersey thought to himself. Dr. Hersey honestly could not tell anyone his true reason for wanting to become Vice-President, not even Frank Richards.

Hersey could think of no other way to bolster his already prestigious status than to enter another realm of power. Fate had provided another opportunity as it did so many years ago with Richards' sister. It did bother him that, once again, it was only because of Frank Richards that he was reaching new levels of prominence.

Rarely did doubt enter his mind, but it did this night. *You are better than that man in every way, yet you are under his shadow.* This thought was soon replaced, incinerated by his mind as a failsafe for negativity, by the dream from the morning. He saw his reflection against the window of the SUV and remembered the way his own eyes glared into his soul from the nightmare. Dr. Hersey was reaching an entirely new level of personal awareness. Dr. Hersey felt unstoppable.

The SUV pulled into an underground entrance to the campaign headquarters just outside downtown Washington at a convention center. The President took an incredible risk before his first election by joining the newly formed Patriot Party. The Patriot Party pledged to fight the medical problems plaguing America and won by a surprising margin. Winning the election also forced all other parties to support Richard so as not to look bad in the case he succeeded with campaign promises. Dr. Hersey was making that initial promise a reality since the distribution of AD1 along the east coast the past two days. Renewed hope from the American people was spreading like wildfire.

Dr. Hersey entered a small but heavily guarded area behind a large stage.

"Bill, good to see you. Hopefully, the secret service went easy on you," the President greeted as he approached from the opposite end of the stage. Hersey remained silent.

"I've got to find out who your tailor is. That suit is exquisite. Well, you definitely look the part, so let's see if you can sound like it," Frank Richards chuckled as he slapped Dr. Hersey on the shoulder.

Hersey broke his silence and asked Tim Harding, "Sir, how did the talk with Vice-President Harding go?"

"Tim took the news well, saying he's going to move to Montana and write memoirs and go fishing."

"Honestly, that doesn't sound too bad does it, Bill?"

"No sir, quite peaceful."

"Just remember to follow my lead. It's better to say too little than too much Bill. These damn media are packs of hyenas always looking for the kill."

Dr. Hersey's pep-talk to himself had not alleviated the anxiety building inside of him. To make matters worse, Secretary of State Renner was already on the stage speaking to high-ranking contributors of the Patriot Party. Before leaving 'The Refuge', Henry mocked up a speech for Dr. Hersey. Hersey in his own right, was a good public speaker. However, normally he only spoke on matters in which he was the expert. Today he was the rookie.

A loud voice began booming out to the crowd, "Ladies and gentlemen, The President of the United States of America." Frank Richards entered the stage waving and smiling effortlessly. Speaking to crowds had become second nature to him. Dr. Hersey walked purposely behind Richards managing a subtle smile and an awkward wave. As he passed Secretary Renner, she narrowed both eyes and stared a hole through Hersey's skull. Renner was still no fan of Hersey, even with the apparent success of AD1.

"Fellow Americans and members of the Patriot Party, allow me to announce my bid for reelection tonight in front of you all." The crowd went ballistic. There were shouts of well-wishers and flashes from numerous media cameras. The President took a long pause before he spoke again. The crowd was molten metal, liquid gold, malleable, and ready to be shaped. Frank Richards began his speech.


*Three years ago, I stood before you a man with one goal in mind. Safety and prosperity for all Americans. Our great nation was staggering under the burden of the illnesses plaguing its citizens.*

*Citizens, like you, I know the pain of having to watch loved ones battle illness, but I, like America, always persevere. I will never tire of making America safer and more secure.*

*I now ask for an opportunity to see the job done for four more years as President. I believe the best is yet to come for America, but we all have to work together as one people, one nation.*

*Now, it is with great pleasure that I present to you my new running mate for vice president. He is a renowned scientist, head of the Center for Disease Control, my current chief medical advisor, and he is the reason America is experiencing this recent rebirth of hope, Dr. William Hersey.*

Frank Richards' words were electric. The crowd continued to shout and people began screaming, "Four more, four more, four more." Dr. Hersey was envious of how the President spoke so eloquently and powerfully. Now, it was his turn to capture the hearts of the American people.

He held the note Henry had constructed for him in his left hand but quickly decided to take the reins and stuffed it back into his blazer pocket. Hersey approached the podium and began.


*Thank you, Mr. President. I am pleased to be here tonight as more than a scientist or a doctor. Tonight, I am a normal citizen just like you all. My goals are to support President Richards in any way I can and to help America remain healthy and strong. Thank you.*


Dr. Hersey's attempt to connect with the people was not completely lost, but not as strong as he would have liked either. The President had been right about his previous comments at 'The Refuge', "Politics aren't made in a lab."

"It gets easier each time you do it Bill," Frank Richards said backstage. The President's chief of staff approached, "Sir, ratings are through the roof! You knocked them dead tonight."

Richards said laughing, "See, Bill, everything's fine. Go home and get some rest because you only have to do this about a hundred more times."

As the two men concluded their conversation, a piercing voice came from behind Dr. Hersey, "Leaving so soon, Doctor? *Normal* citizens normally wait until the President has left before hightailing it back home."

The President said smiling at Renner, "Maggie's been telling me great things about what she saw in Alaska. I'm glad I sent her."

"Yes sir. In fact, you should accompany me next time, Mr. President," Renner said.

Frank Richards looked at Hersey and asked, "How about it Bill? Why don't we go check on your baby? Last time I checked, Alaska has votes too."

Hersey's mind immediately switched to Jake Meyers and Adilene Roth. Under no circumstance was Dr. Hersey going anywhere without apprehending Roth first. Hersey's mind searched frantically for the words to appease both Richards and Renner while saving face. "Sir, you and Secretary Renner should indeed take the trip to my installation. I will have a full executive tour waiting upon your arrival."

Renner interrupted, "Will there be another show like before Dr. Hersey? I think The President would love to see your miracle drug firsthand."

"Yeah, that sounds perfect Maggie," Richards responded. Hersey had no choice but to agree to the terms. President Richards and Madam Secretary Renner would visit Camelot expecting another exhibition like the one before. As Hersey exited, following behind the secret service escort, he heard Maggie Renner's voice float through the corridor, "I'll be in touch soon, Jekyll." With this, she turned on her heel and exited in the opposite direction.

Dr. Hersey spoke not a word for the duration of the ride back to 'The Refuge'. He returned to his chambers still pondering the logistics of how to make everything happen exactly the way it needed to. Dr. Hersey was staring out into the night sky above the fountain when he heard a knock at his chamber door. "Yes," Hersey answered.

Higgins entered the room, "Sir, Dr. Meyers is in his room on the first floor."

"Leave him there until the morning," Hersey said. "He's not going anywhere. Oh, and Major, please make sure Dr. Meyers has plenty of aspirin. I need him in a talking mood tomorrow morning," Hersey smirked, turning once again to peer out over the grounds.

The dream from earlier that morning still drove deeply into Hersey's psyche. *A fire can be better controlled when planned ahead for,* he thought. No doubt, he would have to plan his next series of events carefully to conceal certain matters. Just as he had done so many times before, he methodically rationalized his problems by order of urgency.

"First, Roth, then Meyers, and lastly Renner. All three have Camelot and SAP in common," the doctor murmured to himself, still relishing in the sanitary isolation of his balcony in the cold night air, a perfect place to let loose his intellect as he considered his next move.

In the distance, he could hear the sounds of coyotes yelping as if nearing a kill. The eerie sound chilled the bones of most, but it empowered William Hersey, like electrical energy surging through his spine. His eyes narrowed as his plan slid into focus. Hersey closed the balcony door and smiled once again, "I know exactly how to handle them all."

# 8. Convergence

## The Ride

"Look at the sky, Barry. This is wild, man!" JJ said while moving to the back of the storm chaser. A large storm system continued moving at breakneck speed in a crescent-shaped path up from the Gulf of Mexico. JJ monitored the radar and instruments and calculated that the most severe portion of the storm should impact Atlanta soon. The sky grew darker with the same eerie yellowish hue as the category 5 tornado encountered in Huntsville. Barry was showing much less interest in the storm. He was on the phone with his wife Alice of thirty-two years. She was visiting her sisters in Mobile and called Barry to inform him that she was visiting a doctor in the morning due to abdominal pains.

"You just take care of yourself and explain everything to the doctor, dear," Barry said, placing both hands on the wheel of the massive truck. "I'm sure it's just a stomach bug or something, so keep me in the loop and call as soon as you get out of your appointment tomorrow."

Barry Winters loved his wife. She had spent the majority of her life observing her husband leaving early countless times and getting home late. Barry was no different with his work. There was never an off switch. "Okay, love you too, take care…I will. We are completely safe," Barry ended the call. Alice was not comfortable with Barry accompanying JJ during his storm escapades but enjoyed seeing him happy. JJ was providing further purpose for Winters, and she was alright with that.

JJ turned from the radar screen placing his hands on the back of the front passenger seat to pull himself closer to Barry, "Alice?"

"Just a stomach bug or something. She's sure it's nothing," Barry replied.

JJ smiled, "Yeah, you're right about one thing. She'll be fine. She can survive anything after living with your ornery ass for all these years." The two men shared a brief laugh, but due to the current climate of America with sickness, Barry was secretly worried about his wife.

Barry needed to change trains of thought, so he asked JJ about the fast-approaching storm, "Well, what do you think? Any more solar hiccups detected yet?"

"Not yet, but the lightning strikes are incredible near the center of this system."

"It looks more like a hurricane, Barry, which should be practically impossible," JJ said, returning to the screens near the back of the storm chaser. Hurricane season was a couple of months away but all signs of the instruments pointed to a tropical anomaly. The storm chaser entered Georgia at nine eight o'clock and it was almost dark. The rain continued to intensify.

"Okay, we have about an hour or so until we can set up a base of operations and find a good vantage point from which to observe the storm," JJ told Barry, "I'm going to try and take a nap, so wake me once we've arrived in Atlanta."


## Something Strange

Adi exited the elevator onto the floor above her research lab. She passed various attendants entering and exiting multiple rooms as she continued down the hall to a large lab with patient beds. Adi approached the window and saw the two sisters with sister #1 thrashing about again. Adi paused to check for anyone before entering the lab. The room had a different feeling about it. The air was thick and contained a smell Adi had never experienced before. At about five feet from #1's bed, she stopped and observed. The sister calmed herself and looked deep into Adi's brown eyes. Adi spoke, "I know you're cold."

Adi's senses had become hyper-focused just like with the mouse during the first SAP-23 test. She asked, "How do you feel otherwise? Yes, I tried to help both of you." The sister looked relieved and uneasy at the same time. Sister #2 remained still and motionless. Her breathing was labored, but she was calm.

"When can I leave? What about my sister?" #1 asked.

Adi went around to #2's bed. Adi placed her hand near the injection site and analyzed the area. Sister #2 was exhibiting skin discoloration around where the shot had been administered. Adi heard people talking as they passed by the lab, and she looked up in fear still of the deputy director returning.

Adi knew she had to go but was going to push the time limit given by Fortner to the max. Adi went back to #1 and pulled the sheet back exposing her once-infected leg. The leg was black as coal. "Oh my god," Adi said, loud enough for #1 to hear.

"What? What is it? My leg…what's wrong?" The young woman's leg was disgustedly swollen, and the veins were protruding out from the flesh.

Adi placed her hand on the leg. It was beyond hot to the touch. "How?" Adi ran to a nearby cabinet and grabbed a few empty syringes. She returned to the sisters and almost dropped the needles as the door to the lab swung open.

"Do you have a watch, Ms. Roth?" John Fortner said. "We are leaving. Now!"

"No, not yet. Something's not right." Fortner was trying his best to remain calm with Adi but knew time was their current biggest threat. He had seen it so many times before during combat. Hesitation equates to people dying. "Look," Adi said, pointing to the leg.

Fortner approached the leg and frowned a face of disgust. "You did that," Fortner said to Adi, stepping back.

The sister bellowed again, "Cold."

Adi turned to the sister, "What is cold? You are burning up, so tell me what is cold?"

John was no stranger to the effects of certain biological weapons as he had witnessed the effects of many exposures before. "Is this a weapon, Ms. Roth? What exactly are you making here?"

Adi ignored the questions and began drawing blood into the syringes. The woman continued to thrash, stopping only to repeat the word cold. Sister #2 remained silent and motionless. Fortner grabbed Adi's arm before she could extract the blood sample, "Tell me what this is. I need to know."

Adi gave Fortner an intense stare. "Let go of my arm, Captain," Adi demanded, keeping her fingers on the needle. Fortner turned from Adi and started for the lab door.

"If you are coming with us, you have until we reach the parking garage." Fortner left the room for the elevator.

Adi returned to the samples. She finished drawing two vials of blood from sister #1, and then just before inserting the syringe into sister #2, the lab went dark. Alarms cried out from all directions. The emergency ambient lights came on, partially illuminating the lab. Before she could turn toward the sisters, Adi heard it, "Hurts." Adi's heart dropped.

## Lights Out

(Eight minutes earlier)

Barry parked the storm chaser atop the highest parking deck he could find.

"Wake up, kiddo. It looks like the storm beat us here."

Most of the city lay dark with blotches of lights popping up across Atlanta as emergency generators began to come online. JJ rose from the truck floor and opened the back doors stretching out to look over the city.

"What happened here?" JJ asked, walking over to the edge of the parking deck and looking down.

"Guess the storm knocked out most of the power shortly before we got here," Barry reasoned.

Both men immediately looked up into the sky for more traces of lights but saw nothing.

"This feels different than before, Barry. I don't think it has anything to do with solar flares."

JJ Wilson was right with the assumption. Atlanta's power grid was greatly in need of updating due to recent growth in population and industry. Electrical surge from lightning had caused similar events such as the one JJ and Barry were observing. Nevertheless, they began setting up measuring equipment and readied every camera they had.

The two sat for what felt like an eternity when JJ's phone rang, startling both men. "Mr. Wilson, this is Dr. Julie Reiser."

"My team has just informed me of an enormous pooling of plasma on the sun's surface, so it seems you may get your coronal mass ejection," Reiser said in a firm matter-of-fact tone.

"What should I do?" JJ asked.

"Nothing, if your hypothesis is correct, you may be able to capture footage of another possible aurora."

"EMP possibility?" JJ asked once again.

"Who can say at this point. It depends on the amount of solar radiation thrown Earth's way. I will not be able to help more until I reach my office tomorrow. I can tell you whatever it is, it far supersedes the size of what you experienced before," Dr. Reiser concluded.

"Okay, got it. Thank you," JJ said, ending the call.

Barry continued looking out into the sky. The storm was regrouping and beginning to intensify. JJ looked at Barry, "This is it, Barry, the big one." Barry let out a short laugh as this was what JJ said every time they chased a storm.

"Okay, kiddo, but as soon as this storm blows past, I'm heading home." More power began returning to the city, and the two men retreated back inside the storm chaser with cameras positioned in open windows. Hundreds of millions of miles away, the sun angrily expelled trillions of tons of radioactive plasma particles toward Earth. Eight minutes until impact. Eight minutes until lights out.

## 1st Contact

Adi picked herself up off the floor and tried to reorient her eyes. The dark red lights provided little illumination for seeing, and the sounding alarms caused her ears to throb and ache. She picked up the syringes still warm with #1's blood, and that's when she first saw it. The sisters looked at each other and #2 screamed again, "Hurts," as she began whipping her arms under the restraints. They began to loosen. Sister #1 replied, "Cold," and started to free herself as well.

Adi slowly approached the sisters speaking to #2, "Are you okay? Tell me what hurts." Sister #2 went still and sat up, breaking the other arm restraint. Adi could see her eyes. They were black like a doll's. It was as if the pupil had consumed the entire eye leaving behind no traces of white. Saliva was pouring out of her mouth, and blood began dripping from her nose. Adi did not even notice how close she was standing to sister #1 until she felt a strong pull on her lab coat and quickly fell out of it. Sister #1 began tearing and gnawing at the coat. Her leg was oozing blood from burst veins. The blood began to drip down the side of her bed and onto the floor. The smell was horrendous. Adi ran to sister #2 and injected the syringe deep into her right foot.

"Hurts," the woman bellowed once again deep from within.

"Cold," #1 replied as if responding to her sister.

Adi ripped the needle out of the foot falling backward and scattering all the syringes across the lab floor. #2 ripped her leg restraints free, jumping to her feet. She immediately went to her twin sister and freed her as well. Adi crawled backward toward the lab door, finding only two of the syringes in the process. Both sisters reached for each other's faces and then turned in unison toward

Adi. The blood and looks of their eyes contorted her mind and heart. She couldn't believe the sight before her. She'd been trying to help the women.

The sisters tossed aside everything in their paths with ease and walked slowly toward Adi. They were silent now. The room went dark but for a second as the power was restored to the facility. What little Adi saw in the red hues was compounded tenfold as she saw the sisters in good lighting. The blood continued to fall from their bodies, their eyes lifeless yet fixed on Adi. Every fiber in Adi's body was stricken with fear. She froze in horror.

Sister number #1 reached for Adi's feet, pulling her away from the door. Sister #2 let out one more scream then everything went silent. Adi was in such shock she hadn't heard the sound of John Fortner's massive hand cannon. Sister #2's head was gone. Her body fell to the floor lifeless. #1 released Adi and came for Fortner as he eliminated her too.

"Get up! Now!" John said to Adi. Adi came to her feet and frantically rushed to the elevator. Fortner observed the lifeless bodies, once again picking up the vials of blood Adi had drawn, then dropped before the attack. He entered the elevator with Adi, and they made their way to the garage.

"What the hell is going on here?" Fortner demanded.

Adi, full of shock, just stared.

"Sir, I'm hearing reports of shots fired on the comms," Lt. Mabrey said to Fortner as he and Adi came out the garage security doors. Fortner clutched Adi's arm in one hand and two vials of fresh blood in the other.

"We're leaving. Now!" Fortner said. All five individuals entered the SUV, and before they could pull away from the garage, another alarm, different in sound than before, rang out. "Go right," Fortner commanded. "Where to, Captain?" Lt. Mabrey asked, pulling out into traffic.

Fortner began giving him Adi's parents' address. She stopped him mid-sentence, "No, go north. I know a place we can go." Adi was referring to her father's cabin in the mountains. The cabin was about a two-hour drive north east of Atlanta near the gorge Dean took Adi to as a child. The traffic in Atlanta was notoriously bad on good days, so on a day like today it was a nightmare. The SUV came to a red light near one of the busiest intersections in downtown. While the team waited for the light change, Fortner looked at Adi and spoke very slowly, "Those women were not well. They looked possessed."

"I'm going to ask you again. What exactly are you working on?"

Adi looked at Fortner with tears still in her eyes, "I told you it's a chemical compound that is supposed to help people."

"Like you helped those two young girls back there," Fortner replied with disgust.

"You…you killed them. You killed them both," Adi said.

"Whatever happened to those girls was already killing them."

"I've seen death, and they had it written all over their faces," Fortner said. The rest of the Echo Team gave each other inquisitive looks, but no one spoke.

Adi continued, "I did notice where I injected the serum looked different than before, like nothing I've ever seen."

"The blood was oozing out of the veins and nose, and the smell was horrible," Adi paused again, becoming physically ill once more. Fortner was still unsatisfied with the conversation with Adi but suppressed himself from asking further questions about the matter until they were out of the city.

"Sir, you have to hear this," Sergeant Sims said, turning the volume up on the radio.

*Dr. Adilene Roth, age 32 and Johnathan Fortner age 38, are wanted for murder and domestic terrorism. Roth is 5'5", 135 pounds with brown hair and green eyes. Johnathan Fortner is 6'4", 250 pounds, with blue eyes and black hair. The police urge anyone that has seen the suspects to call law enforcement immediately as they are considered armed and dangerous. Do not approach the individuals. Call 911 if you have any information as to their whereabouts.*

Everyone in the SUV turned and looked at each other without speaking as everything once again went dark.

**The Big One**

The rain poured so heavily that it came down sideways as the wind blew at gale force.

Lightning illuminated the city for a few seconds at a time. JJ checked the cameras, then the radar, and then the cameras once more. "Barry, do you see anything?"

"Rain, kiddo, lots of rain," Winters responded.

JJ smirked at Barry then the storm chaser began to sputter. The equipment started the same flickering patterns as the van had done earlier in the week. JJ looked down at his watch. The second hand was not moving. JJ tried his cell phone, but nothing. Barry wore an old Rolex he inherited from his father. The watch was better than fifty years old but still worked flawlessly. JJ asked Barry, "What time is it? How long has it been since I talked to Dr. Reiser?"

Barry responded, "I'd say, about ten minutes ago, maybe."

JJ was about to ask another question, but the wind and rain suddenly stopped. JJ opened the storm chaser's doors and exited the truck. "Do you feel that, Barry?" The air grew colder, and then everything went completely dark. The wind began to blow violently again. And in the distance, lightning partially illuminated two massive tornadoes. JJ ran back into the truck. Barry threw his hands behind the wheel and looked at JJ. "Dead, just like last time." JJ and Barry started arguing about everything not working and the cameras being off. Lightning continued flashing across the sky as the tornadoes fast approached downtown Atlanta.

Car horns and people shouting could be heard in all directions. There were sounds of glass breaking and loud booms echoing around the city. Atlanta was in complete chaos. Most people ran into the closest building, while others stood in the streets looking at the aurora filling the night sky.

"Who is shining that light our way?" Barry asked.

"Somebody's out there," JJ observed. "It must be a flashlight or something."

The men were not viewing a flashlight, or any other man-made light for that matter. The coronal mass ejection struck heavily, distorting the magnetic field of Earth. The solar event caused an EMP to be felt hundreds of miles away in all directions. Most modern electronics were created to rebound from an EMP attack, but the initial impact of encountering the electromagnetic waves renders them useless.

"Green, Barry, it's green," JJ exclaimed. JJ was referring to the lights covering the night sky. The lights became bright enough to see most of the city, including the tornadoes still en route to their location. JJ was elated that his theory was true, and he wished he could speak with Dr. Reiser, who he was sure was watching the events from wherever she currently was.

"The truck isn't starting this time," Barry cried above the storm. "We have to go lower. We have to get underneath for protection."

"Okay, okay, let's go," JJ said, grabbing his pack. The two men ran into the nearest door with stairs leading down to the safer levels below. After descending another five levels of the parking deck, JJ and Barry stopped to rest and reassess the situation. The tornadoes began pounding the city. JJ and Barry looked with mesmerized horror at the tornadoes moving swiftly through the city wedged between the magnificent green sky above and the dark earth below.

**Change of Plans**

Echo team and Adi looked out from the window of their SUV. Vehicles gridlocked the roads, and nobody was going anywhere anytime soon. Even without the effects of the current EMP, traffic would not allow for travel due to the storm and tornadoes. Fortner looked across the road and saw a concrete structure. He pointed ahead while turning to Adi, "Alright, on me. We make for that building."

Adi tied her shoelaces tight and prepared for running. People were frantically running by the SUV. A few people even ran into the SUV as they tried to find safety from the storm. "Sir, all equipment is down," Lt. Mabrey said.

"I know it is Lt. Looks like we've encountered an EMP, but I am unsure of the cause or severity."

Corporal Gunn, who had remained silent for most of the mission up to this point, looked at Captain Fortner and broke his silence to ask, "Sir, is this the end of the world?"

"Corporal, focus. All you need to worry about is getting to that building," Fortner said, throwing open his door. "Everybody stay together and follow my lead."

"Ms. Roth, you stay between us," Lt. Mabrey said.

The short run across the two lanes felt like an intro to an apocalyptic survival video game. The team pushed past numerous people running and staring up at the sky. They maneuvered around stranded cars until finally reaching the entrance to the ground floor of a parking deck. "Here," Fortner said, pointing to the stairwell. Everyone made their way up.

The tornadoes were right on top of Atlanta by this time. The green lights still shone across the night sky, but the tornadoes blocked the view of most of the city.

"Keep going," Fortner said, pointing to the next level. After climbing two more floors, Fortner stopped everyone; he heard voices closely above.

Fortner threw his right hand up. The team stopped, and everyone was completely silent and motionless. The captain ascended one final flight of stairs and turned the corner to observe two men holding the fifth-floor parking deck door open, observing the storm. Before Fortner could speak, Barry Winters turned, and JJ let out a startling yell. Echo Team and Adie converged on the scream.

## Unlikely Band

"Who the hell are you guys, security? We haven't done anything," JJ shouted.

"No, not security, just trying to get out of the storm," Fortner said, extending his hand to shake JJ's, "Captain John Fortner, Army Ranger, and this is Echo Team."

"Um, she doesn't look like an Army Ranger," JJ said, nodding toward Adi. "Never mind her; who are you two?" Fortner asked.

"Excuse me," Adi said, turning to Fortner as she walked past Echo Team. "What do you mean, never mind me? I may be on the verge of having a nervous breakdown, but no one, not even you, Uncle Sam, speaks for me."

Barry and JJ gave each other a funny look as if reading the other's mind. *What has this storm gotten us into now?*

Before anyone else could say a word, a tornado crossed over the top of the parking deck; the train-like sound was deafening. Everyone covered their ears as Barry pulled the garage door close. The structure was more than sufficient for withstanding the natural disaster, so Adi continued where she left off. "Dr. Adilene Roth, Atlanta…I mean Alaska CDC."

"Doctor of?" JJ asked.

Adi said, looking at John Fortner, with a proud stance, "Microbiology, biochemistry, and molecular biology."

Barry laughed and slapped JJ on the back. "Well, all we have here is a washed-up reporter, Barry Winters," he said, pointing at himself, then JJ, "and soon-to-be out-of-a-job meteorologist, Jeremiah Wilson."

JJ pretended to ignore Barry, held up his dead device, and asked, "You guys wouldn't happen to have a phone that wasn't fried?"

"Negative. An apparent EMP attack has rendered them useless," Fortner said.

JJ looked at Barry again, "You hear this guy? Look, Captain, right? You're correct about the EMP part, but it isn't an attack unless the military had the sun on a hit list or something." JJ paused, then said, "You guys aren't planning on blowing up the sun, are you?"

Mabrey entered the conversation and asked, "Are you saying the sun did all this? The storms, the green lights in the sky?"

"Precisely," JJ responded.

Mabrey pulled Fortner aside and whispered, "Captain, we must get out of here now. I don't know how long we can wait before they start looking for you and Dr. Roth."

Adi went and sat beside Barry, "You look tired. Do you need anything?"

Barry looked at Adi with kind eyes and a gentle smile, "No, kiddo, I'm fine, Thanks for asking."

Adi turned her attention toward JJ and began a line of inquisition regarding the sun being the cause of the EMP. "You're talking about a CME, aren't you, Mr. Wilson?" Adi said, looking through a small window in the door out at the wavy green lights.

"Oh, let me guess. You minored in astrophysics too?" JJ asked sarcastically.

Adi shot JJ a dirty look.

JJ immediately apologized to Adi, "I'm sorry, that was uncalled for. It's just been a very long day."

"You have no idea," Adi said. "My dad has only watched three channels his entire life: History, Discovery, and Outdoor. I used to get caught up in all of those conspiracy theories about the end of times, space dangers, and hidden treasure."

JJ said, laughing, "Well, some of those are true."

What seemed like a long time had, in fact, only been around thirty minutes since escaping the lab, and the events of the night were beginning to wear on Adi. Fortner finished his private conversation with Lt. Mabrey and decided that now was a good time to find transportation to leave the city before power returned. The tornadoes were long gone now, but their destruction was not. Generators were, once again, powering some structures throughout the city. Sounds of sirens and horns continued to fill the night, and Fortner knew it was only a matter of time until either authorities or Hersey would be after Adi.

"It's time to go, Ms. Roth," Fortner said, standing with Echo Team.

"Where, how are we going to get up there? We don't have a ride now."

Fortner replied to Adi, "Just give it a few minutes, and the cars will be fine."

"It would take a tactical nuke to cause enough disturbances to fry everything permanently."

For some reason, as if he were the EMP expert in the room, everyone looked at JJ.

"Hey, we don't mind dropping you guys off somewhere if needed," JJ began walking up the stairs with Barry.

Adi glanced at Fortner, for the first time, with the same idea. Echo Team and Adi could not return to the SUV as law enforcement would already be looking for it by now.

They needed a new ride and couldn't afford to turn down JJ's offer. Everyone reached the top of the parking deck, and saw that only about a third of the city was still experiencing outages. It was impossible not to hear responder sirens now. Emergency service vehicles raced around the city. Barry looked at JJ and announced, "Well, that's a good sign."

Adi and Fortner both looked at each other with extremely concerned faces. Barry said, climbing into the driver's seat, "Let's try it."

JJ noticed the headlights coming on and knew the storm chaser would start. It did. The truck V8 engine roared to life, and everyone climbed in.

"Where to, gang?" Barry asked. "Back to Alaska, Dr.?" he added, looking into the rearview mirror.

Adi tried to display a little charm as she answered Winters, "Well, it depends on how much gas you have in this thing." Barry smiled and began down the parking garage.

"North, drive north," Fortner said.

JJ responded, "North it is, as long as it's not too far north." There was a brief period of awkward silence as the truck pulled out from under the last floor of the parking deck. There were accidents on every street. Some people had even begun looting stores, and there were hundreds of others still staring at the sky while holding their cell phones up into the air. Fortner reached into his pocket and brought out his phone. It flickered for a moment, then powered on.

Fortner turned to Sergeant Sims, "Sims, check comms."

"Everything is operational, sir. We are back online," Sims said.

JJ turned on the radio to listen for updates. He clicked through a few until he found one for the Atlanta local news. An announcement aired on one of the channels, leaving everyone speechless.

*Authorities are enacting a mandatory curfew until 6 a.m. tomorrow. Please refrain from going outdoors until then. If you have an emergency, please dial 911.*

Adi and Fortner both hoped the storm had created a distraction, buying them enough time to escape the city. The news announcement continued.

*Law enforcement is still searching for Adilene Roth and John Fortner, both wanted for murder. Their last known location was the Atlanta CDC. The individuals are considered armed and dangerous. Do not confront them. Call 911.*

Barry raised his eyes to the rearview mirror and stared at Adi, Fortner, and his team but continued driving north. JJ, on the other hand, was dumbstruck. He turned to Adi, "Murder!"

"Barry, stop the truck. Stop the truck," JJ told Winters. Barry pulled into a side alley and turned the truck off. Adi tried to explain some of the situation but to no avail. JJ, unhinged about the news announcement, started mumbling wildly to himself.

"Murder…wanted."

"Murder, murder."

"Call 911."

He paused, looked at Barry, and said, "Barry, we have to call 911."

John Fortner kneeled between the front seats, "Listen, both of you, we are not murderers because this is all just a big misunderstanding."

Adi called out to JJ and Barry from the back of the truck, "Please, listen, JJ. We're not lying. Please, trust us." Barry remained silent, never taking his hands off the wheel. He began thinking about Alice and worse-case scenarios of how this situation could play out.

"I don't have time to explain what happened. I don't think, even I fully understand what happened, but I can't let you call the police," John said calmly. "Do you understand?"

Barry finally spoke, "JJ, let them go. We don't need this. I have to make it home to Alice. She isn't well."

Adi approached the front of the truck pulling Fortner back. She began to feel deep remorse for Barry, "Is Alice your wife or daughter?"

"Wife," Winters responded.

"Barry, I've dedicated my entire life to trying to help people who aren't well. Please help us, and I promise we will make sure you get back to Alice."

JJ looked at Barry, "Are you seriously considering this, like, really?" Watching Barry express concern for his wife brought out all the empathy Adi had left within her. Her mind flashed back to Camelot again, Meyers, and her parents. *My parents*, Adi thought.

The possibility of anything happening to her parents was more than she could bear.

"This must be exactly how Barry feels about his wife, Alice," Adi contemplated. The gravity of even thinking the worst for Dean and Ethel caused Adi to fall with her head into the seat of the storm chaser. Ethel Roth filled every synapse of her head; every happy memory, every argument, every sad moment, and every fight. She began to sob, telling herself out loud for everyone to hear, "I'm sorry, Mom. It's all my fault. You were right about everything! So many people have suffered because of me!"

Everyone in the truck felt her brokenness and couldn't help but have compassion on Adi for the torment she was enduring. There was no faking pain like that. Her realness and conviction had swayed JJ and Barry into giving her the benefit of the doubt, for now, at least.

JJ tapped Adi on the shoulder, "Look, I don't know what happened to you guys, but if you promise not to kill us, we'll take you to your parents." Barry shook his head and started the truck. JJ never really learned to read the room, and this mistake usually resulted in him making a fool of himself.

The storm chaser left the alley as Adi gave the directions to Dean and Ethel's home. Adi was only thinking about her parents right now. Adi needed to know with certainty her mom and dad were unharmed by the storm, and then she would worry about having to explain the entourage invading their house. Adi looked out the rear windows of the truck, gazing at the wild scene of flashing lights, fast-moving clouds, and people moving about. The remnants from the storm lingered as drizzle and scattered flashes of lightning could be seen and felt around the city. The green aurora was fading with every approaching minute.

Fortner sat silently, pulling his sidearm out of its holster and staring at the splatters of dark, human blood around the muzzle. "I've never seen anything like that in my life," John said quietly, wiping the semi-dried blood blotches off the barrel. Fortner turned to Adi, pulling her attention from the events outside the truck, and said, "We need to talk about what that was back in the lab."

Before Adi could squeeze out a single word, Barry pulled the storm chaser into a narrow driveway.

The address on the porch read 3282. "This it?" Barry asked.

Adi kept her eyes on Fortner as she opened the rear door and replied, "Yes, this is it." There were no lights on in the home. Adi took her key and unlocked the door. Now came the most inconvenient situation of the day, explaining everything to Dean and Ethel Roth.

Adi went into the kitchen and saw the faint lighting of several small candles. Adi continued down the hall and knocked on her parent's door. No one answered, so she immediately returned to the living room. She heard multiple voices talking loudly.

"Adi, what is going on here? Who are all these men?" Dean and Ethel had reemerged from the basement, confronting the gang filling their den.

"It's okay, Dad, they're all with me, and we needed a place to go after the storm."

Dean rubbed his forehead, "All of them needed a place to go?"

Ethel remembered Captain Fortner and turned to Dean, "Of course, your friends can stay the night here, sweetie."

Adi approached her father and grabbed his right hand, "I'll explain everything in the morning, but right now, we are all extremely worn out and need rest."

JJ looked at Barry and said to everyone, "Well, I guess we should be moving on. We got a long ride back to, well, we really should be going."

Adi immediately replied, "You two should also rest, at least, until daybreak comes, and traveling is less dangerous."

"Thanks for the hospitality, but I think it's best we get going," JJ said, and motioned his head toward the door at Barry.

"No, we insist," Fortner said.

Dean caught a feeling that something more was going on here but remained silent. His years of interrogating people and exposing them in lies heightened his sense of knowing when something was wrong. Ethel returned with a stack of blankets and pillows.

"Barry, are you really going to say nothing?" JJ asked, losing his temper.

Barry had been texting his wife this entire time and was blocking out everyone else. He received a single message from Alice, "Feeling a little better, still going to the doctor in the morning. Take care, love you." Barry placed the phone into his coat pocket and said, "I'll take a blanket, and y'all mind if I commandeer that couch?"

JJ threw his hands up, "Fine, but soon as the sun is up, we're gone."

Everyone found a place and eventually settled. Dean and Ethel retired to their bedroom. Only Adi and Fortner remained awake and alert. A much needed and overdue conversation with John had been put on hold since the events from the lab. Adi and John sat in the kitchen examining each other. Neither spoke for what seemed like a lifetime. Fortner placed a hand on the table and turned it over, revealing the contents remaining in his palm. Fortner allowed two vials of blood to roll gently out on the table and said, "Tell me everything."

Adi took a deep breath and let it all out. She told John about Camelot, the mice test subjects, the exhibition with the panel, and Hersey. Adi explained why Hersey brought her back to the Atlanta CDC and about SAP-23 being rushed to human trials by Dr. Hersey due to his political ambitions. Adi told Fortner everything. "You think I'm evil, don't you?" Adi said, staring at the vials.

"No, but I think this is all coming back on you unless we can prove Hersey made you conduct illegal tests on those sisters."

"You don't get it, do you?" Adi said irritably. "Hersey has thousands of doses of SAP-23 now. If he has already distributed them, more of what we saw tonight may be out there."

Adi fixed her eyes on the vials and continued, "Hersey took the SAP-23 vials two days ago. Meaning that in a few short hours, anyone who has received an injection might develop into whatever the sisters became."

Fortner's flexed arms began stretching his sleeves to the brink of tearing as he responded, "In the morning, I have to call my commander and try to explain all of this, and I don't know how that call will turn out. In the meantime, nobody leaves this house."

"I suggest you get some sleep, while you can because I have a feeling that things are about to get a lot worse," Fortner said, standing and returning to Echo Team.

Adi remained at the table, holding the vials of blood in her hand. She pulled a third vial out of her front pocket and showcased them against the light from the candles. The light illuminated the dark blood into a semi-transparent solution. "Whatever happened to those girls is in this blood," Adi said, growing drowsy. Adi put her head on the table and, before drifting off to sleep, murmured, "I can fix this."

# 9. Conversations Kill

## The Talk

Before daybreak at 'The Refuge', Hersey emerged from his chambers and descended down the long spiral staircase to the first level. One of Higgins' men sat beside an ornate wooden door with a beautiful wood carving inlay. The man saw Hersey approaching and stood to attention.

Dr. Meyers was lying in a bed adorning the same clothes as he had on the flight from Alaska. Hersey grabbed a nearby chair. It made a harsh screeching sound as he dragged it across the floor, stopping next to Meyers. Hersey sat, never saying a word, and waited. Dr. Meyers must have felt the hole being bored through his skull because he swiftly turned toward Hersey and sat up. "How long have I been here?" Jake knew where he was but had lost all notion of time after sustaining the blunt-force trauma to his head.

"A few hours now, Dr. Meyers."

"I know what you're planning, Hersey," Jake said, sitting up against the back of the couch.

"Really? Please enlighten me then. You have my curiosity," Hersey said, sternly yet somehow retaining a cheerful tone.

Jake lightly rubbed the back of his aching head for a moment before the words trickled out, "I know you want SAP-9 to infect everyone."

"Please continue," Hersey encouraged. That was never Hersey's plan, but he enjoyed humoring Meyers.

"I know the only reason Adi is in Atlanta is so you can use SAP-23 to cure everyone after you infect them with SAP-9." Jake's words were beginning to come out strong now. He was more confident as he regained focus. "You separated us, hoping we couldn't figure all of this out."

"Interesting hypothesis, Doctor, but if I wanted to keep an eye on you two, I would have brought both of you here together," Hersey responded leaning forward in his chair. "First, allow me to say, you are wrong. Next, I don't need you, Dr. Meyers. You need me to help save your friend, Ms. Roth."

The shock on Jake's face was apparent to Hersey. Jake remained silent on the couch, contemplating Hersey's last statement. "What's wrong with Adi?" Jake asked. "Is she alright?"

"It seems Ms. Roth decided to distribute an untested, unproven medical compound to various health departments to speed up her trials," Hersey responded.

"Bullshit," Meyers said, standing up from the couch. "Adi would never inject SAP-23 into anyone without conducting tests first."

"As a matter of fact, it was me who told her we should speed up trials back in Alaska," Jake said. He had known Adi for months now. Not once had she ever conducted any experiment or trial without proper preparation. At this moment, Jake made it apparent that he had no idea what Hersey was up to.

"Is it too hard to think Ms. Roth felt SAP-23 was ready for human injection?" Hersey asked.

Now Jake started to become confused with Adi's motive for returning home. *She did tell me that she had to go and for me to stay,* Jake pondered, turning away from Hersey as if the doctor could read his thoughts by looking into his eyes. *Maybe she wanted to distribute SAP-23 before I could get results from SAP-9...but how would she know what I was doing? Unless...*Jake blurted out the words without even knowing he had opened his mouth, "Adi is working with you." Jake repeated louder so Hersey could hear, "Adi is working with you, isn't she?"

Hersey smiled as if to signify Jake had cracked the code and sorted the matter out. The fact was that Hersey had no idea what he would say or how he would react to Dr. Meyers upon arrival at 'The Refuge'. Hersey's only plan was to allow Jake to manipulate his own perceptions with conspiracy theories and what-ifs. Hersey just provided the final push over the edge. Dr. Hersey knew Jake could now be controlled, with no further need to threaten. As long as Hersey could preserve the lie of Adi going rogue, Meyers would not try to contact her.

"Well done, Dr. Meyers," Hersey said, clapping his hands sarcastically. "However, I believe it is an unfair case of judgment for you to say I am associated with the actions of Ms. Roth." Jake returned to the couch and listened intently to every word spoken. The idea of Adi circumventing Jake to distribute SAP-23 was inconceivable, at least, until the seed of doubt was planted well enough by Hersey.

"How many times did Ms. Roth worry about funding?"

"How many times was money the reason for the many disputes and stress between you two?"

*How*? Jake thought. *How could he know these things?*

Hersey was, in fact, taking strong liberties in hopes of being correct, which he was. Meyers had just dug his own mental grave, and now, what would have been impossible a few short days ago, had become a reality. Jake Meyers trusted Hersey more than Adi.

Jake stood again and asked, "So now what?"

"I want to show you around the grounds, Dr. Meyers. Henry will get you some clean and acceptable clothing."

"Afterwards we will discuss your next course of action over lunch." Hersey opened the door and motioned for Jake to enter the foyer as Henry hurried down the stairs. "Henry, show Dr. Meyers to the lower suite and send for clothing from my personal tailor," Hersey said, ascending the steps.

Hersey reached the second floor and looked down at Jake and Henry, "Whatever you need, Dr. Meyers, please ask Henry." Henry showed Jake to a massive suite and took his measurements.

Jake took a shower and crawled into the large canopied bed. He planned to sleep until his new clothes arrived. The last few minutes were a blur. Jake, still with a mild headache, wondered if the conversation had happened at all.

Dr. Hersey returned to his chambers and began cackling with delight. Although in a few minutes, laughter would never be so far from his mind again. SAP-23 would make sure of that.


**Crisis**

The morning daylight caught everyone by surprise. Adi remained asleep face down on the table. Even John Fortner was reeling from the effects of the day before. He slowly came to, stretching his back against the front door. JJ and Barry were completely comatose on adjacent couches. Lt. Mabrey caused the first commotion as he answered the satellite phone, "Yes, sir, right away."

Mabrey approached Fortner and handed him a phone. John Fortner was agitated as he had never liked being caught off-guard with unknown callers. Echo Team's commanding officer had finally made contact. Fortner took the phone, "Yes, sir, General Baskin." Fortner stood abruptly and went out onto the front porch continuing the conversation in privacy, "Sir, we both know I'm innocent."

"Echo Team has footage of a highly dangerous and classified chemical serum stolen by associates of Dr. William Hersey."

The general spoke to Fortner and informed him that FBI and NSA agents were searching for him and Adi. Fortner then began explaining the woman thief and how it all went down in the lab, "Sir, you would have to have seen them to believe it. Both of them were chemically enhanced with some form of mind-altering hallucinogen." Fortner continued, becoming even more agitated, "I had no choice but to neutralize the threats."

"Yes, sir, right away."

"Thank you, sir, out," Fortner concluded the conversation and went back inside to inform Echo Team and Adi of their next course of action.

John entered the kitchen about the time Dean was in the act of pouring a cup of coffee. "Coffee?" Dean asked, walking to the table.

"No, sir, we will be out of your way in five minutes."

Adi groaned to life and began sitting up in the chair, rubbing her neck, "What time is it?"

John reached the room threshold and announced, "Echo Team we're heading for Ft. Benning in five minutes."

Echo Team entered the kitchen, choosing to partake in Dean's coffee. JJ and Barry also stood, then squeezed into the small kitchen. In a matter of a few seconds, Dean and Ethel's small kitchen was having trouble containing the nine adults. Dean decided it was becoming too crowded for his liking and went to check on Ethel. Her coughing had worsened throughout the night.

Dean planned on taking Ethel to the hospital this morning to see her doctor. The pneumonia symptoms were intensifying.

JJ, Fortner, and Adi looked at one another as if to wait for the other to speak first.

Fortner cleared his throat and began, "I spoke with my commander at Fort Benning. Yes, authorities are searching for Ms. Roth and myself as I speak. My commander informed me that I would fall under his jurisdiction if I could make it to base." Echo Team all stood in unison as if to show support for Captain Fortner. Fortner looked at Adi and continued, "The footage of Hersey's men stealing the serum could also help exonerate Ms. Roth."

"Could, how about better," Adi said.

"There are no guarantees here, including for myself," Fortner said. "But we have to get to the bottom of what happened to those two girls," he said, looking straight into Adi's eyes.

"You're right, Captain," Adi began down the hallway to her room.

"So why are Barry and I still here for all this?" JJ asked, looking at Barry. Everyone looked at JJ as if he was the only person that hadn't figured out the plan.

Barry turned to Fortner, "We would be happy to give you a ride to Ft. Benning."

"Aww hell no," JJ blurted out, and went to take the keys of the storm chaser from Barry.

Barry refused to give JJ the keys and said, "Look, kiddo, these people aren't killers. I can feel it."

"It's not that far out of the way going back home, and then we never have to see any of these people ever again," Barry concluded.

"It's called aiding and abetting, Barry. The cops aren't going to ask us if we think they did it."

"If we are caught, we go where they go…jail." JJ concluded, throwing his hands up with disgust.

During the conversation between JJ and Barry, Adi emerged from her room with a backpack and a small secure container for the vials of blood. She began taking ice cubes from the freezer, preserving the integrity of the vials as best she could. "What's going on now?" Adi asked.

Fortner replied, "We are leaving."

"No, we are not," JJ said.

Ethel heard the commotion and entered the kitchen with Dean. Adi felt terrible for bringing this into her parent's home but was relieved they had remained safe from Hersey and the storm. Everyone thought Ethel was about to speak, but she instead walked past them into the living room and turned on the television.

They saw news reports of random people in local communities attacking each other. The attacks were deemed random acts of violence, but deep down, Adi knew the source of the chaos.

"Please, don't be," she said to herself.

The news report continued, "We have reports that one of the perpetrators of these violent random acts has been apprehended just outside of Charlotte, North Carolina."

The camera panned to a young man in handcuffs fighting while being dragged by six police officers. They began having trouble keeping the man secure and placed a belt around his face so he could not bite them. His eyes were black, just as the sisters' in the lab, and blood oozed out of his nose.

Adi stumbled into her father's arms but continued to watch. Just before the live footage panned away, the belt came loose from around the man's face. He let out a high-pitched scream. "SHARP!" The man continued to bite one of the officers on the face, tearing a large piece of flesh from his cheek. The officers opened fire on the man, killing him on live television. His lifeless body lay in the street. The dark blood pooled around his chest. The transmission stopped. Everyone was dead quiet.

"SAP-23?" Fortner asked Adi.

Adi freed herself from Dean's arms and nodded, picking up her pack and container. Adi looked at the container and then threw her head up at Fortner, "SAP-23, it's still in the car." Due to the storms and worry for personal safety, Adi and Fortner had forgotten about the remaining boxes of SAP-23. Now the threat was time. Echo Team pushed Barry and JJ out the door and into the storm chaser.

JJ asked, "Where are we going? What car are you guys talking about?"

Adi paused at the front door and turned to her parents, "I'm so sorry, please forgive me, but I have to go."

"You are our daughter, and we love you," Dean said, tears pooled up in his eyes.

Adi hugged her mother, "You were right, Mom. It's evil."

Ethel looked into her daughter's eyes, "I'm proud of you, and everything will be okay."

The weight of those words reinvigorated Adi. A feeling of calmness came over her, and she found renewed strength to carry on.

"I'll call you when it's safe," Adi said, climbing into the truck. "Don't trust anyone." The door closed, and the storm chaser was gone.

"Did you see his eyes?" JJ asked Barry. "I've never seen anything like that before." JJ was asking what everyone else was thinking. The man on the television looked like a possessed demon. Barry turned onto a major intersection near the parking deck from the night before, "Drugs, kiddo, the stuff kids are on these days is pure evil." Barry's investigative mind reverted to the most logical explanation. Drugs were rampant in various areas of America.

Fortner viewed Winters' statement as a positive. News outlets and most citizens would agree with Barry blaming drug use for the recent random attacks. Near the back of the storm chaser, Adi looked at John and said, "The storm cleanup and news of the attacks might buy us enough time to make it out of the city." The storm chaser came to a red light and stopped. Sergeant Sims cried out, "Look at that. What is that, Captain? Look." The sergeant pointed to a woman just outside the truck, ripping a small dog apart on the sidewalk. Bystanders came to the animal's rescue but were too late. The woman began screaming some inaudible words and then rushed to attack.

The light went green. "Drive," Fortner commanded Barry.

The storm chaser pushed through the light as the woman ran out into the road and into the path of a large bus. Her body lay motionless in the street. The woman showed extreme strength but could not endure the impact of the bus.

"Oh my god," Adi said, clutching the container of vials tighter.

Lt. Mabrey turned to Fortner, "Captain, is that what attacked you in the lab last night?"

Corporal Gunn added, "What was that Captain? I've never seen drugs do that before." Everyone in the truck looked at Gunn except Barry. "I mean I've never *heard* of drugs doing anything like that before." Gunn sank further in his seat.

John Fortner let out a deep breath. He wasn't sure how to answer either of the men's questions. "I honestly don't know what we're dealing with here, men," John said, unclipping the strap to his sidearm holster. "We will stay together. If attacked, be prepared to defend yourselves."

"Those are people out there, real people," Adi said.

"You are in no position to lecture me about what they are," Fortner said.

The storm chaser pulled beside the large parking deck from the night before. The tornadoes must have passed directly over the area of the street where the SUV was left, as it lay under a pile of cars and other structural debris. Sirens still abounded in many places within Atlanta. Other people were also returning to check on their vehicles.

"Lt. Mabrey, you and Gunn go secure the boxes." John did not want to show his or Adi's face to the public unless absolutely necessary.

The storm chaser truck provided the perfect cover for transport due to the logic of it being on-site because of the storm. Fortner felt very confident that as long as he and Adi stayed inside the National Weather Service truck, they could move freely on public roads.

Mabrey and Gunn exited the back of the truck and walked toward a pile of cars, spotting the SUV wedged between a blue minivan and a red sports car. A large metal pole penetrated deep through the top of the van and into the hood of the SUV. People could be heard close by, cursing on their phones with their various insurance companies. Gunn, who was much smaller in size when compared to Mabrey, squeezed between the minivan and car, slowly approaching the SUV. He opened the trunk and pulled the first bag out. Mabrey positioned his body sideways to reach the bag. "Got it," Mabrey announced to Gunn.

Gunn returned for the second bag when he felt a strong tug on his right ankle. A bloody hand was clinging to the corporal's leg and was not letting go. Gunn screamed out, "Something's got me."

"What is it?" Mabrey responded, trying to lower the bag so he could see. Fortner and Sergeant Sims watched from the storm chaser. JJ and Barry continued looking ahead and playing with camera equipment attempting to look as unassuming as possible.

"Dude, this is taking way too long," JJ said to Barry.

"Just stay calm, kiddo," Barry replied, looking into the rearview mirror at Mabrey and Gunn.

"It won't let go," Gunn said, shaking his leg.

"It's probably someone trapped. Try and see if you can pull 'em out." Mabrey had almost worked his way to Gunn, where he finally got a clear look at who was attached to the hand holding the ankle. "What the…" Mabrey saw an older man whose right arm was broken and jammed into the front dash of his car. The left arm clutched Gunn's leg. The man's eyes were coal black, and the veins in his neck were beyond swollen, dripping with blood. The veins looked like a den of snakes, pulsating in all directions, and were an eerie dark bluish hue. "Get away from him," Mabrey screamed out to Gunn.

"What, get away from…what?"

The merged man began screaming loudly, "Stop!"

"Stop what?" Gunn said to the man kicking free from his hand's grip. The corporal knelt down. He saw the black eyes and blood oozing from the veins and fell backward, slamming his head into the SUV. Corporal Gunn was out cold.

Mabrey pushed into the cars until he bent enough metal to work his way to Gunn. He approached the corporal and saw blood.

Fortner was becoming concerned. The simple task was taking two of Echo Team's best men much longer than expected to procure a couple of bags. "Sims, go check on them. We need to get out of here," Fortner commanded the sergeant.

Sims exited the vehicle and walked about six feet when he heard the screams.

People began circling the group of mangled cars. Sims ran toward the commotion and was startled by gunshots. "Lt. Mabrey…Corporal Gunn?" Sims continued shouting, looking for the men.

"Here!" Mabrey, throwing the bags out to Sims. Behind the bags, Mabrey emerged and started pulling the corporal by his legs.

"What happened?" Sims replied.

Mabrey picked up Gunn and threw him over his shoulder. Blood ran down Mabrey's back. "Go, now!" Mabrey commanded.

Sims and Mabrey, with Gunn in tow, ran back to the storm chaser. The truck doors flung open, and Mabrey threw Gunn into the back as Sims placed the bags near the front beside Adi. Barry wasted not a second. He pulled away from the scene before people could approach the storm chaser truck.

"You think they got our tags?" JJ asked Barry.

Lt. Mabrey responded, "The gunshots and dead body probably took their minds off looking for some tags."

Fortner turned Gunn over onto his back. A large portion of his side near the liver was gone. The corporal began convulsing, and blood poured from within the giant torn hole in his side. Adi checked his pulse while Sims stuffed the wound with a shirt. Everyone was hands-on, pressing here and elevating there. Fortner began CPR as Adi had detected no pulse. Fortner continued compressing the chest, stopping for a breath and a look from Adi. JJ turned and went to the back of the storm chaser to help, but there was nothing anyone could do. Corporal Tim Gunn was dead.

Two days before, the older gentleman had received an injection of SAP-23 from a hospital three blocks away. He was fighting symptoms from strep throat and heard about the new free procedure, AD1, touted as a cure-all for an assortment of ailments and was injected in the neck.

"Captain, he had him with one hand…one hand," Mabrey told Fortner.

"I saw him rip the flesh right off his body." Lt. Mabrey fell back against the rear doors of the storm chaser, "He started grabbing for me, my god, his eyes."

"What about his eyes?" Adi asked, interrupting Mabrey.

Mabrey turned to Adi with a blank expression, "His eyes were black as death itself. He kept saying stop or something like that."

JJ pulled a blanket from a compartment in the truck and gave it to Fortner. He placed the dark cover over the lifeless body, and everyone remained quiet. Barry turned south onto the interstate.

A few minutes passed, everyone looked and stared at Adi. She was thinking about the events and what Hersey must have done. "Dr. Hersey must have distributed doses of SAP-23 to various locations." This response did not satisfy the group. Adi would have to do better because playing the blame game was not bringing Corporal Gunn back from the dead. Unfortunately, Adi, once again, had fallen into the terrible cycle of having to explain her work and SAP-23 after experiencing another tragic event. The storm chaser continued south as Adi did her best to explain everything to everyone inside.

Everyone took the news differently, but they were all in agreement that something terrible was causing people to lose their sanity.

Barry had heard enough and turned the radio on. More news reports of people becoming hostile and attacking others. Then the radio made a long beeping sound.

*Multiple reports now confirm a possible biological attack is to blame for the deaths of two young women inside the Atlanta CDC.*

The news update detailed Fortner and Adi again and provided a reward of 50,000 dollars for any information of their whereabouts.

*Checkpoints are being set up all along the perimeter of Atlanta. All traffic will be stopped and searched.*

JJ shook his head and looked at Barry, "They're no killers, kiddo."

Barry responded, "I agree this looks bad."

JJ snapped back, "Looks bad? We're driving a car that does not belong to us. We have two fugitives from the law, wanted murderers no less, and we're holding a dead body."

"So yes, pretty bad. So, how does that get any *worse*?" JJ asked.

Fortner responded to JJ, "If we get caught, that's how."

Adi told Barry, "Take this exit. I know some backroads that might get us through."

Barry continued to drive as the morning wore on, and the recent events made everyone forget about the lab and the storm. It seemed that each occurrence was becoming worse than the last.


## Eagle has Landed

By this point of the day, Dr. Hersey was well aware of the news reports. He and Higgins remained glued to a series of screens. Higgins spoke, "Sir, is it still wise for me to apprehend Ms. Roth now that law enforcement is also searching?"

"You can never have too many hounds in the hunt," Hersey said, switching to another screen.

"And Dr. Meyers?" Higgins asked.

Hersey was growing tired of Higgins and was beginning to feel apprehensive due to what he viewed on the news. Hersey whipped his head around, "Major, you have your assignment. Take your team and go get my scientist."

There was no response this time, and he turned and left the room. Within the hour, a team of dangerous men was on a helicopter heading for Atlanta.

After Hersey's attendant in Atlanta had taken the vials of SAP-23, he told his men to take them up and down the eastern US, picking at random health departments and hospitals. Each container of SAP-23 also bore a letter from Dr. Hersey. As CDC director and Chief Medical Advisor, there would be little pushback from doctors to refrain from administering the injections.

Hersey had no idea the effects of SAP-23 would be so dramatic. Certain side-effects, yes, but turning people into wild mindless beasts, no. The scientist went to work, "It must be some mutation at the cellular level." Hersey turned from the screens and stepped onto the balcony overlooking the fountain for clarity, his favorite place to think. "It's as if the serum merged with the patient's cells, creating a zombie-like effect," Hersey said haphazardly. The doctor was correct about the zombie-like effects, but these were not what people had grown accustomed to in old horror movies. The merged was a reality. The look of the eyes confused Dr. Hersey the most. It was the only feature every injected individual shared and exhibited.

Hersey continued hypothesizing what could have caused this, but he knew the answer, likely, lay with Dr. Roth. Without her, finding an explanation and solution would be almost impossible.

Or would it?

"Dr. Meyers, you are becoming more valuable by the minute," Hersey said, heading for his suite.

Henry met the doctor halfway down the spiral staircase, "Sir, the President is on his way here."

"Now?" Hersey asked as he continued down to find Jake Meyers.

Henry provided even worse news, "Sir, Madam Secretary Renner is accompanying the President. I tried to inform her that she was not on the guest list, but she insisted."

"No matter, Henry. Send them to the balcony upon arrival." Hersey made his way past a guard and knocked on the door of a suite. Jake was currently still sleeping off his headache. Hersey opened the door and let himself into the room. "Time to work, Dr. Meyers," Hersey said, placing a single vial of SAP-9 beside Jake's head.

"What? Work on what? Where?"

"There is a lab under this manor, and I want you down there as soon as you get dressed." Hersey opened every curtain in the room, exposing the blinding bright sunlight against the manor this time of day. Jake came to his feet, grabbed a new suit, and disappeared into the bathroom. A few minutes later, Jake emerged from the bathroom wearing a perfectly form-fitting gray suite. "How do I look?"

Hersey wasn't amused, "You look like a man preparing for a funeral." The childish smile was immediately gone from Meyers' face. Jake went over to pick up the syringe and hesitantly asked before extending his hand, "SAP-9?"

Hershey did not respond. He stood by the door stoically, intent on making Meyers continue asking questions until becoming uneasy enough to wait for instructions.

"It has come to my attention that Ms. Roth may have jumped the gun with her research," Hersey said, leading Jake to an elevator. A nearby security guard was relieved of his post, and Hersey, trailed by Jake, entered the elevator and descended into the lab area. The lab was a little dated but by no means was unequipped to conduct various scientific research. After final construction of the manor, Hersey used the lab as his base of operations until accepting the position of CDC director. The new appointment and funding allowed Hersey to begin construction on Camelot. He had not been in this sector of 'The Refuge' in many years.

"How do you know it was her? Why would she do this?" Jake asked as he pulled back thick plastic sheets from numerous lab tables and equipment. "Turn that screen on, Dr. Meyers, and see for yourself." Hersey pointed to a large screen over a row of stainless steel cabinets. Jake powered on the screen and witnessed the chaos unraveling around numerous American cities.

"Holy hell! What have you done?" Jake saw the live reports of people losing their minds and attacking, at random, anyone within the vicinity.

One news interview showed a young woman after a recent attack. "Ma'am, can you tell us what happened?" the reporter asked. The woman, in shock, explained, "He just came at me. His eyes were gone, and there was blood coming out his mouth. It's like he merged with a demon or something. Then they shot him, and now he's dead."

"There you have it, America. Merged demons are out there attacking at random." The screen panned back to storm updates from the southeast. Jake turned to Hersey, "That's horrible, but what does it have to do with Adi?" As on cue, another news report flashed on the screen, and Jake saw photos of Adi and John Fortner. The captions ran, "Dr. Adilene Roth and Captain John Fortner, wanted for murder and carrying out a biological terrorist attack at the Atlanta CDC." Jake almost fell as he read and heard the words on the screen.

Hersey folded his hands behind his back and slowly approached Jake, "I told you Ms. Roth is not who you thought she was. Now, I believe *you* hold the key to *stopping* this."

"How?" Jake asked.

"I am going to find one of these merged, and you're going to use SAP-9 to cure them. Understood?" Hersey said, returning to the elevator.

"Where's the rest of my serum, Hersey?"

"I'll have it brought down later. As for now, prepare for human tests or whatever those things are."

Henry called into the lab intercom, "Sir, the President and Madam Renner are waiting for you on the balcony."

"The President? Here?" Jake asked.

"Focus, Doctor, be ready by tonight." Hersey left the lab and headed toward the balcony.

The story to appease both Frank Richards and Meggie Renner was iffy at best. Hersey was more intent on distraction techniques than having a solution to the questions sure to be asked in a few minutes. Time was once again the main threat. Time for Hersey to think. Time for Meyers to find a possible SAP-9 solution. And most importantly, time to catch Adilene Roth.

Hersey entered the balcony. Numerous secret service agents remained in the room monitoring every window and door. Unlike any other time before, the manor was full of agents and military personnel going in all directions.

"Can you explain any of this, Bill?" Richards asked.

Renner interjected before Hersey could respond, "I'll answer it for you. One of your scientists is part of some covert terrorist cell hell-bent on causing another biological pandemic."

"Dr. Roth is acting alone. I can tell you that," Hersey responded.

"You knew she was going to do this?" the President asked.

"No, sir. After the exhibition in Alaska, Ms. Roth pleaded to be brought back to Atlanta for human trials. She used Captain Fortner to forge documents bearing my signature, then began sending her biological weapon out into society." Hersey was adept at taking what others said and using it against them. Even Renner was buying this lie, as it was a very plausible scenario.

"So, what do we do now? How do we fix this, Bill?" the President asked, folding his arms and surveying various military personnel circling the perimeter. "I have people being shot dead in the streets because they are losing their minds and attacking innocent Americans." Richards was becoming angry.

"Alaska," Renner said, looking at Richards. "Whatever is going on here, must have started there," she said, nodding.

"Would you stop with the Alaska conspiracy, Maggie?" Richards said, throwing his hands at her with disgust.

Hersey took this unexpected opportunity to buy himself more time, "Madam Renner may be right, sir."

Maggie Renner almost fell out of her seat. She had never been so surprised in her life.

"You're agreeing with me, Hersey?"

The President interjected, "Go ahead, Bill. What are you proposing?"

"Sir, for your safety, it may be best for you and Madam Renner to visit Alaska and see the lab for yourself. You can call it a show of strength, visiting many states along the way to show unity and reassurance," Hersey concluded, feeling good about the plan he had just conjured.

"You expect me to leave Washington when I have intel about an aurora borealis in Georgia and a bus driver eating one of his passengers in Boston?" President Richards would need much more convincing if he were to leave the Capitol.

Hersey held a glass of water close to his chest as he answered, "Sir, I believe Americans will see your traveling differently. It shows that you are confident that officials have the situation under control."

"He's right, Mr. President," Renner added, looking even more shocked that she just agreed with Hersey.

Richards scoffed and looked at Renner and Hersey like a father giving in to their children after much badgering. He turned to Secretary Renner, "So, you want us to check out this secret lab in the Alaskan wilderness, then campaign as we head back to the east coast?"

Renner and Hersey responded in unison, giving each other a weird look, "Yes, sir."

Richards motioned for a secret service agent and whispered something into his ear. The President stood abruptly, "Okay. We leave now, then."

"General McMillan will accompany us to Elmendorf then we will visit the lab."

"Bill, I want you to find out what's going on with the CDC and get back to me in an hour," Richards said, walking behind Renner toward a door leading out to the stairs. He turned just before touching the first step, "And for god's sake, Bill, don't talk to the media until I get back."

"Yes, sir, not a word."

Hersey followed the President down to the front door of the manor. And even though the tension in the air remained palpable, Hersey felt confident about buying enough time to sort this matter out. Regardless of the situation, Adilene Roth had to be apprehended. Only then would this nightmare end. As the President's motorcade pulled away from the compound, Hersey dialed Higgins, "What is your location, Major?"

# 10. Exit Plan

**zongshot**

The Atlanta metropolitan area contained an interstate perimeter encompassing nearly sixty miles of city and suburbs in addition to millions of people. The odds of finding a way through the wall of checkpoints were surprisingly good as long as the storm chaser stayed off the major interstates and highways. The distance between the downtown area and Ft. Benning was straight forward and could be covered in just a few hours. The close proximity of the fort and their ability to blend in, thanks to the weather truck, provided hope they could make it without being stopped. They hoped!

Fortner continued looking at Gunn's covered outline, "Do you think you can stop this if I can get you to a lab?"

Adi took a few seconds before answering, "I don't know. Before the sisters, SAP-23 was performing as was intended. They were healing." The conversation continued back and forth in the back of the storm chaser for a few miles as JJ checked his phone and saw numerous missed calls from Julie Reiser.

JJ put the phone to his ear, and John Fortner sounded off, "No phone communication."

"Look, you can't tell me what I can do. If you want to try hitchhiking, go ahead and be my guest," JJ said, waiting for the line to connect. Everyone in the truck suddenly became interested in JJ and his phone call.

"Hey, Dr. Reiser?"

"Yes, I was in Atlanta when the storm hit."

JJ continued the call switching ears, "Yes, it was spectacular. Well, except for the tornadoes almost killing me."

Dr. Reiser's voice could barely be heard, but not understood, as she responded to JJ. His tone was light and bubbly. Barry looked once again into the rearview mirror at everyone and smirked. JJ was being a little too friendly with Dr. Reiser. "Well, of course, I'd be honored to. Yes, I will call you soon as I return to Huntsville. Thank you." JJ ended the call, not realizing everyone had been listening intently to his conversation with the astrophysicist. JJ looked at everyone, "What?" The back and forth between JJ and the group proved to be a nice reprieve from the traumatic situation experienced earlier that morning.

Barry turned to JJ, "Got a date?"

"No, Dr. Reiser seems interested in seeing some portions of the storm footage."

Lt. Mabrey sat back into his seat, nodding his head with approval to Sims. Anyone eavesdropping on the group's current talks would never have guessed that Adi and Fortner were wanted for murder. Or, more importantly, that a dead, bleeding body remained amongst everyone. Unfortunately, the lighthearted moment vanished as the storm chaser approached a roadblock containing FBI and local sheriff deputies. All cars were being searched from front to back, top to bottom.

"And would you like to explain about how we're getting through that?" JJ asked Barry. There were about fifteen cars ahead of the storm chaser, and each search was about three minutes or so. Fortner turned and began looking around for escape routes. By this point, cars lined up for almost a mile. The situation seemed like everyone else leaving the downtown area had the same idea as Adi. The backroads and alternate streets were packing out and bogging down traffic.

Barry sat-up straight in his seat, pulling the seat belt tight across his chest, "There's always a chance they won't check the back." Barry was known for his trademark pearls of wisdom during difficult situations, but even Adi felt that this was one he'd like to have back.

"They're checking every crevice of each car. I don't think we can take a chance like that, Barry," Adi said in her most reassuring voice.

"Okay, this is what we have to do. Lt. Mabrey will open the side doors. Sims, you will help me with Gunn." Fortner turned to Adi. "I want you to grab one of those cameras and follow behind us like you are setting up for a video shoot."

"Oh, I see. You're going for the, Hi, I'm about to film a funeral documentary trick," JJ said, turning toward everyone.

The cars continued to move forward. A large brown van stopped at the checkpoint. FBI agents approached the vehicle from the front while two deputies went around to the rear. The agents began pointing to the back doors, shouting at the driver. The sheriff's deputies pulled the rear doors open, finding numerous blue fifty-gallon barrels. The FBI agents ripped the driver from his seat and placed him face down on the pavement. Everyone in the line of cars began exiting their vehicles, trying to get a better look at the commotion. A female FBI agent continued down the line of vehicles instructing everyone to get back into their cars and remain calm. The agent approached the storm chaser, and Fortner placed one finger over his mouth to signal, "Everyone remain quiet."

"What's the hold, miss?" Barry asked, pulling his sunglasses up.

"Nothing, sir. Please remain in your vehicle and stay calm." The agent's words were robotic in nature, as if recalling certain pages in her training handbook.

"Will do, ma'am. Thank you for keeping us safe." Barry quickly rolled the window up.

Adi followed the agent across the windows, "Okay, I think we can try it after she returns to the checkpoint."

"I don't know, Captain. There's a lot of eyes out there now," Lt. Mabrey said.

Fortner was not used to covert operations. He would, normally, bull rush his way through most engagements. Fortner had always believed that the best defense was an even better offense. However, there was no way to avoid this conflict unless they all could successfully sneak away.

Adi turned her attention back to the brown van and the contents within the barrels, "It is odd that a van would have so many barrels as cargo, don't you think?" looking at Fortner. He did not have an answer, but he did notice the horns beginning to honk from behind the storm chaser. A large eighteen-wheeler was accelerating, smashing in and out of the gridlocked cars.

"Oh my god, what is that idiot doing?" Adi said, pointing at the big rig through the back window. The driver inside the semi-truck had received his inoculation of SAP-23 at a local health department just outside of Atlanta two days ago. He was experiencing complications from a staph infection. He had cut his stomach while moving some old sheet metal behind his workshop. The merged driver was trying to exit the truck but had no fine motor skills or mental capacity to complete the mundane task. His mind was gone, but his foot remained glued to the accelerator.

People began running left and right away from the path of the large truck. Some made it to safety in time, and others were not so fortunate. The agents and deputies opened fire on the large truck but were unsuccessful at slowing it down. The blue barrels inside the van were full of diesel fuel, stolen earlier that morning. In addition to the current health crisis in America, fuel prices skyrocketed, allowing pirated fuel to become a very lucrative enterprise for criminals.

The merged man continued clawing at the seat belt, trying to free himself and was struck numerous times by the incoming fire from the agents and deputies. The explosion busted out every window within the immediate radius. The diesel fuel created an atomic bomb effect with large plumes of billowing smoke reaching hundreds of feet in the air. Most of the agents and deputies died on impact. The man inside the semi was engulfed in the explosion and instantly vaporized. Large pieces of metal and rubber began falling from the sky. The intense heat from the blast was felt by many rows of cars behind the explosion.

Fortner slapped Barry on the shoulder, "Go around it. That way. To the right." Fortner was thrown back into his seat as the storm chaser roared to life.

"Don't look. Just keep moving," JJ said to Barry. The mangled mess left by the explosion was almost too unbearable to fathom. Charred bodies lay all around the initial impact. The fire continued to rage. The smoke choked the atmosphere where the van had existed just minutes before.

Fortner looked at Adi, "SAP-23?"

Adi continued looking down as she knew that was a question no one needed to ask. Everyone knew without having to be told what had caused that horrendous sight.

"Pull behind there. We have to make a better plan," Fortner said, pointing behind an old warehouse. Barry turned the radio on again to catch any updates that might provide beneficial future travel intel. The bulletin sounded off.


*Officials continue to deal with uprisings of hostile individuals committing heinous acts of violence. The perpetrators, now referred to as 'The Merged', are said to be on a newly discovered hallucinogenic drug of some sort. The drug causes all users to lose cognitive control and become extremely violent. We now have breaking news of a large explosion north of Interstate 20-West.*

*Traffic is backed-up for miles, so please use alternate routes. Heavy delays are expected.*

Barry turned the radio off once again. Everyone sat quietly. As though they hadn't enough to deal with, soon, there would be another variable to navigate. Higgins was drawing close.

## Vulture

Major Higgins touched down at Dobbins AFB and handed the base commander a piece of paper given to him by Hersey in case of events such as these. The letter was an authentic document from the President's office with certain contact information and classified language to repel anyone from asking too many questions.

The commander allowed Higgins access to any help and resources needed to complete his mission. Airmen began refueling the helicopter as Higgins looked through a database on a large tablet. The first point of contact would be Dean and Ethel Roth's address.

"You're all set, Major," one of the airmen said, giving him the thumbs up. Higgins saluted the commander and climbed back into the helicopter. He called out the address, and the men disappeared out of sight. In less than ten minutes, Higgins should arrive at his first destination.

Dean was helping Ethel into the old green Ford when a violent sound hovered above them. The helicopter landed in the middle of the road outside the driveway. Higgins quickly jumped out to approach the Roths. The helicopter remained on. Its propellers creating an awful, deafening ruckus.

"Dean and Ethel Roth?" Higgins asked, showing a photo of Adi.

"Who are you, and why do you have a picture of our daughter?" Dean responded, eyeing the Major suspiciously with narrowed eyes.

"I'm here on behalf of the President of the United States. I have been tasked with finding Dr. Roth and escorting her back to Washington."

"Liar," Ethel said, loudly over the helicopter's propellers chopping through the air.

"Mrs. Roth, if you know where your daughter is, please tell me. She may be in danger."

"I'm not saying another word to you or anyone else." Ethel began opening the old truck door. Higgins extended his arm, stopping the door from opening.

Dean became enraged, reaching for the Major's arm. Higgins grabbed Dean, throwing him down beside the truck. There was a time Dean Roth would have folded the Major in half like a dollar bill, but time and age had changed his once strong and broad body into a lesser form. Dean remained on the ground.

Higgins pulled out his pistol and pointed it at Ethel. She stood firm, never blinking an eye. The Major was impressed by Ethel's resolve. She had not given him a single useful piece of information.

Higgins removed the gun from her face slowly, pointing it at Dean. Ethel's eyes changed. "I don't know where Adi went," she finally responded, "They left this morning."

"Who left this morning? Which direction?" Higgins fired a warning shot inches from Dean's head.

Ethel began to shake and cough before speaking, "The soldier and two other men, but I don't know who they are."

Higgins fired another shot, even closer than the first, "What were they driving?"

Ethel took a deep breath and fell to her knees, protecting Dean with her body, "Some kind of weather van like the ones you see on TV. That's all I know. That's all we know."

Higgins holstered his weapon, "Thank you for cooperating. Have a nice rest of your day." The Major entered the helicopter and was gone.

Dean returned to his feet, visibly shaken but surprisingly unharmed. Ethel opened the door and sat in the truck as she began to cough uncontrollably. Dean phoned Adi as he climbed into the old truck.

Adi was listening to Fortner go over possible routes on a tablet screen when her father Called, "Some army man came for you. Said he was taking you to the White House."

Adi became manic, "What? Are you okay? Did he hurt…Mom?"

"We're fine, but he threatened…" Dean was cut off by Ethel shouting into the phone while crying, "I'm sorry, he had a gun pointed at your father."

Fortner took the phone from Adi, asking Dean, "What did the man look like. Did he give you a name?"

Dean Roth continued talking to Fortner for a few more seconds. Adi left the storm chaser and began walking around in circles beside the truck with her hands placed firmly on top of her head. Fortner finished the call and stepped out from the truck, finding Adi, "Higgins, it was Higgins, and he's in a helicopter."

Fortner stuck his head inside the storm chaser, "Pull under that awning over there." Barry did as he was told. The storm chaser wedged itself between a partially broken wall and a row of pallets. There was barely enough room under the tin roof to cover the truck, but it should be undetectable from the sky.

"Lt. Mabrey, I need you to tap into local air flight control comms," Fortner said. "You go to that tree line and keep a lookout for anything coming down this road." Sergeant Sims ran into some thick bushes near the entrance of a warehouse and waited.

Fortner, Barry, JJ, and Adi stepped inside the building connected to the awning. JJ pulled water out of his pack, "So, this Higgins, he's not with you?"

"Negative," the captain responded.

Adi asked Fortner, "Just how did you get assigned to me, Captain?" Fortner never had mentioned that the Major was the one who contacted his commander to get Echo Team assigned to Adi.

Fortner began, "I was tasked by my commander per Major Tom Higgins to be your security detail and keep intel on you while at the CDC."

"Keep intel on me. Like what?" Adi asked, growing paranoid.

"It means they were spying on you while you worked," JJ said, with Barry nodding in agreement.

"I did not know anything about your work. My assignment was to keep an eye on you and report my findings back to Higgins when contacted," Fortner said. The captain's situation was becoming more perilous by the second. JJ and Barry were also starting to feel that they were following the orders of a traitor leading them in circles, so Higgins could catch up and apprehend Adi.

Adi walked across the room and stood beside Barry and JJ, "How do I know you aren't lying to me?"

The next words out of Fortner's mouth would need to eliminate all doubt, or this would be the end of the traveling entourage. He called out to Mabrey, "Lt. bring me the satellite phone." Fortner's tone was brutal.

Everyone watched as the captain punched numbers into the phone, "This Higgins?"

"Good, now listen to me carefully. Dr. Roth is under my watch, and she will be taken to the proper authorities."

Adi's face almost melted. She looked at Barry and JJ like she was seeing a ghost.

Fortner continued, "No, you don't understand. Dr. Roth is staying with me." Fortner began squeezing his free fist tightly as he listened to Higgins.

"You and Adilene Roth are wanted fugitives Captain. However, I can make all your problems go away. You have to give me the girl. I will only offer you this opportunity once, so be smart and do the right thing."

"Or what? What will you do?" Fortner's tone was as dark and ominous as the eyes of the merged.

"You and your team will be hunted by every agency in the country until caught or killed. Either is just as well with me."

Adi moved closer to Fortner, trying to hear Higgins speak. She had never trusted Higgins not since her first time laying eyes on him at Camelot. He always looked like he was up to something because he 'was' always up to something.

Fortner paused. The following words for Higgins were as heavy as a sledgehammer striking a thumb tack, "I choose death. See you soon, Major." The call ended. Fortner tossed the phone back to Mabrey and told him to continue monitoring the skies. He looked at Adi, "Higgins wants me to turn you over to him. In exchange, my team and I walk free." He pointed to the storm chaser holding Gunn's dead body and said, "We're beyond that point now."

"What was all that 'I chose death stuff' about?" Adi asked.

"Don't worry about that. Higgins got the point," Fortner concluded.

The morning had transitioned into evening during the events and aftermath of the explosion and the phone call with Higgins. The last phone call with her parents scared Adi more than anything that had happened so far. Ft. Benning felt a million miles away, an oasis in a vast desert with no guarantee of safety.

"We will wait until nightfall. Try to rest," Fortner commanded, walking outside to speak with Mabrey.


**Enemy of my Enemy**

Jake Meyers was focusing on a glass slide while holding a small syringe. The needle slowly penetrated a red blood cell, and a small amount of SAP-9 was injected through the membrane into the cell. The organelles all responded to the compound differently. As before in Alaska, the ribosomes showed the most severe mutation. The part about SAP-9 that left Jake in the dark was why it began attacking white blood cells days after contact. "If only I had more time with the patients at Camelot," Jake wished aloud. He wondered every so often how they were holding up. Jake shook his head and continued looking at the slide, "I should have asked for them to have been brought here too, so stupid."

Jake had been stuck inside Hersey's lab with no food or water for over nine hours now. He was a cyborg hell-bent on figuring out further mysteries of SAP-9. SAP-9 was the first project he and Adi worked on together at Camelot. The first eight variants of serum remained ultimately unchanged. The random healing properties of SAP-1 through 8 had to be isolated and reduplicated. Jake let out a sigh and stepped away from the microscope. He couldn't help but tell himself that SAP possibly would have remained safe and effective for burns and scars if not for the push to change and modify and enhance it.

Jake thought, *why did we have to be so greedy?*

Nature has shown, through time, that things that cannot sustain homeostasis must either adapt or die; those rules do not change. Adi viewed SAP in that same manner. However, the laws of nature were thrown out the window when SAP-9 and 23 were created. It seems Adi and Jake had made the same mistake countless other scientists had made before them. Jake mumbled the words quietly while readjusting his eye to the slide containing a drop of Sap-9, "Just because we can, doesn't mean we should."

Suddenly, the elevator came to life, bringing down Dr. Hersey, a nurse and a man in a hospital bed. The man had a leather muzzle covering his mouth, and the rest of his body remained secured by a thick canvas material locked in place by chains. Jake turned from his slide and asked, "Let me guess, he's one of those merged?"

Hersey pointed to a corner in the lab, and the nurse rolled the man over. She found a stool and sat down.

"Quite merged, if you must ask," Hersey informed, walking over to the slide Jake had been observing. "Are you ready to begin, Doctor Meyers?"

"Now? As in right this minute now?"

Hersey approached the man and looked deep into his black emotionless eyes.

"Come look at this man, Dr. Meyers," Hersey said.

Jake walked over to the man. He was dreadful to look at. The way the eyes never blinked, always open, always watching. The eyes were so dark they produced a glisten as if coated with clear oil.

"What do you see here?" Hersey asked.

Jake covered his mouth but, somehow, managed a response, "I don't know. It looks like he's possessed."

"He is possessed. Possessed by what you and Dr. Roth created." Hersey leaned over merely a few inches from the man's face. The man tried with all his might to free himself and most surely would have attacked and killed everyone in the lab.

"You have an opportunity to make this right, Dr. Meyers, so make it right before your colleague turns more people into that," Hersey commanded, pointing down at the abomination. Hersey returned to the elevator, stopping just before entering, "I will return in a few hours. Henry will bring down food and drinks soon."

Jake returned to the stool beside the microscope he was working with before, "Okay, I'll get started."

"Oh, one more thing, doctor, you might want to view the mitochondria again." The elevator doors slid shut and slowly ascended up and out of sight.

Jake immediately looked down to view the mitochondria of the cell. He switched the slides with other cell samples from various merge infected tissues. The mitochondria were not releasing enough ATP to adequately power the vesicles. Therefore, not removing cellular debris or unwanted matter from the cell. The cell was becoming contaminated by itself. Even more shocking, the ribosomes were then infusing the excess waste with cellular DNA creating an anomaly.

Jake was furious that he had missed something as basic as this when observing cellular function at Camelot. He was even more upset with Dr. Hersey. "That man has never once looked at my work, and just by taking a five-second glance at one cell, finds something I've overlooked for months!" Jake exclaimed.

Although it could be said William Hersey was a ruthless man, his genius never would be denied. SAP-9 needed to increase mitochondrial effectiveness to theoretically destroy the infection while, hopefully, uncompromising white blood cells, which up to this point, had not been achievable.

Jake spent the next hour or so mixing chemicals into vials of SAP-9. Some of the vials boiled and became volatile, while others did nothing. Jake was so enthralled in his efforts he never saw Henry bring the platter of food and containers of different drinks down to the lab. The sun began to fade, yet he continued to work until, finally, stopping and holding a vial up to the lights. "SAP-9 vial 17," Jake said.

He laid the vial down in an aluminum tray and went to get a drink. He drank water, trying not to take his eyes off the vial.

Jake finished the glass of water and drew the solution from vial 17 into a new syringe. The serum was more orange in color now than its earlier bluish hue. He walked over to the merged individual, examining for a possible injection location.

"No way I'm touching any of those chains, especially that mask," Jake said, startling the nurse awake. Jake noticed the man contained freakishly large jaws, providing a perfect injection site. "Cheek it is. Mr. Merged," Jake said, plunging the syringe into his face, emptying the solution. And just like countless times before, with the mice subjects, nothing happened for a few minutes. The man began thrashing and muffled screams belted from underneath the muzzle. Then, after a few more minutes, calmness. The eyes had faded and resembled normal ones. The dark black pupil receded and changed to hazel. The man fell into a deep sleep and lay motionless.

Jake ran to the elevator, almost falling and sliding into the door. He frantically pressed the button and tried to regroup his thoughts. Jake could not wait to show Hersey the results of the procedure. However, Hersey would not be surprised as he had been watching the entire time.


**Re-Merged**

Dr. Hersey met Meyers at the bottom of the grand spiral staircase, "You have news?"

"Um, yes, how did…whatever, you have got to see this." Jake was already moving back into the elevator before he finished his statement.

Hersey would never show his excitement as it gave away his intentions, but he was delighted by how the events of the evening had transpired. The most difficult task was finding a merged person without causing a scene for investigation. The man in the hospital bed had made the unfortunate mistake of opting for AD1 instead of a more traditional pill-form antibiotic. The infected tooth in his mouth was becoming more than he could bear. The likelihood of an injection acting quicker was his ticket to becoming mutated and merged.

Hersey could not help but to think a little ironic sick humor as he followed Meyers into the elevator, "Funny to think that a tooth cost him the entire body. Now, chew on that."

The nurse continued caring for the man by dabbing a cool towel on the man's forehead as Hersey and Jake approached the bed. The merged effects seemed to remain a bay, but neither Hersey nor Meyers was bold enough to remove any of the security precautions in place. Jake observed the injection site and said, "You were right about the mitochondria. The ATP output was not sufficient."

Dr. Hersey was actually tolerating the company of Jake as a scientific contributor. The man was un-merging before their very eyes. "Yes, well, at one time, there wasn't a cell that could hold its secrets from me, young man."

Jake could not help but give the doctor a hesitant look. "Young man. What was that all about?" Jake asked himself.

"How long until you feel satisfied with the results of your inoculation?" Hersey asked, stepping back from the table.

Jake took a step back. He smiled at the nurse, then turned to Hersey, "I don't know. In Alaska, today would have been the third day. The patients at Camelot were still fine the second day, but I wasn't injecting merged subjects either."

Jake's answer was the correct one, but that still did not stop Dr. Hersey from immediately becoming agitated. The man could not be satisfied. He never let anyone find peace at his expense. Either way, even Dr. Hersey wasn't willing to endanger his home by releasing the man yet. 'Mr. Merged' would remain a prisoner until absolute safety could be guaranteed.

"I believe that will be enough for today, Dr. Meyers. You've earned some rest." Hersey opened an arm to show Meyers to the elevator first. Hersey turned to the nurse and said, "If he changes in any way, press the red button on that phone."

The nurse settled in for her nightly duties. The red button remained in clear sight, but she would never need to press it. The man remained normal. Hersey returned to his chambers. He was having concerns about who to contact first.

The President was all set to leave out in the morning for Camelot, while Higgins had not reported back with an update on Adi.

As for Camelot, Hersey had not received one phone call from anyone at his hidden installation since the departure of Dr. Meyers, but this wasn't totally unusual as most people stationed in the building were terrified to think about Jekyll, let alone contact him at his home. Still, after viewing what he had seen that night, fear of the worst-case scenarios began playing out in his mind. There was no guarantee that the new SAP-9 formula would counteract the merged effects of SAP-23. The problem of Dr. Roth was the most important but did not require immediate attention. The President reaching Camelot and finding merged creatures would destroy everything he had accomplished, so it became priority number one. "Becoming merged would be too good for you, Madam Renner. If only I could be so lucky," Hersey said out loud on the balcony. The fountain water was fluorescent blue tonight against the dark tree-line shadows. Hersey took a few moments to observe the beautiful scene, and for a few minutes, nothing else mattered.


## Night Riders

Sergeant Sims approached the warehouse from the road to switch over watch duties with Lt. Mabrey. The gentle chirps of crickets provided a quaint, ambient sound to break the dead silence between Echo Team, Adi, Barry, and JJ. Seven people, who less than a week ago were living out their separate lives as they had done day after day, were now forming an unlikely but mostly unwanted alliance.

Fortner would meander out from under the awning, every so often, to check for sounds of helicopter blades cutting the air. He found an old chair that had to be at least a hundred years old, that made an awful creaking sound every time he sat down on it.

Barry was texting his wife, Alice. Her doctor's appointment went well. She was feeling much better after receiving her shot of AD1. If only Barry knew that was the terrible pseudonym Hersey created to mask the SAP-23 moniker. Barry would only have one more conversation with his wife, but as it had been said many times before, ignorance is bliss.

Jeremiah Wilson downloaded every file and scientific article published by Dr. Julie Reiser. *Incredible*, JJ thought, stumbling upon one of her earliest planetary discoveries, 'Reison-892'. He was looking forward to calling and scheduling a trip to Houston once he got home. JJ also couldn't help but laugh to himself seeing the sixty missed calls from Jack Crowder.

Mabrey and Sims were doing what they did best, supporting their captain. However, both men were still reeling from the tragic loss of their late comrade, Corporal Gunn.

Adi was experiencing the most trying time of anyone. The people she cared about most were now in grave danger. Her calamity was further exacerbated by the thousands of people who had, or who would soon, become merged from SAP-23. She felt Jake Meyers either gave up on her or was dead.

Adi's parents recently experienced the ordeal of being strong-armed by one of Hersey's most diabolical henchmen, and Fortner had been working on his own accord because she had no idea what went on in that man's head. "He's so stubborn," Adi mumbled, standing to go sit beside him.

"It's getting pretty dark now, so you think we can leave soon?" Adi said, finding an old five-gallon bucket to sit on. Fortner got up to give Adi his seat, but she refused. "I can find my own seat, thanks."

"That's part of your problem, Roth. You won't let people help you," Fortner said, stretching his feet out.

"Help? I never asked for your help to begin with."

Fortner let that comment slide. However, Adi was right about not having asked for his help in the first place. But the more Fortner thought about taking the high road and dropping the matter, the more he realized there was nothing to lose, "Has it occurred to you that the man you hate most just so happens to be the very person that had me sent and saved your life?"

Adi's self-control had never been tested so hard after hearing those words from the captain. It was not the fact that Fortner insulted her but because of the words he chose were true. Adi was a conqueror. She lived for being told, "You can't do that." It provided all the motivation she could ever need, but sometimes she was her own worst enemy. There were many burnt bridges in the subconscious of Adilene Roth. Yes, she hated being wrong. Especially if it meant the other person was right.

"Nothing, huh? Did someone finally figure out how to keep you quiet?" Fortner said, extending his legs out even longer, letting out a sigh of victory.

Adi tried a different approach. Perhaps reverse psychology this time, "You're right. I have nothing to say." This response caught Fortner off-guard. His mind immediately became skeptical. John Fortner had only known Adi about four days, and she always had something to say, some clever comeback. He squinted his eyes at her, but it wasn't the best choice to show distrust, as it was almost completely dark outside. On one side of the conversation sat Fortner, steadfast but unaware, and opposite Roth, confident yet broken. Their empty silhouettes were visual representations of how much the two really knew about each other. Adi continued, "No, I have nothing more to say. Everything's fine."

Fortner was becoming actually concerned now because one thing having three sisters had taught him, 'everything's fine' coming from a woman was anything but 'fine'.

Fortner turned to address everyone, "Are you all ready to try and find a route out of here?" This question was, of course, a formality as everyone, including Adi, counted on Fortner already having a plan drawn out. Fortner stopped to wait for Adi's reply, but she said nothing. After a few seconds, she stood and walked over to Barry and JJ.

Everyone came together inside the warehouse. Fortner held up a map and used a flashlight to illuminate the route outlined with a red marker.

"You know we have GPS and maps on our cellphones, right?" JJ asked. "Right, but what happens when the lights go out again?" Fortner asked.

"Just saying," JJ mumbled to himself.

"I've outlined the route that, I feel, gives us the best chance of making Ft. Benning by morning. Upon arrival, I will contact my commander, and we will prepare further arrangements for everyone. You all will make it home safely," Fortner concluded his speech, and everyone climbed back into the storm chaser.

Corporal Gunn's outline under the blanket was a staunch reminder of how, at any time, plans could unravel. Fortner spoke with Mabrey and Sims about burying Gunn behind the warehouse but decided against it as they felt Corporal Gunn deserved a proper military burial. Sadly, even more burial discussions would be needed soon.

# 11. Shattered Forces

## The Accident

Barry continued driving down a densely wooded two-lane road. The dull orange glow of Atlanta's downtown lights still shone in the distance. The unlikely band formed through tribulation would soon test what little bond earned so far. The effects of SAP-23 were now reaching critical mass around multiple towns and cities. After the events of Hersey's insider stealing the vials at the CDC, Higgins already had a network of smugglers in place to distribute AD1 quickly up and down the coast. Each SAP-23 mule received Hersey's official letter to dispel any inquiries from local officials, along with enough vials to merge scores of individuals. The total process for distributing all 400 vials took less than twelve hours. Even the 'Pony Express' would have been proud.

Adi, too, was thinking about a worst-case scenario of possible merged victims. She began estimating the math in her mind, "400 vials…twenty shots per vial, give or take. That's at least 8000 people." Adi placed her hand over her mouth and tried not to draw attention to herself inside the truck. "That's so many," Adi said, staring up at the moon as she had done earlier that month in Alaska. Also, the numbers she conjured did not take into consideration for the merged having the ability to spread whatever mutation had formed.

No one, including Adi, Meyers, or Hersey, knew that the infected cells could probably only transmit through blood-on-blood contact, or so she believed. Adi continued holding on to the small container of the sisters' blood in her hand. These three vials were the key to figuring this all out. Adi thought, *if only I could get to my lab in Alaska and have a little time.* Time, she would not get. The next course of action was making it to the military base, then hopefully, being proven innocent of her current charges. "I can't save others if I'm sitting in prison," Adi said, too loudly, and Fortner heard the words.

"You're not going to prison, Ms. Roth," Fortner said, checking his bootlaces. Adi did not answer. She had invoked the quiet treatment from the captain and wasn't planning on breaking anytime soon. Fortner sensed this and let the matter go.

JJ turned to Barry, "Hey, ma. You okay? Is Alice, okay?"

"Feeling much better, she said," Barry answered surprisingly calm as he continued on with Wilson. "I think we will be done with all this mess in no time."

"How you holding up, kiddo?" Any more news from Houston? Barry was secretly interested in knowing how JJ and scientist were getting along.

JJ deduced his friend's question correctly, "I think she's very nice, you know, like…someone who's passionate about the same things as me." What Barry did not know; Wilson was happier he had met Reiser than he was about the electromagnetic storm. Wonder and awe of the phenomena out in space was replaced by something more powerful, the human element. JJ was smitten.

The friends continued to talk for another minute or so as the wooded two-lane road opened onto a large exit bypass. Cars were on fire, and people were frantically running in and out of stores. Chaos reigned around the strip malls lining the streets of the exit.

JJ turned to Fortner and Adi, "Merged?"

Adi answered, "Can't be…the probability of more than a few infected at any given area is extremely unlikely."

The truth was that due to the storms, conspiracy whack jobs took the aurora as a sign of the end of times. Looting and destruction increased around larger cities. The merged were scattered amongst them, hiding in plain sight.

Barry turned south at the exit, and people began running up to the truck, looking into the windows. Fortner and Echo Team removed their side arms and prepared for the worst. "Keep moving," Fortner said, sliding a round into the chamber of the ridiculously large gun.

"Is that thing really necessary?" JJ said, staring at the chrome barrel. Fortner carried a Smith and Wesson 500 magnum, and no, it wasn't necessary, but like Adi, Fortner was either all in or not at all.

"They're starting to climb on the hood," Barry said.

The group could also hear faint voices outside the truck, "Hey it's the weatherman." Barry and JJ said nothing. The storm chaser was barely moving forward now. "What you got in the truck, Mr. Weatherman." A group of men began pulling on the rear doors. Adi switched her attention to John, "Are you just going sit here and let them rip our transportation apart?"

"C'mon, Mr. Weatherman, we just want to know the time and temp." The voices from outside continued talking, louder and closer than before.

Fortner approached the rear doors and flung them both open, exposing the enormous revolver's barrel. The sheer horror in the eyes of the men scattered the crowd in all directions. Fortner turned to the others and smiled. Even Adi found this amusing. Every day, people encountered hoodlums and criminals working to make innocent lives miserable. The desire to get vigilante retribution had been satisfied by Fortner's current actions.

Fortner reached to close the doors placing his gun into the holster first. He should have waited. A large hand grabbed the captain and yanked him out and onto the pavement from the moving truck. A large, hulking man, who had received his AD1 injection to counter a staph infection contracted at the local gym, began clawing and pounding Fortner. Sims and Mabrey opened fire, striking the man several times, but he wasn't going down. Years and years of steroid abuse had left the man a raging emotional mess. SAP-23 had enhanced his strength and rage. His cells were regenerating faster than ever.

Adi looked out at Fortner in horror. This enraged monster was her first time seeing an infected up close since the episode back at the CDC.

"Stop the truck, Barry. Go back. Go back," JJ yelled frantically. Mabrey and Sims jumped out of the truck forcing their way toward the captain.

Fortner was holding his own the best he could. The strength of the man was incredible. Very rarely did John Fortner come across a man that could beat him, but right now, he wasn't fighting a man and was getting his ass whipped. Mabrey landed a crucial hit on the left knee, causing Fortner to be released. The knee healed almost instantly.

"What? How?" Sims screamed out, reaching for another magazine from his belt.

Fortner regrouped, pulled his gun, and began unloading the five-shot chamber. Large pieces of flesh were blasted away, immediately replaced with gaping holes of space. The man screamed in a bellowing growl, "Hot." The merged began approaching Mabrey and Sims when a white cloud engulfed the merged man. Adi had sprayed the entire contents of the fire extinguisher disorienting the hulking beast. Echo Team had but a moment of time to reorganize and reload their weapons.

Fortner commanded, "Sims, chest. Lt., stomach. On my fire." The echo team fired over thirty shots into the body in less than five seconds. The shock and stress of trauma overcame the ability of SAP-23 to heal the man. It also helped that the man no longer had a head. He fell with a thud. Crowds in the distance had caught it all on video, the footage already receiving millions of views on social media.

Barry saw the various flashes from the groups of people and knew this was about to get a lot worse for everyone. "Get in. It's already on the news," Barry said. The storm chaser was on the move again, and so was Higgins.

Fortner checked himself once back inside the truck. Adi dropped her mental wall and asked, "Are you hurt? Did you see his eyes?"

"Black like death," Fortner replied, loading fresh rounds into the chamber.

"Um, they know what we're driving now," JJ said.

"Who does?" Adi asked.

JJ slowly raised his phone while Barry turned the volume up. A short video clip from a prominent social media website played, showing the firefight and Adi running with the fire extinguisher.

"Oh my god," she said, covering her mouth.

"The Extinguisher," JJ said randomly to Adi.

"What about it?"

"That's your new name, girl," JJ said and replayed the clip of Adi in slow motion, spraying down the merged man. The look on her face was pure ferocity. Adi was embarrassed at her appearance on the camera.

"And you," JJ said, pointing at the captain, "They're calling you Jacked Ryan." Fortner's clip showed his bulging arm absorbing the recoil from the hand cannon.

Fortner asked, "And what is the news calling us?"

"Murderers, terrorists, you know…same as before," JJ concluded, returning to his phone.

"Welcome to the club." Fortner's words soon made their way into JJ's mind for understanding. He and Barry were now on the most wanted hit list too. "We need another ride," Fortner said, surveying the surroundings. "Pull into the next parking lot."

The storm chaser came to a stop. Everyone exited the truck and began looking around for a new suitable mode of transportation. Fortner began walking toward a large shadow.

"A school bus, riding through town at midnight? Really," Adi questioned.

"I've got to agree with her on this one," Barry said to everyone.

Fortner opened the door to the bus and fired it up, "School buses have good radio comms, and they can withstand a lot of damage." The captain was absolutely right about the bus. He knew Higgins wouldn't be too far away. It would have to do. "We use the bus until we can put some distance between us and Higgins," Fortner concluded by pulling the air brake.

Sims and Mabrey retrieved the corporal's body and the two duffle bags containing SAP-23 vials. JJ and Barry pulled the license plate tag from the storm chaser with all other documents linking them to Huntsville and piled them into the bus. Adi plopped down in the front seat closest to the door, looking at her phone now as well, "The Extinguisher…ha!" The bus set out into the darkness.

Not too long after leaving the school, the CB radio began picking up traffic reports of increased police presence near their location. Helicopters filled the sky. Some of the choppers were news crews reporting on the looting, though the majority remained FBI and state law enforcement on the hunt for Fortner and Adi.

The media continued touting the random attacks of the merged as random drug-induced psycho-maniacal activity. A few prominent news networks even jumped on the merged nomenclature to boost ratings. Dumb teenagers were seen in the background of the newscasts wearing t-shirts with 'Merged' or 'Merge Me' written on them. Others wore black makeup around their eyes and started shouting one-word idiocies.

The drug was said to cause severe adrenaline output and the inability to remain rationally, cognizant.

The blood oozing factor, however, were not reported. The coverage of those symptoms would most certainly have caused a national panic and health crisis.

"This is getting crazy. It looks like a hornet's nest up there," JJ said, observing the lights from the helicopters zipping in all directions from the helicopters.

Fortner had given Barry a break from driving and began having second thoughts about choosing the large school bus. The safety reflectors gave the large yellow target away like a Christmas tree at night. Fortner swirled the truck, took a sharp turn onto a dirt road and pulled into a thick patch of forest. He told everyone, "We aren't going anywhere right now with all that up there."

"So, we sit in a bus in the woods?" Adi said.

Fortner ignored Adi telling Mabrey and Sims to, once again, set up a perimeter and monitor traffic near the dirt road. He turned to Adi, Barry, and JJ, "Look, I know this isn't what you want to hear, but we need to wait until the patrols move to new coordinates."

"It will be daylight in five hours, Captain. At our current pace, we won't make it to base before daybreak, will we?" Barry asked, propping his feet up on the long brown faux leather seat.

The cycle of riding a few miles, stopping, then repeating over and over again began taking a toll on everyone. The vice was closing tightly, and it was only a matter of time until the group would deal with either Higgins or the police. Barry was the first to think of using the glaring weakness of the bus to their benefit, "Tomorrow is a school day, right?"

"Barry, what does that have to do with anything? You got homework from the 70s to turn in?" JJ asked, looking at the local weather radar on his phone.

Adi interrupted, "No, he's talking about camouflage. Brilliant idea, Barry." By waiting until the proper hour in the morning, the school bus could move about with little concern as it would appear as nothing more than any other bus carrying students to school.

"This could work," Fortner added.

"Okay, so we just wait until first light, then stay on the back roads as long as possible. I like it." Adi said to everyone.

The cleverness of Barry's idea suggestion renewed the purpose of action within Adi. She was also surprised that the great John Fortner had not thought of this first. "Doesn't the army teach you guys the art of blending in?" Adi directed the jab at Fortner, and everyone on the bus was well aware Adi was trying her best to be petty, even though it was not in good taste.

Fortner huffed but did not respond, and he continued plotting a new course on the map. The pendulum of pettiness had swung back in favor of Ms. Roth. The two had far too long been enthralled in this game of 'correctness gotcha' since day one at the lab. JJ, who rarely asked Fortner many questions, could not help but do so after witnessing the fight between him and the large, merged man.

"Have you ever been thrown around like that before?"

"Negative." The Captain's single-word response did little to appease JJ, prompting him to continue asking questions.

"I just figured a guy like you would enjoy getting into fights with large objects," JJ said.

Fortner was completely unprepared for the wild ride through JJ's mysterious memories which were about to be unloaded on him. "Watching you throw down with that thing tonight made me remember this boxing match I saw during a snowstorm."

"Here we go," Barry said, giving Adi a peanut butter cracker from his pack. Barry had experienced this before many times with JJ's memory bank, an assortment of unbelievable truths and excellent lies.

Fortner continued looking at JJ the same way a squirrel looked before crossing a busy road. The indecisiveness was what usually killed the animal, not the car. Fortner wasn't sure if he should run away or remain still.

JJ continued, "No, I'm serious. Fine. I'll spare you details of that one, but I really did see a guy wrestle a bear once." JJ turned to Adi and Winters, "Yeah, this guy was getting crushed by the bear, kind of, like the captain was tonight by that merged dude and…"

JJ tried to continue but was abruptly cut off by Fortner, "Okay, that's enough."

Barry and Adi were rolling. Mabrey and Sims could hear the laughter at their post near end of the dirt road.

*So much for keeping a low profile*, Mabrey thought.

"Alright, be honest. What do you like to do for fun, Captain?" JJ was persistent if anything. He wasn't going to be satisfied until he pulled something out of Fortner to lighten his mood.

One might have thought Adi and Winters were at the movies. They ate their snacks and hung on every word, relishing this moment. It was quite the entertainment, a gentle to and fro between a mosquito and wildebeest.

Fortner looked JJ dead in the eye as seriously as any man has ever looked at another and paused briefly. The ambient lighting of the bus made the Captain look like he was about to tell a cheesy ghost story at summer camp, "I like to wake up in the morning and see which way the American flag is blowing outside so…"

Adi and Winters stopped chewing; their eyes frozen wide open. JJ had also become enthralled with Fortner's words.

JJ became overly excited, and he couldn't take the pause anymore, "So?"

"So, I know which way to start running. I only run the way Ole Glory is blowing." Fortner completed his grand statement and truly dumbfounded everyone on the bus. Barry, for the first time in his life, saw JJ completely speechless. The comment from Fortner was comically absurd, so it had to be true. Fortner was incapable of lying when he was serious.

*Oh no, he's telling the truth. No lie could be that bad*, Adi thought.

Fortner calmly returned to his map, and JJ never asked him a stupid question again.

*That shut him up*, Fortner thought, chuckling to himself.

The unexpected comedic relief of the night turned out to be much-needed. The heaviness and pain of death and destruction remained in the back of everyone's minds. Surprisingly, none of the group slept. The adrenaline rush continued throughout the night. The sunrise would come soon. The bent but not broken group was ready to move on in more ways than one.


## Air Force None

President Richards awoke at 4:00 a.m. to sign a few last-minute directives and receive the agenda for the day. The President's Chief of Staff delivered the itinerary with every minute of every hour detailed and accounted for. Secretary Renner would meet POTUS on Air Force One at 6:00 a.m. The seven-hour flight would provide time to cover any newly found problems of the merged, EMP storms, to discuss any mundane bureaucratic issues. Richards would then give a press conference at Elmendorf AFB, have lunch with Alaska's governor to discuss the upcoming election, and then travel to Camelot to tour the facilities. The President would immediately leave Camelot for Seattle, thus completing his tour.

It was an extensive and busy schedule. Frank Richards, like many other presidents, had aged drastically during his first term due to the stresses of world affairs and the crunch of time to perform all the duties. The last few years had helped Richards condition himself for the job, but even he was being slowly worn down. It was inevitable. Soon after liftoff, President Richards, Secretary Renner, or anyone else aboard would not have to worry about those inconveniences again. The Eagle would go down this morning in a remote wooded area of Minnesota.

Richards boarded Air Force One, "Morning everyone. Let's get started." The President made his way through to the executive office. Renner was already present and waiting as the President always boards last per custom. Richards passed by the press corps, smiling and waving. Some of the reporters he had grown to like, and he would stop by to talk with them if time allowed, which most times it did not.

"Mr. President, welcome aboard, sir." Richards' chief of staff announced, handing over the packet. Everyone else present stood and acknowledged as The President entered the room and sat at his desk. The ornate desk could never be mistaken for anyone's except that of POTUS as it was the only one littered with numerous phones and dossiers. Many screens on the opposite wall provided strategic command information while others tuned into various news outlets.

Renner and McMillan opened a classified folder, and Richards began, "As you all know by now, a new drug has leaked out into the public, and the terrorist attack on the Atlanta CDC resulted in two citizens dead, and numerous hazardous, potentially deadly chemicals being unaccounted for."

Renner asked, "Sir, don't you feel a little worried about the leadership at the CDC? Dr. Hersey hasn't released a statement or any information about the terrorist Dr. Adilene Roth, a scientist he had hand selected to work in Alaska and Georgia."

"I talked to Bill myself. He has people working to contain the situation."

General McMillan was excited about the opportunity to return to Camelot. "I hope you get to see how it worked. The injection brought that mouse back from the dead. Just imagine a battalion of soldiers without fear of getting sick," the general said, flipping through more pages in the folder.

Renner added, "I still don't trust anything that man does."

Richards slapped his folder down onto the desk and looked at both of them, "Look, I'm not discussing my vice-presidential running mate and friend anymore on this flight, understood."

Renner and McMillan responded in unison, "Yes, sir," and continued the debriefing.

"General McMillan, what are the reports from the EMP storm over the southeast?" the president asked after reading item three in the folder.

"Sir, there are still a few cities suffering power outages. All military installations and personnel remain unaffected and fully operative. Borders remain secure," the general concluded his report.

The climate, national security, and lastly, Alaska were pressing topics covered during the debriefing. The other passengers of Air Force One worked on news bulletins and questions for the upcoming conference. The pilots were checking gauges and monitoring flight systems. Everything was business as usual until it wasn't.

"Saw you were a little late for inspection this morning, Randy," the co-pilot Adam Connors said.

"Yeah, I had to swing by the hospital. I burned my hand last week grilling, and the damn thing got infected," Pilot Randy Morris replied.

"You're supposed to cook the food, not yourself." Connors laughed, twisting a small dial near a series of lights in the cockpit.

Morris laughed, nodding in agreement, "Best burger I've had in years though, so I guess it was worth it." Randy Morris held his hand up for the copilot to see, showing it as a trophy for the pain he endured.

A strong gust of wind had blown the grill cover shut on top of Morris' hand. A long scab shown strung along the knuckles tapering off behind the pinky finger. Randy Morris received his injection of AD1 two days ago to fight the infection. AD1 performed wonderfully in healing the hand. The scabbing vanished within mere minutes after injection. However, the veins around the knuckles were already becoming darker than before, and Morris had to blink constantly. AD1 was taking control.

"Doctor said he had some new miracle drug. I don't know what that stuff was made of, but it cleared my infection in an hour. And my hand probably won't even have a scar."

Connors responded with a cackle checking his watch, "Now, if it could just cure your stupidity, you'd be golden."

Morris shook his head and continued updating ground control and other military contacts in the air and ground. The pilots would switch primary flying duties every hour. The time was now 6 a.m.

The President went to meet with other members of his staff. He needed to stretch his legs and show his face. Richards enjoyed all the perks that came with the seal, flying in the safest airplane in the world being one executive perks he coveted the most. The President was smiling for a photo with General McMillan when the plane began to shake violently.

"Randy, what are you doing? What's wrong with you?" Connors asked, grabbing the wheel.

Morris began to merge and was currently more focused on attacking the copilot than keeping an airplane in the sky. People began knocking on the cockpit door. It was locked.

Connors began screaming for help as Randy Morris ripped patches of clothing and skin from Connors' body. He kicked Morris across the cockpit and they made for the door. His hand grasped the handle, but for a brief moment, when his entire body slammed against the floor, breaking his back. Morris began biting and clawing the face of his dead friend.

The plane spiraled into a nosedive. Secret agents finally breached the cockpit door, but their efforts were trivial.

The President was preparing to try a tandem parachute jump with one of his secret service agents. More agents piled into the cockpit fighting with Morris. The SAP-23 continued merging with his cells, creating added strength and adrenal rage. Morris killed them all and continued hammering their lifeless bodies.

President Richards attached himself to the secret service agent and made their way to the nearest hatch. "Okay, sir, when we jump, stay calm," the agent said, checking the straps one final time.

"It's going to get really loud when they open the door…just…" That was the last word Frank Richards ever heard. Air Force One crashed in northern Minnesota; there were no survivors.


## Quicksand

Back in Virginia, Dr. Hersey was startled awake for the second day in a row by another nightmare. Unlike the wildfire dream from before, this dream produced no positive illusions. The terror of what he had seen allowed, for the first time, doubts about making it through the current situation with Dr. Roth unaffected. He continued replaying the events of the new nightmare.

Hersey dreamed two hands were reaching through an opaque streaming veil of water. The two hands were on course straight for each other and would collide unless one altered its path. A cloud stood between the hands, obstructing the visuals of the other. The cloud concealed some hidden truth and sustained itself by pulling vapor from both veil of water. The first hand was Hersey's. It continued forward, plunging itself deep inside the cloud. The second hand began circling the cloud, never touching it. Hersey's hand emerged withered and decrepit. The second hand left the cloud, crossing through the veil the first had entered, disappearing forever.

Hersey was left distraught by this nightmare since he could not decipher its meaning. He put great discernment into analyzing each detail, but this was not a case for the mind but the soul.

The two hands in the dream belonged to Hersey and Adilene Roth. The cloud only revealed its contents to those who were worthy. Hersey's hand was deemed uncertain as it was harmed but not destroyed. Roth's hand never found out because it did not try. The truth of the cloud was life. Hersey would lose himself unless he changed his destiny, and Roth would not have life without trying.

Hersey entered the balcony. The weight of every skeleton in his closet began pressing down like a submarine stranded in an abyssal trench. The new list of problems was reaching critical mass.

All of the following were constantly on his mind now: Jake Meyers was downstairs sleeping, not knowing he was being lied to, Roth was somewhere with evidence proving he was to blame for everything, President Richards and Maggie Renner were headed to his lab chopped full of secrets, and SAP-23 was turning people into the merged.

"I need another miracle." The doctor turned to check his morning reports on the many screens. Hersey did not get a miracle. Nevertheless, the next event bought him more time to contemplate a solution. Dr. Hersey fell to his knees when the emergency captions ran across the screen.


*Air Force One crashed near the Canadian border. President Richards and Secretary of State Renner are presumed dead.*


Hersey remained frozen to the screen and captions. Vice-President Tim Harding was in the process of being sworn in at the White House when the rapping on Hersey's door came.

"Sir, Dr. Meyers is downstairs and has requested an audience," Henry said, entering the room.

"Dead," Hersey whispered.

Dr. Hersey turned to Henry with a broken, sullen face, "The President is dead."

"Sir, how?" Henry asked, placing a coffee cup on a small round end table near the door.

Henry was quite fond of Richards. He always enjoyed his short talks with Frank Richards, and for years Henry would walk Richards up the stairs to the second-floor balcony having quick conversations and talking about various topics.

"How terribly awful, sir."

"Air Force One went down in a Minnesota forest. No reports as to why. Henry, I want you to prepare a vehicle for me. Also, phone President Harding's people at the White House."

Hersey turned his attention back to the screen. Tim Harding stood at the presidential podium surrounded by his and Frank Richards' family.

Harding was a man twenty years senior to Frank Richards. At one time, he was a fine horseman and wrangler from Oklahoma. Harding's reputation helped swing blue-collar voters toward Richards. Tim Harding was a good man, and even though he and Richards could not have been any more different. Regardless, the two became good friends. Another bold, red caption bar ran across the screen, *President Harding addresses the nation.*

"This morning, America has lost a great Patriot. I am deeply saddened to learn of the tragic news of my dear friend Frank Richards. He truly loved America and its people. I also want to send my condolences to the families of Secretary Maggie Renner and General Nathaniel McMillan's families. At noon today, I am asking for twelve minutes of silence across America, one minute for each American lost." Harding concluded his statements and left the podium.

The newscast concluded. Hersey powered the screens down and went to the coffee cup near the door. He drank it down with one gulp.

"Thirty minutes, Henry." Hersey approached the stairs and headed down to the lab.

Jake did something that morning he hadn't done in a long time. He awoke early before sunrise and went to work. The patient, injected with the new SAP-9 formula remained stable. The pigmentation of the injection site was as if it had never occurred.

The nurse spoke for the first time, "He slept most of the night. I gave him water through the straw and kept a chart of his temperature changes."

Jake walked over to analyze the eyes and drew a small amount of blood from the man. "Do you know his name?" Jake asked.

"No, I was contacted by an associate of Dr. Hersey to arrive here and administer normal intensive care unit services." The nurse took another look at the gentleman on the bed. "I was paid 100,000 dollars for one night's work and told to never speak of any of this."

Jake returned to a microscope. He placed one drop of fresh blood onto a glass slide.

The elevator door opened, startling Jake and the nurse. Hersey had to put away the terrible news replaying inside his mind and compose himself. Meyers could not see him in a weakened state. He approached the patient. "It seems the serum was a success doctor," Hersey said with a pleased tone, turning to the nurse. "My dear, you may exit the premises."

The nurse gathered her bags. Henry summoned another driver for the lady, and she left 'The Refuge'.

Jake joined the doctor beside the patient. The man's eyes provided the assurance to release him from the muzzle. Jake unlatched the thick leather restraint covering most of the face. The eyes of the man followed the hand movements of Meyers. The patient was fully aware of his situation. Jake loosened the last strap, pausing to prepare for the worse. "Can you speak? Do you hear me?" Jake asked.

"Where am…I was—What happened?" The man had no memory of SAP-23 overcoming him while shopping at a grocery store. The serum merged his cells and a brutal rampage had ensued.

Hersey had already begun contacting local detention centers looking for inmates incarcerated for extreme violence due to drugs.

"You were ill, but you're good to go now," Jake said.

"Can I go home?"

Dr. Hersey interrupted, "Sir, you are to return home and stay there until you receive a call releasing you from quarantine."

"Quarantine, why? Oh my god, what's wrong with me?"

"Sir, you will comply with our instructions and remain indoors until released. Dr. Meyers, a word in private," Hersey said, leaving the man restrained in the hospital bed. "I must leave for urgent business at the White House."

"Your orders are to stay and continue the synthesis of the new formula and prepare single doses for mass distribution."

Jake looked confused. The orders were extremely careless, "I don't understand. Did you not see what that man was last night?"

"He was sick, really sick." Jake had forgotten an important lesson as he stood in front of Jekyll. He was still basically nothing more than a prisoner without bindings.

"Let me remind you why you are here Dr. Meyers. You are not my guest, and that (Hersey pointed at the man) is the work of Ms. Roth. So, you will do as you're told and prepare my medicine," Hersey concluded, entering the elevator.

Jake's heart sank. He sat, looking at the man for another few minutes pondering his next move. "I need to try and contact Adi. Something is not right." The harshness of Hersey's words was unnerving. Unlike his first night at 'The Refuge', Jake would never trust Hersey again. He kicked himself for ever believing Adi orchestrated this mayhem. Hersey's men still had Jake's phone and continued to monitor his every movement. Jake Meyers was no better than Moucious Clay, trapped in a cage.

"Can I please go home now?" the man asked again. His tone was pitiful.

Jake began writing something down, and he placed the note beside the man, then released him from all of his restraints.

"Thank you," he said, rubbing his wrists and ankles.

The man took Jake's note. It read: *Write down your phone number and wait for my call. Do not tell anyone about this.* The man slowly met eyes with Jake and continued checking his arms and legs without acknowledging the paper's contents. Both men understood that each would be in danger if anyone found out.

"Here are your clothes," Jake said, throwing a bundle of clothes, including a pen, onto the foot of the bed and returning back to his microscope. The man wrote his number down, and slid it under the blanket.

Henry reappeared from the elevator with two large men, and in the blink of an eye, Jake was alone in the lab again. Impulsive decisions made by Hersey would result in even more catastrophes.

The improved SAP-9 formula did not neutralize SAP-23. It enhanced it, creating an even more volatile compound. The man's cells began mutating the instant Jake applied the serum. And to make matters even worse, the new incubation period was reduced to twenty-four hours. Twelve hours now until something worse would terrorize a community. SAP-9 sped up the regenerative properties of variant 23, making the new merged harder to kill.

However, just like Adi at the CDC, no one knew this, and by that night, Jake would have thousands of doses ready to expedite across the country. The only detail Jake had not figured out yet was how Hersey was going to get people to agree to using yet another unknown medicine.

By the time Hersey reached the hospital, he had already contrived a plan to answer the questions Jake was asking himself back at the lab. After showing his respect for Frank Richards, Hersey would get, newly sworn in, President Harding to allow an emergency CDC broadcast. He would use this to prey on the fear of the public about the ongoing coverage of violence due to sickness and drug abuse. Hersey would then have no need to hide the new serum from the public. This would increase his ability to mass distribute the injections. The SAP-23/AD1 infected participants would be cured for good, and Hersey would be lauded as a national hero. Hersey thought all of this through during his ride to Washington.

*Hasty but inevitable*, he thought, looking down at his hands. Despite the recent dream remaining fresh on his mind, Hersey felt cautiously optimistic that his new plan would be a success. The glaring issue with this stunt was that if it failed, Dr. Hersey would essentially be committing political and professional suicide.

There would be no one to blame except himself. Hersey would be ruined and held liable for countless American deaths.

Hersey arrived at the White House and was led straight to the Oval Office. Tim Harding met him at the door, "Dr. Hersey, please come in. We have much to discuss."


## Hounds of War

Higgins' pilot hovered the chopper over an intersection outside of Atlanta, "Sir, this is the last known location of Captain Fortner." Higgins looked down at random cars on fire and the dried bloody pool where the gigantic merged man lay.

"Put it down over there, private," Higgins commanded, pointing to an open parking lot. People scattered away from the helicopter. Law enforcement was on the scene, and other news vans began rolling up.

The Major had used the news traffic to make it within an hour north of Fortner and Adi's current location. Higgins along with three heavily armed men, approached the dead body riddled with bullet holes.

"Jesus," one of the men said, poking the body with the muzzle of his rifle.

Higgins looked over the man and turned back toward the helicopter to rally his men. He told the pilot, "Circle the area. They would have switched transportation by now. Find that weather truck."

Major Higgins was an excellent soldier. He was a superb marksman and well-adept in hand-to-hand combat, but the Major's greatest attribute was his intuition and brutality. He knew he was close to finding Captain John Fortner and Dr. Adilene Roth.

"There, by the school," the pilot rang out.

The storm chaser stood out like a sore thumb beside the yellow buses. Drivers had already begun showing up for their routes. Some busses were pulling out of the lot as the helicopter hovered ominously nearby.

The pilot asked, "How do you want me to play this, sir?"

Higgins surveyed the school and the buses still on location. The plan became obvious for Higgins to decipher. "A school bus, bold, even for you, John." Higgins turned to the pilot, "We are looking for a school bus now, private."

"Sir, there are hundreds of buses out there by now. Which way should we go?" The helicopter was starting to draw attention from school officials arriving for work. The buses leaving the school were all heading north.

"South, go south, follow that road." Higgins knew Fortner would try and make it back to Ft. Benning because that's what he would have done. Military investigations superseded local law enforcement matters. Higgins contemplated contacting Fortner's commanding officer but did not want to draw attention to himself during the hunt.

Higgins was essentially a fugitive without official affiliation with the military or law enforcement. Exposing his current location and plan would not be good publicity.

As the helicopter followed the rod recently traveled by Fortner, Higgins mumbled to himself, "Very close, now Captain, I'll have you soon...real soon."

# 12. Reckoning

**Found You**

The sunrise was as bright as it was beautiful. Fortner brought the old bus to life, kicking up gravel and dust as he pulled onto the paved road. The plan was to continue down this path for ten miles then turn onto the interstate and make for Fort Benning.

"I thought you said no interstates?" JJ was not liking the new route drawn up on the map.

The captain was not overly confident about putting everyone at risk driving on the busiest roadway in Georgia, Interstate 85. Nonetheless, these were desperate times. Fortner felt the speed advantage of the interstate was worth the hazard of potential exposure.

"It's a calculated risk," he responded.

JJ instinctively gripped the leathered upholstery ahead of him, bracing for what lay ahead as the bus roared through a green light.

Adi saw the large air control towers of the Atlanta Airport, the busiest airport in the world. Every day thousands of people departed and arrived through its gates.

"We might be able to find a less conspicuous ride in one of the remote parking lots." Adi's hypothesis was valid as plenty of shuttle vans and large SUVS parked in various places around the airport, but problems lay with navigating security. Adi must have been extra spry this morning as she continued encouraging Fortner to try the airport, "Since you're already feeling bold this morning. Why not go for the gold?"

Mabrey and Sims secretly hoped the captain would do what he had become very good at, ignoring Adi. The crew did not get a chance to hear Fortner's final answer because a large black helicopter began hovering above them, interrupting all conversations.

JJ screamed out, "Cops! Feds!"

"No, worse." Fortner recognized the helicopter as a military-style Black Hawk.

Police didn't have the budget for such a chopper. No, this bird of prey was dispatched by someone with too much money and power, Dr. Hersey.

"It's Higgins." Fortner floored the bus causing a huge black cloud to engulf the cars behind. The chopper continued lowering itself until it flew just a few feet above the bus. Onlookers were videoing the chase like a crazy action scene from a movie. Many motorists actually thought it was a film crew making the next blockbuster.

"Are they crazy?" JJ said, trying to get a better look from one of the side windows. "It sounds like they landed on the roof!"

The airport was less than two miles away now, and everyone inside the bus was uncertain about what to do. There was no way the slow cumbersome school bus could evade the helicopter.

A voice boomed out from within the chopper above, "Captain John Fortner and Dr. Adilene Roth, pull the bus over. Comply and you will not be harmed." The chopper's PA system went quiet for a moment and then again erupted, "This is your only warning."

Lt. Mabrey pulled a rifle from a pack and loaded a fresh magazine. "I can engage the target Captain. Give the word."

"You can't start shooting on a highway. There are people around us," Adi said, running to the front of the bus toward Fortner. "Go to the airport. He can't enter airport airspace." Adi's suggestion was brilliant.

"Alright. Everyone, hold on." Fortner almost flipped the bus, swerving into the far-right lane headed for the airport off-ramp.

"Do not let them reach that ramp," Higgins commanded, for he also knew flying the helicopter into forbidden airspace would trigger FBI and law enforcement. "Take out the bus, now."

The helicopter door slid back, and two men began firing down upon the school bus. At first, they aimed for the tires and hood, hoping to disable the vehicle. However, the ruggedly made bus was not slowing.

"Everybody, under the seats," Fortner said as he continued driving in a zigzag pattern. The exit was only a few hundred yards away. "Stay under the seats."

Higgins saw the exit and commanded, "Shoot them, kill them. They cannot get away." Bullets began impacting the bus roof, sending shrapnel and fragments to bounce inside. Some bullets went clean through the roof and down to the floor.

"Oh my god! oh my god!" Adi was screaming with her hands over her head. She crouched in the middle of the bus near the wheel well. The sounds of the wheels whining on the road and bullets ricocheting around inside the bus drove her insane.

"Lt., return fire, return fire," Fortner said.

Mabrey unloaded his magazine into the helicopter, killing one of the men. Higgins began firing into the bus as well.

*Almost there*, Fortner thought. Sweat was pouring down his face, and his heart was pounding. He had been in many firefights during countless deployments, but this was different. Fortner wasn't used to being the prey. He hated the feeling of being hunted in such a defenseless vehicle.

The bus made it to the airport off-ramp and took on a dozen or so more shots until the helicopter had to pull back before crossing the airport's boundaries.

"Pull back! Pull back! Put it down in that field." Higgins pointed to a field close to the west gate of the airport. He was livid that the bus had made it to safety. "Sir, law enforcement is en route, and not they're happy," the helicopter pilot said.

"Alright, fly south. Find the next small airport. We'll refuel and regroup there. I need to make a phone call."

Fortner pulled into a parking deck. The man collecting money was flabbergasted by the appearance of the bullet-mangled machine. Fortner smiled and handed the man a wad of cash, "Keep the change. Not a word."

They came to a creeping stop. Fortner stood and made his way down through the bus aisles. "Lt., sitrep."

"Barry. No, no! Barry!" JJ was the first to find Winters under a seat with two gunshot wounds in his chest.

"Hey, kiddo," Barry responded, barely awake. Adi helped JJ pull Barry from under the seat out into the aisle.

"He's going into shock." Roth turned to Fortner, "He will die unless we get him to a hospital."

"Sims, go get help," Fortner said.

"Captain, are you sure? We're done for soon as I explain this."

Fortner was in no mood for discussions. He kicked the back door of the bus open, clean off its hinges and repeated, "Go find this man some help, now!"

"Sir." Sims jumped out of the bus, running toward the airport entrance.

"What can I do? Tell me what I can do." JJ looked frantically back and forth between Adi and Fortner.

Barry began coughing blood, and his breathing purled with a gurgling hiss. His lungs were filling with blood.

Adi ran to one of the duffle bags, pulled out a vial of SAP-23, and drew the shot. She returned to Barry, but it was too late. Barry Winters, a man loved by everyone, died on the floor of that bus.

Adi overcome with grief, shattered the syringe against the wall of the bus and screamed for what seemed to be forever. Then she fell into one of the seats, head in hands.

JJ watched the translucent blue solution trickle down the side of the bus. He wasn't ready to come to terms with Barry's death yet.

"What are you doing? Help will be here soon. We have to get him off the bus!" JJ pleaded, frantically looking around at everyone.

"JJ, I'm so sorry!" Adi cried out.

An ambulance pulled behind the bus. "This is it," Fortner said. "You all need to get out of here. I'll stay and wait for the police."

John Fortner was willing to sacrifice himself to save others. That was the difference between him and Higgins. The Major, given the chance, would have killed every last person on that bus.

"I'm with you, sir," Mabrey said.

"So are we," Adi said, holding JJ's hand.

The ambulance slammed shut, and there never was a more surprised group of people than when they saw Sergeant Sims rounded the corner from the side of the vehicle. "Let's go. I snagged this ambulance idling by the front entrance."

The body of Barry Winters joined Corporal Gunn's in the back of the ambulance. The bags of SAP-23 beside their dead bodies may as well have been the grim reaper. Adi and Lt. Mabrey climbed into the back and closed the doors. As Fortner drove away, JJ broke down in the passenger seat. Everyone boarded the ambulance, leaving the airport and the torn bus behind.

Meanwhile, back in Alabama, out at Dauphin Island, Alice Winters fully merged on the beach and ran out into the water after a man parasailing offshore. She drowned before reaching her goal. If any positive could have come from Barry dying so suddenly, it would be that he never knew the terrible fate of the love of his life.

Even though it was still early morning, the day had already levied a heavy toll. As the ambulance drove on through the congested area, several people around the airport merged and began attacking innocent bystanders. Many SAP-23 recipients were going about their mundane lives until they changed. Some were coming in on flights, and others were preparing to lift off.

The scene was chaotic. Security opened fire on some of the merged, killing a few, while others continued the rampage throughout the airport. The more time the solution had to *merge* with the victim, the stronger and more resilient they became.


## Duty Calls

Dr. Hersey entered the Oval Office and greeted newly sworn-in President Harding.

The President approached Hersey, "William, thank you for meeting with me. We have much to discuss."

"Sir, please allow me to express my condolences," Hersey said, bowing his head solemnly to President Harding. He knew how close Hersey and Frank Richards became through the years.

"I'm getting reports it was a case of the pilot going crazy on some drug-induced frenzy," Harding informed Hersey. "The Secret Service was going to try a tandem parachute jump with Richards when they ran out of altitude."

"Drug-induced frenzy?" Hersey asked, checking his watch. Higgins should have made contact with him by now, and this lateness caused concern for him.

"This merged-drug stuff that's been going around the last few days, I'm told. It's getting out of hand. Stopping it will be my first executive order. The reason why I wanted to talk with you so soon is that I need a Vice-President." Harding walked back to his desk and sat. "I want you to fill that role, William."

Dr. Hersey wasn't sure what to say. The news of how the crash had happened revealed that is was entirely his fault. By bringing Dr. Roth to Atlanta, everything after that point was his fault. "Sir, can I have a few hours to think the matter over before giving you a decision?"

"You have until noon, William. Just remember this is still an election year. If you were good enough to be Frank Richards' pick for running mate, you're good enough to take the nomination yourself."

"Thank you, I'll be in touch before the day's end." Hersey stepped onto the White House front lawn, contemplating his next moves. He began to think,

Harding basically stated that he has no ambition of continuing as president after his current term. If I should become Vice-President, resources to capture Ms. Roth and dispel any evidence of my involvement improve exponentially. Hersey's thoughts were interrupted by Higgins.

"Major, pray tell you have useful news this morning." Hersey was beginning to lose trust in Higgins. For many years the Major had stood ready at a moment's notice to execute any order. Up to this point, he had a flawless resume. His recent inability to apprehend Ms. Roth was increasing cause for concern.

"Sir, we engaged Dr. Roth and Captain Fortner near the Atlanta airport."

"What do you mean by engaged, Major? And don't speak to me about this Captain. He is your problem, not mine." Hersey's voice took on an unusually, deeper tone.

"Sir, we took shots. We fired back in response, and we pursued. However, we had to abandon the pursuit when they entered the airport."

Hersey walked further away from the surrounding secret service agents, beginning to raise his voice at the Major, "So, you're telling me you shot at them, not knowing if you hurt or even killed them. You then allowed them to escape as you flew away to call me? Is that what I'm hearing?" Hersey had a way of repeating what people had just said to him but completely turning it back on them. This style of embarrassment to his minions was especially favored when dealing with recovering disappointing news.

Major Higgins was becoming angry at himself, not because he was mad at Dr. Hersey, but due to looking like a buffoon in front of his men. "Sir, I just need a few more hours, and I'll have Ms. Roth, dead or alive."

"Fine. I'd prefer alive, but if that's what it takes to cover your incompetence, then so be it." Hersey ended the call without waiting for a response from Higgins and immediately returned to the oval office.

"William, I didn't expect you so soon," President Harding said.

"I accept your gracious offer. Thank you, sir. When do I start?" Hersey asked.

Harding picked up a phone on his desk, and within minutes, a lady appeared with a bible. Dr. Hersey took the oath and was now, after a brief ceremony, Vice-President William Joseph Hersey.

"Congratulations, Mr. Vice-President," Harding said as he, and a few other people, clapped in the background.

"Sir, what would you have me do first?" Hersey asked.

"I want you to start a campaign showing our allies that America is strong and working through this drug epidemic and Frank Richards' death. After that, do what you deem necessary for keeping Americans safe," President Harding concluded.

Hersey left the White House and went to meet his new staff. Hersey also wanted to examine his new office. Keep Americans safe and secure, he thought as the car passed by the Washington Monument. I know one citizen that will never be safer than when Ms. Roth is dead.


## Get to the Chopper

The ambulance came to a stop in an abandoned shopping mall. Twenty years earlier, this mall was a sprawling mecca for shoppers delighting themselves with the newest fashions or catching a movie on IMAX screens. The evolution of the digital era slowly wiped these establishments from the map. Only a few malls remained in operation. It also helped that Fortner chose one of the roughest areas in metro Atlanta to stop.

"I'm done being chased like a rat," Fortner said, stepping out of the ambulance. The latest altercation was enough for Fortner to put escaping on hold. He decided to change his mode of thinking. "We need to find our own helicopter and go hunt that maniac down," Fortner said, pulling another rifle from a bag.

Lt. Mabrey said, "Sir, where and how are we going to find a helicopter?"

"Yeah, it's not like we can just go to the store and pick one up, and no airport is going to let us get within a thousand feet of one before calling the cops," Sims added.

JJ was inside talking to Adi. "I can't believe he's gone. He's just dead now."

"I know it's hard. Barry was a great person, inside and out."

"What was that, stuff you were about to inject him with before he died?" JJ's tone switched to a more serious and ominous one.

"It was…it was going to help keep him alive," Adi said.

"Just what exactly are you guys running from? Don't lie to me, for Barry's sake, don't lie to me." JJ was starting to shake with anger.

"It's my work…it was what I was working on at the CDC."

"I'm going to ask you again. What exactly are you a doctor of?" The words reminded her of the first questions JJ had ever asked Adi, and she had given him the academic response. Now he wanted the truth. Adi was becoming frightened by JJ.

"Fine, it was me. I'm the reason Barry is dead. Is that what you want to hear? I know it, you know, everyone does. The stuff going on out there in the public changing people and killing them, I created it…and I was going to put it inside Barry."

Adi began to cry and returned to the back of the ambulance. Fortner ran around to check on the commotion. He saw JJ still shaking with rage and Adi in the back crying.

"Listen, she did not kill your friend. The man that shot him did. Ms. Roth can't change that now, and neither can you." Fortner continued, "Barry Winters died admirably, and now you have the chance to make sure he didn't die in vain by helping us take down the people that committed this heinous act."

Fortner, deep inside, would have never admitted it to anyone, but he blamed himself for Winters and Gunn's deaths. Under his guidance, two people had died, and he was no closer to accomplishing any of the goals.

Mabrey approached the captain and said, "Sir, what about a police station? Maybe we could sneak in, and I could steal one?"

"Steal one what? What are you trying to do now?" JJ asked.

Fortner interjected, "We need a helicopter. It gives us our best chance of getting out of here and finding Higgins. That's the man who shot Barry. His name is Major Tom Higgins."

"Weather station," JJ said.

"What about it?" Mabrey asked.

"God, how are all 'you' military and doctor people so damn smart yet stupid at the same time. All weather stations have at least one helicopter," JJ said, checking his phone for the nearest weather installation. "Here, the nearest one is in the city of LaGrange. It's about forty-five miles from here," JJ said.

"Are you sure?" Fortner asked.

"I trust him, and so should all of you," Adi said, emerging from the back of the ambulance. Roth looked at JJ and hoped he would forgive her for Barry's death.

"Look, Barry was my best friend, and I know it's not any of your faults. It's just that I really miss him." JJ paused and took Adi's hand, in apology.

JJ turned back to Fortner and Mabrey, "If you can get me to that weather station, I can use my National Weather Center badge and credentials to get us a helicopter. Of course, that's assuming we can find a pilot," JJ said.

"We've got that covered," Lt. Mabrey said, smiling. Bernard Mabrey had been a Blue Angel pilot for the US Navy before joining the Army and finishing Ranger school. He was a man of many talents and could fly basically anything with wings or propellers.

Fortner met with Echo Team for a few minutes alone. Adi wanted to contact her parents but resisted as she knew turning her phone on would bring unwanted pings on nearby towers risking giving away her position. After a minute or so, the urge to check on Dean and Ethel was more than she could ignore, especially after what had happened to Barry. "JJ, can I borrow your phone?"

"Now? For what?" JJ asked.

"I need to call my parents and make sure they're okay. No more than a minute."

JJ reluctantly handed over his phone, and Adi called her father, "Hey, Dad, are you okay?"

"Yeah, just left the hospital again. Your mom's pneumonia is picking up. The doctor said it was some infection in the lungs."

"Nothing too bad, I guess. He gave her this new stuff, supposed to clear it up in no time," Dean said.

"New stuff? What new stuff?" Adi asked in a low voice.

"Your mom laughed when she saw the name of it. She told the doc it looked like her daughter's name, AD1 was what they called it."

At that moment, Adi understood what Hersey had done. She felt it deep inside her soul. *He named it after me, that sick son of…* Adi's thoughts were interrupted by her father.

Dean turned to Ethel in the car and asked, "You feeling better already, aren't ya?"

"Did she get the shot? Did she get it?" Adi screamed.

"Calm down, dear, she's fine. Of course, she got it. About thirty minutes ago," Dean answered confidently.

"I love you both, but I have to go now," Adi barely got the words out of her mouth.

Dean and Ethel said in unison, "Love you too. Bye. Be careful."

Adi handed JJ back his phone, and immediately powered hers on to phone Hersey. "My dear Ms. Roth, where have you been? I've been looking for you?" Hersey said.

"AD1, you did this. Why?" Adi asked.

"No, you did this the moment you cured that mouse."

"I swear to god, I'll kill you myself," Adi said. This was the first time Adi had ever threatened to take a life.

"My, my, you have descended into the deep end, haven't you? You can stop all of this by coming to my home so we can sit down talk through our problems," Hersey coaxed in his usual coy tone. Adi could hear voices in the background. Staffers and were referring to Hersey as Mr. Vice-President.

"Where are you?"

"My dear, I'm in my new office at The White House. You can come here as well if you like. I'll pencil you into my schedule right now. Give me a time. Better yet, tell me your location, and I'll send someone to get you right now."

"White House!" Adi exclaimed.

"You really should catch up on the news, Ms. Roth," Hersey said.

"I swear I'll find you and make you pay for all of this."

"Please do. Find me, sooner rather than later. How many more of these merged things are you willing to be responsible for?" Hersey ended the call.

Adi ran to Fortner, "We have to warn everyone about AD1."

"What is AD1?" the captain asked.

Adi went into a trance of dialogue with everyone. She spoke clearly and concisely so as not to sound confusing. She told them how Hersey had renamed SAP-23 to AD1 as a hit to Adi and that the merged were being infected by AD1. Lastly, Adi told everyone about her mother. Who now had two days before merging unless Adi could figure out a way to stop the change from happening.

Fortner remained dead serious about hunting Higgins. He knew they would not be safe until Hersey's hounds were off their trail. "We get the chopper, then we kill Higgins. After, we make for Adi's parents and get them to a lab."

"Sir," Mabrey and Sims responded, loading into the ambulance.

JJ climbed into the driver's seat, staring at Fortner, "I'm driving, don't ask."

Captain Fortner looked at Adi, "We can do this. We kill Higgins then we can save your mother. Hersey will just have to wait."

The ambulance headed toward LaGrange and the weather station. Adi couldn't help but think of Jake Meyers, "If only you were here, we could fix this."


**Accept No Substitute**

Jake paced from one end of the suite to the other, pondering his next course of action, *I've got to get to a phone. I need my phone.* He held the number from the man injected with the new SAP-9 formula and wasn't sure if he would help, but it was his best chance of finding Adi. Jake was smart to believe Hersey was taking liberties with his story about her going rogue and stealing SAP-23 to infect civilians.

"I'm so stupid. How did I ever believe that man?" Jake asked himself, walking to the suite door. "Hey there, Mr. Guard. I need a phone. Umm…got a craving for some pizza. What ya say? I'm buying."

"Hersey's orders are no phone calls for you, Meyers, no questions."

"C'mon, man, You guys have to be bored and hungry. Think about it, large, extra cheese, maybe some wings. I know I could go for some hot wings," Jake said, tapping on the door. Jake began hearing whispers on the other side of the door, if anything, the guards were at least considering the proposal.

One of the guards cracked the door open and said, "Tell us what you want and give us your card."

"Wow, I can tell you guys were first in class in interrogation school. I'm not giving you my credit card."

Henry approached the guards, and one of the men left to answer a call from Hersey. A young man, new to 'The Refuge', remained on watch.

"Hey, man, what's your name?" Jake asked.

"Robert, I mean private." Robert wasn't the brightest of the bunch. Hersey usually disliked men like the private, but simpler minds were less likely to second-guess the questionably commands of late.

Jake shook his head because he knew Robert was way out of his league at 'The Refuge'. "Okay, private, give me your phone, and I'll order the pizzas. You can tell the other guys that you placed the order, so problem solved, and everybody gets what they want." Jake waited patiently for a few seconds. A phone slid under the door bouncing off his foot.

"Thanks, buddy! Give me a minute."

Jake desperately wanted to call Adi. But like most of the population, he only knew her contact when it popped up as her name on his phone. The only time he ever saw her number was when he entered it on the phone the first time. "Great, I can't make the most important phone call of my life because I don't know the number," Jake said.

He then opened the little piece of paper to the man's number, punched the digits into the phone, and waited for the call to connect.

"Hello, who is this?" a voice asked hesitantly.

"This is Meyers from the lab. Are you ready to help?"

"Tell me what to do. I'll try. You saved my life."

*Don't thank me yet*, Jake thought, then asked, "I need you to find Dean and Ethel Roth. They live in Atlanta, Georgia. Tell them their daughter is in danger and to call this number and ask for Dr. Jake Meyers. Are you getting all this?"

"Okay, I'll find them and deliver the message."

"Tell them to call this number as soon as they can. If I don't answer as Jake Meyers, hang up immediately and try later," Jake concluded and ended the call.

Jake called a local pizza company and ordered a plethora of pizzas and wings. "Here you go, buddy. Hey, they might call back and make sure it wasn't a prank order. I'm really hooking you guys up tonight. If the phone rings, just give it back to me so I don't miss the call," Jake said, sliding the phone back to Robert.

"Okay," Robert said.

"Okay," Jake said to himself, making a funny face.

A few minutes passed, and the other guard, who clearly was in charge, returned. "Who ordered pizzas? Did you give him your phone, idiot?"

Jake shouted through the door, "Hey, go easy on the guy. He did you a solid. You and the boys are eating well tonight. You'll see." Jake returned to lie on the bed, folded his arms behind his head, and waited.

The man Jake previously injected with SAP-9 was in good spirits. His infection was gone, and in fact he hadn't felt this good since his college years almost twenty years ago. After a quick search on the internet, he found the only Dean and Ethel Roth located in Atlanta and made the call.

Dean answered, "Hello, Roth residence."

"Yes, I am calling on behalf of Jake Meyers. Adi is in trouble. Please call him at this number 202-…."

"Who is this? Dr. Meyers is in Alaska, and that's a Virginia number."

"Just call it." Then the man ended the call.

Dean turned to Ethel and told her about the call and how Adi was in trouble.

"Must be that man that came here," Ethel said.

"How are you feeling, dear?" Dean asked.

"Great, I haven't coughed once in an hour. I'm thinking of doing some gardening this evening."

"Well, I'm going to give this number a try. Maybe it was Dr. Meyers. I know Adi was looking for him earlier this week." Dean paused to look at a picture of Adi on the refrigerator. It was from one of their past fishing trips in the mountains. Adi held a small rainbow trout up with a huge smile, missing one of her front teeth. Dean smiled went and sat down at the kitchen table. He dialed the number, "Yeah, I need to talk with Dr. Meyers."

Robert held the phone and turned away from the other guards, "Okay, one second." The private slid the phone back under the door, "Pizza guy on the phone for you."

Jake almost broke his back, jumping out of bed to reach the phone, "Hello, Mr. Roth is that you?"

"Yeah, what you doing in Virginia? Adi called you yet?" Dean asked.

"Mr. Roth, I need your daughter's number. Please, hurry."

"Adi's number, let me see here…Okay, think I've got it for you. You ready?"

Jake was having a hard time not being rude and telling Dean to hurry up again, "Yes, I'm ready."

"404-…" Dean gave Jake the number, and before he could ask another question, Jake closed the phone. The door to the room flung open.

"Who are you calling, Meyers?" the lead guard asked, checking around the room.

Jake held up a finger, "Yes, that's two cases. Alright, thanks." Jake turned to the guard, "Sorry, I wanted to surprise you guys with some extra refreshments." Jake had called one of those services where they deliver alcohol right to your door. Eight large pizzas, ten dozen wings, and two cases of the stoutest beer known to man were on their way to 'The Refuge'. It would be a party to remember and, more importantly, one that Jake could escape from.

While waiting on the events of the evening to unfold, Jake couldn't help but think about SAP-9 and the man he hopefully had cured. The new SAP-9 was unproven, even with mice or other animal test subjects. The original SAP-9 never turned the mice merged, but then again, SAP-23 didn't either. *There's something in people that causes the mutation.* Jake thought as he tossed a small rubber ball up in the air to break the monotony. He wondered about Camelot and the patients that he had injected with SAP-9. They might be cured, dead, or worse for all he knew.

Something had changed in Jake since arriving at 'The Refuge'. He had matured so much over the last few days. He had no choice but to grow up and become a leader, something he never dreamed about happening. Adi would have been impressed and surprised by a long shot over Meyers new mindset. Jake was living up to Hersey's previous words when he casted him as the *dark horse*. Adi would need Jake Meyers if they were to get out of this craziness alive.

Jake returned to the bed and waited. He kept checking the time every few minutes, knowing that Hersey would return at some point. Jake was hoping to be long gone by then.


## The Wheels on the Bus Don't Go Around

"Sir, we found the bus," one of Higgins' men reported.

"I'll be right there," Higgins replied, leaving the helicopter and headed toward the airport. Higgins arrived and searched the battered bus. There wasn't much roof left attached to the bus frame, and many windows shattered by gunfire. Glass covered the floor, and at the rear, blood covered everything.

"Somebody got really busted up, Major," a man said.

Higgins found the broken syringe and saw the residue of SAP-23 on the wall of the bus. "Busted indeed," Higgins said, showing the needle to the men.

"What now, Major? They have to be close."

Higgins went up to the man in charge of the parking area. He held up a photo of Fortner and asked if the man had seen him. Higgins would know if he was lying due to the bus's proximity to his booth. "I'm looking for this man. He had others with him. They are wanted criminals. Where did they go?" Higgins asked.

"I've never seen that dude." The man's mind made his eyes look directly toward the money in Higgins' front pocket, giving away his intentions.

Higgins was not one for follow-up questions and drew his sidearm, sticking the muzzle an inch deep into the man's chest. "What did they leave in? I'm not asking another question."

"Ambulance," the man said slowly.

"That wasn't so hard, was it?" Higgins and his men left for the helicopter.

"Sir, an ambulance?" Higgins' man asked.

Higgins smiled, turning to his men, "Perfect! They're going to need it after I'm through with them." The helicopter spun to life, and Higgins was again off in hot pursuit.


**House Party**

Jake was still waiting in his room. He began reflecting on recent events. Any cordial headway he and Hersey had established had quickly vanished after he'd healed the man with SAP-9.

*Nicest prison on earth*, Jake thought.

Most news outlets were still running non-stop coverage of President Richards' death. Secret Service agents tried their best to limit access to the crash site, but drones and satellite footage began leaking out all over the internet.

Only one network was carrying the merged story more extensively than others. Short clips of enraged people, oozing blood from various areas of their bodies, were shown attacking anyone in their paths. The eyes of each merged black as death itself.

Jake was amazed that a solid black pair of eyes could contain so much emotion yet appear so empty. He thought, *my god, their eyes, I can't look at them.*

Pictures of the merged eyes were interrupted by a "Breaking News" special:

*We have reports that a cruise ship leaving Miami, destined for the Bahamas, was attacked, leaving thirty-seven dead. The attacks were allegedly carried out by a recently discovered drug gang known only as the merged. Information of more attacks by other Merged continues to pour in. It seems that the new drug is quickly turning into an epidemic. Authorities are unclear*

Jake was in a trance. He was unable to come unglued from the screen. This news report was to be the first time he could focus and take in the full gravity of the merged. By this point, everyone who had received the first shots of AD1 was already fully merged and continued attacking at random. Jake turned the screen off and walked over to a row of large windows overlooking the grounds of the vast compound. "Adi would never do this."

The guards outside the door were startled by Henry. "Is Dr. Hersey aware you ordered food from an outside source?" Henry asked. The guards were stammering and trying to come up with an acceptable answer but instead elected to open the door and let Meyers talk to Henry.

"Because I have two vehicles at our front gates with orders for Dr. Meyers," Henry continued stepping into the suite.

Jake said, "Alright, I know I'm the new guy around here, but this place could use a little excitement. I figured the guys would like some good food and cold drinks."

Henry tried not to get caught up in the intricacies of Dr. Hersey's personal business matters, but he knew Jake Meyers was currently confined against his will. "This one time, I will allow it. I don't know Dr. Hersey's plans for you, sir, but if my time here has taught me anything, it is that when guests fail to remain useful, they are *gone*." Henry closed the door.

Jake understood the coded language from Henry. He knew that the longer he stayed at 'The Refuge', the more likely he would end up a wanted man, or worse, dead. "Gone is just what I plan to be."

Shortly after Henry left the room, the food and beverages appeared. Numerous voices filled the foyer of the manor. Jake's plan was working. He watched as guards left their posts from the grounds outside. Jake did not have to wait very long until the guards returned.

"Here you go, Dr.," one of the guards said, handing a pizza and some drinks to Jake. "You got some kudo points from the guys, that's for sure," he said, closing the door.

Jake waited to hear the door lock. It never came. The commotion of guards having fun, which never happened around 'The Refuge', provided holes in the strict protocol for Jake to exploit. Jake cracked the door ever so slightly, peeking through the sliver of space down the hallway. He saw who had to be,

Robert standing with a small slice of pizza facing the foyer. Robert was a young, slim man and stood with an unsure posture. The more seasoned guards gathered together, laughing and chugging drinks, stopping only to tear away at the wings and pizzas in the boxes.

Jake closed the door and went to the row of windows. They were all sealed and did not have the option to be opened. "Of course, your windows don't open. That would be too convenient," Jake said to himself in frustration. He went back to the main door and peered out once more at Robert. "Okay. Sorry, buddy, but this is going to hurt." Jake waited for a roar of laughter to come from the lobby. He went to the bathroom and grabbed a towel, twisting it until it took the shape of a whip. He slowly opened the door and crept toward the young man.

"Chug! Chug! Chug!" rang out from the foyer. Jake sprang to action. He flung the towel over Robert's head and pulled tightly, cutting off his air supply. Jake pulled with all his might. Robert gasped and pulled frantically on the towel. Jake switched the towel into one hand and struck Robert in the back of the head one good time with his free hand, knocking the young guard out cold.

Jake took the all-black uniform and cell phone from Robert, taking time to check himself out in the mirror, nodding with approval, before he headed down the hallway. Jake pulled the cap down, covering most of his face, and made his way to the front door. Other guards began shouting obscenities at Robert (or who they thought was Robert) as he walked by.

"Where are you going, Big Time?" one of the guards yelled.

Jake threw up two birds and continued walking, never saying a word or turning to acknowledge the crowd. The unexpected gesture from Jake drew a response from the other guards.

"Looks like someone's finally growing up."

Jake continued holding both hands up, only dropping the expressions to open the front door. He immediately ran to the first car in the driveway and checked for keys, and to his surprise, found a set, "Yes!"

The large Mercedes' exhaust caused quite a ruckus as he floored it, heading for the front gate. It remained closed and locked.

"There has to be an activator or clicker in here somewhere." Jake began pushing every button near the rearview mirror. The SUV was only a few feet from the gate when it opened. The guard on post never thought about checking anyone leaving the compound because, in 'The Refuge's' totality of existence, no one not allowed to vacate the premises ever had. That is, nobody escaped and lived to tell about it.

Jake Meyers had escaped.

Two things began haunting him as he turned south toward Georgia: Hundreds of thousands of SAP-9 doses remained at 'The Refuge', and Roth's guitar was still on Hersey's private jet. Neither of the two was beneficial for the well-being of Jake Meyers.

# 13. Changing Tides

## Good Help is Hard to Find

Dr. Hersey took one final look at his new office before leaving for the evening. The White House bore a clean limestone appearance that Hersey agreed with. The architecture of the building was simple in nature yet inspirational. "Every brick has a purpose, not one out of place or unnecessary," Hersey said, approaching his motorcade.

His staff wasn't sure how to respond to many of his sayings, and perhaps they felt the prior Vice President was more approachable. Nevertheless, they all agreed that Hersey was a brilliant man and would bring many innovative ideas to the office.

Thus far, today was more eventful than Hersey could have ever imagined. By lunch, he had been sworn in as Vice President, relinquished his duties as CDC director, and had directed the release of a man back into society pumped full of an untested SAP-9 serum. Of course, he was keeping that last bit of information privy to himself.

"Never have I gained so much by losing so much," Hersey said. He perceived the death of his friend Frank Richards as a necessary loss. Any power he gained today from Tim Harding quickly and undeniably added to Hersey's maniacal ego. His downward moral spiral continued at an alarming rate. The seesaw of power and morality would never be equal again.

"At this rate, I'll become president by doing as little as anyone in history."

Hersey arrived home a few hours before dark to find no guard details patrolling the perimeter of his grounds. In all his time since constructing the manor, this was the first time he had felt uneasy coming home. He entered the manor and immediately noticed the food and drink remnants scattered around the foyer.

Henry ran to meet Hersey, imploring that he tried to stop them, but to no avail. Henry said, "Sir, things have gotten well out of hand."

"Where are my men, Henry?" Hersey asked, flipping the lid to one of the pizza boxes.

"Sir…" Henry's response was cut off by gunfire coming from behind the manor. Hersey ran with Henry to the back of the home and saw men throwing cans and bottles into the air, shooting at them. The men had long lost their reasoning skills. Things had 'gotten out of hand' as Henry had previously put it.

Hersey immediately reentered the estate and went straight to Meyers' room. He found only the unconscious body of Private Robert and a pile of clothes made from Jake's previous wardrobe.

"Incompetent fools," Hersey muttered, storming back to Henry. Hersey dialed the number to his contacts at the secret service. This agency is responsible for protecting the vice president and other high-profile members of the U.S. government. Hersey initially declined their services but now deemed them necessary.

"I need a full security detail at my home immediately. I believe I may be in danger from fugitives of the law," Hersey said, alluding to Meyers and Roth.

The guards were given two choices. Either be loaded into a large van and taken to a remote airstrip to be shot or head down to the nearest bus station and never be heard from again.

"Bus," they all responded in unison and loaded Robert's body into the van. Hersey went next to the guard at the gate, "Who has exited the premises today other than me?"

"A delivery from Mr. Powchos Pizza Palace, Sud Shack, and one of your guard detail SUVs, sir," the guard replied, sinking into his shirt collar.

Hersey's face became locked into an unrecognizable distortion, frozen in place like trying to conduct a video conference with a terrible internet connection. Meyers would have loved to have heard this conversation. It was the strangest combination of comedic gold and raw rage ever seen by anyone at 'The Refuge'.

"Get in the van," Hersey ordered the guard.

"Sir, maybe we should return to the manor and wait for your new security to arrive," Henry said, holding back a smirk with all his might. Henry was pushing his tenure to the max. He knew Dr. Hersey would not likely send him away, but over his years as the caretaker of 'The Refuge', Henry was well aware no one was irreplaceable.

Hersey reentered the manor and went to the lab. "Good," he said. The coolers of SAP-9 all remained full.

Hersey dialed the number to the newly appointed head of the CDC, who just so happened to be the deputy director of the Atlanta location during Adi's short stint there.

"I believe I have a solution for these merged drug abusers. I am sending you a compound that negates the effects of the drug. Distribute it immediately upon delivery, understand?" Hersey commanded the new director.

"Yes, sir. I wanted to thank you again for the recommendation." The new director had cleaned up the mess from Roth's encounter with the sisters. He could not hide dead bodies, but he could hide the SAP-23 research. The problem with men like the new director was as long as they could obtain new power, they cared little about the destruction. From this moment forward, whatever new problems SAP-9 would create would be blood on his hands.

"Don't let me down, director. The American people are counting on you," Hersey concluded. Hersey was still the de facto power head at the CDC. The deputy director was a 'yes man' and would fulfill his role as such with unflinching loyalty to the person who put him there, Hersey.

Dr. Hersey stepped out onto his balcony to phone Higgins, "Major, once you've tracked down and dealt with Ms. Roth, I have another task in need of your services. Call me when you are ready to complete the next obstacle." Hersey ended the call. Jake Meyers would soon be back in his crosshairs.

Hersey had, like so many times before, analyzed the situation and set into motion his end-game plan to strategically deal with each of these obstacles. Without SAP-9, Meyers would pose little threat, for now at least. Hersey just needed to put Dr. Meyers on the wanted list along with Roth and Higgins or the authorities would do the rest. Dr. Roth still remained the highest priority for his concern. *You are proving to be quite a hindrance, my dear.*

Hersey soon received word from Henry that the new security had arrived and was awaiting duties. Many of the secret service agents had never heard of 'The Refuge' and were quite astonished by the magnitude of security problems the compound presented.

Everything appeared fine on the surface in front of the men, but Hersey was beginning to feel the pressure from the many urgent areas surrounding his life. He looked down again at his hand, extending the fingers out, examining each digit. The dream remained fresh in his mind from earlier that morning. The withered fingers and knuckles took shape, disappearing as fast as they had formed.

The evening quickly into a few hours before twilight, and even though he would never admit it, what Hersey had gained that day was replaced by the loss of Jake Meyers. The scale was tipping, but to whose advantage?

## The Posers

"Crap, everybody shut up." JJ saw the call from Jack Crowder. For almost three days now, Crowder had been unaware of JJ and Barry's whereabouts. He did not know if they had survived the storm or if the two had even made it to Atlanta from Birmingham. JJ was not in the mood to talk with his boss, and he surely wasn't ready to tell anyone he knew about Barry's demise.

The phone stopped ringing, "That's my boss, Jack. He can't know I lost the storm chaser or that Barry died. I'm toast if he finds out."

"You need to talk to him and let him know you're okay. Just leave all the other stuff out," Adi said.

JJ was in no mood to get professional lying advice from Adi. "Oh, like my best friend dying, losing a new truck from work, stealing a school bus, getting shot at, helping a mad scientist and soldiers of fortune escape the law. Did I mention getting shot at?"

Mabrey and Sims knew the comment should not be funny, but JJ Wilson was a hilarious man, even when he was trying to be dead serious. They hid their faces, turning toward the back of the ambulance.

Adi did not push the measure any further. She got the point loud and clear. "Yeah, I wouldn't tell him any of that." Adi sat back down in her seat, placing her hand over her mouth. *Too soon*, she thought.

JJ did not hate Adi, but she wasn't his favorite person in the world right now. Yes, Barry's death was partly her fault, but he had made the decision to drive Echo Team and Roth. He was a grown man and did what he felt was right. And yes, Barry Winters would still be alive if not for meeting them at that parking deck during the storm, but that was too little and too late.

Fortner's trusted paper map made a reappearance. He was calculating the time and distance to reach the weather station and was paying no attention to JJ or Adi.

JJ's phone rang again. He sighed and accepted the call, "Hey, Jack. Sorry, I haven't called you back yet."

The ambulance became filled with the sound of Crowder's voice, "Wilson, where are you, and where is my storm chaser? The storm has been gone for almost three days."

"Did you see the aurora, Jack? Tell me you didn't think it was amazing?"

There was a pause, then a much calmer version of Crowder, "Yes, you were right about the solar flares, and that's why I need you back here so we can go through the footage."

"There is no footage Jack. It's called an EMP. All of the equipment was destroyed during the CME."

"What? Then what have you and Winters been doing all this time?" So much for the calmer Jack Crowder. JJ's boss had risen through the ranks at the National Weather Service. Starting as a janitor, then a technician, finally completing meteorology school and putting in twenty years of fieldwork before being promoted to director. He was a short, stocky man with a Friar Tuck hairstyle (from Robin Hood). If there ever was a poster child for a Napoleon Complex, Crowder was it. But he wasn't stupid and knew something was up with Wilson.

JJ shook his head because his next words may well have brought Barry back from the dead to strangle him. "Barry had an accident, and I'm with him in an ambulance. We're heading to the hospital." Every jaw in that ambulance was on the floor. Even Fortner thought JJ's last statement was over the line.

"No JJ…no," Adi said. She was in shock and hadn't realized her words made it out loud.

Crowder heard the voice, "No? JJ? What happened?"

"Uh, nothing, sir. Look, I really have to go. As soon as I get checked in, I'll call you back. Remember, don't call me. I'll call you." JJ ended the call as he had done so many times before. He did not give Crowder a chance to respond.

The silence after JJ ended his conversation with Crowder was interesting. Within just a few seconds, JJ went from having everyone's sympathy to telling the harshest lie in history.

Mabrey called up to JJ from the back of the ambulance, "That was cold."

"What? Barry is technically in the ambulance and…" JJ tried to justify the situation.

Adi said, "Just stop. Please, stop."

"There, I see the satellite," Fortner said, folding the map. The weather center in LaGrange was not an affiliate of the National Weather Service but all stations communicated with each other, so the prospects of JJ getting access to a helicopter was not out of the question. It would, however, depend on how well he could embellish his story.

The ambulance pulled into the parking lot. It was nearing the time of day in spring when darkness came at around 8 p.m. Management and directors would most likely have left for the day by now, leaving cleaning crews and low-totem weather monitoring staff on duty. Getting past these workers should not be too difficult. However, they were about to meet one of their most formidable foes at the station, an old security guard in no hurry to do anything.

Fortner turned to everyone, "Okay, we can't all go inside. That would draw way too much attention. JJ, Lt. Mabrey, and Ms. Roth will go together. Wilson, you will use your badge to gain access to the helicopter. Mabrey you're a cameraman, and Ms. Roth, I need you to become a reporter."

"I'm impressed, Captain. Break into weather stations frequently?" Adi asked.

"Best looking cameraman you have ever seen," Mabrey said, holding the camera on his shoulder and exiting the vehicle. Bernard Mabrey standing beside most men, excluding Fortner, would have been a giant in his own right. He was ruggedly handsome.

JJ stopped before leaving the driver's seat, "What do we do after we get the helicopter?"

"C'mon, man. Let's go," Mabrey said. Lt. Mabrey inferred the rest of Fortner's plan without having to be told. The Lt. would fly the helicopter down to the parking lot, land, and pick up the Captain, Sims, SAP-23, and the dead bodies. Then, they would be off to find Higgins.

The newly formed news team approached the main entrance of the weather center. The helicopter's propellers extended out and over the top of the building. JJ turned to everyone, "Told ya!"

The three entered the main lobby and walked over to a single security guard who was not in his best mood that evening. The Braves had already given up a three-run homer, and it was only the second inning against the Dodgers.

JJ spoke first, "Hi, I'm Jeremiah Wilson from the National Weather Service. I spoke with your director earlier today about borrowing a helicopter to cover the recent storm."

"Storm was two days ago," the guard said.

"Yes, it was. We need the helicopter to report on the aftermath."

"Who's the reporter, because I can tell it ain't you."

JJ and Mabrey looked at Adi and nodded their heads toward the guard.

"I am the reporter, and my name is Dr. Roth," Adi said, extending an arm to shake the man's hand.

"Dr.?" the guard asked with a confused look.

"Well, I was a doctor, then I became a reporter because I didn't like to look at blood." Adi turned and smiled at Mabrey and Wilson.

JJ thought. *I need to teach this girl how to lie. Has she ever lied before? Probably not. They don't teach that in a textbook.*

"Yeah, I reckon you can't be a good doctor if you don't like a little blood every now and then," The guard said. The current pace was going to have to pick up. The three did not have all night. However, the guard did.

"Show me the badge again."

"Here you go, sir," JJ said.

"Hold on, I have to call this in. Boss really loves that helicopter."

"While you're calling it in, would it be okay if we tour this fine facility?" JJ asked.

"I reckon," The guard said, pulling out an old Rolodex. The guard was of the old variety and was not caught up with the digital age. He relied on paper records for everything. This archaic system proved useful for the three con artists.

The group exited an elevator out onto the fourth floor. There was a cleaning crew of two vacuuming over on the other side of the floor. JJ walked past the screens. Some were showing the local news, some the current time and temperature of LaGrange, Georgia, and others replayed the storm just before the EMP disrupted the footage.

"I didn't realize there were two tornadoes," Adi told JJ.

"Worst storm I've ever seen, and I chase them for fun," he said.

"Never seen a green sky before," Mabrey told Adi and JJ, pointing at a screen near the top of the wall.

JJ noticed one final monitor that contained future projections for the area over the next few weeks. Another massive system was coming up from the Gulf of Mexico, making landfall near southern Texas. The storm was projected to impact the southeast Unites States in a month or so.

*Another month*, JJ thought.

Mabrey walked past JJ and Adi, "Let's go. We are wasting time." The stairs led up to a door and onto the roof containing the helipad. The helicopter wasn't the most up-to-date, but it looked well-kept and in good operational order.

Fortner and Sims waited below as patiently as they could, but times were always tense when waiting on others to complete their part of a mission. Not having eyes on the current situation was one of the most stressful parts for Captain Fortner. His mood lightened when he heard the helicopter start.

"Okay, we'll put the SAP-23 in first, then bodies," Fortner instructed Sims. Mabrey checked fuel levels and ran a few pre-flight diagnostics as Adi and JJ climbed aboard.

"Should I close the door?" Adi screamed.

JJ reached over and pulled the door shut. The security guard emerged, running toward the group and helicopter. He was shouting, well they had no idea what he was saying and did not care to find out. The helicopter hovered over the side of the building and landed near the ambulance. Fortner and Sims loaded the bags of SAP-23 and bodies and were gone. Of the many recent tragedies that the bunch had encountered, getting the helicopter proved effortless. It had only taken fifteen minutes to get in and out.

JJ was high-fiving Adi and Sims. Fortner sat up front with Mabrey, plotting a course toward Higgins' last known sighting. That's when the first bullet ricocheted off the fuselage. Major Higgins had caught up with them, doing their job of finding him for them.

"Shots Captain, Higgins, behind us, seven o'clock," Sim called out.

Adi and JJ huddled in the middle of the helicopter between the bodies of Gunn and Winters. Adi was shielding the bags SAP-23.

"Swing it around, take him out," Higgins said.

The pilot of Higgins' craft maneuvered quickly above and to the left, exposing a clean shot at Lt. Mabrey. The shots missed their target, cracking the front windshield. Mabrey had the controls in one hand, firing back at Higgins with the other. Bullet casings from Mabrey's sidearm bounced around inside the front of the helicopter.

Fortner grabbed his rifle and began shooting through Mabrey's window. Years of working in tandem, Fortner and the Lt. knew exactly what the other was thinking. It was chaotic poetry in motion, terrible beauty, a syncopation of minds working as one.

"Get above them Lt," Fortner said.

Sims busted out the rear window and began firing at Higgins. Hundreds of shots were whizzing by both aircraft. The army had not provided training for helicopter dog fighting.

Mabrey was literally flying by the seat of his pants. The Lt. pulled back on the controls jolting the craft violently past and above Higgins. Fortner began shooting down onto the other chopper, hitting the tail near the rotor. It wasn't enough. Higgins continued in pursuit.

"Sir, we're heading back over the city. Do you want to keep engaging?" Higgins' pilot asked.

"If they get away, you're a dead man." Higgins' directive was clear.

Both helicopters were now back over downtown Atlanta. The chaos of the gunfight caused Mabrey to lose track of direction. "Sir we can't turn around. We only have about forty-five minutes of fuel left," Mabrey said, checking the gauges.

"Go north," Adi called out from the back.

"Where north?" Fortner asked.

"Give me your map."

Bullets were impacting the helicopter but not as frequently as before.

Higgins was losing altitude, and the rotor of his craft was failing. They could not continue in the pursuit and landed near, of all places, the Atlanta CDC on top of a nearby building.

Adi circled the location on Fortner's map. She circled Dean's old cabin located in the mountains with a red marker like a sunken treasure from a long-forgotten Spanish galleon. It had been many years since she visited that place. It was a treasure all its own.

Adi couldn't help but see the irony of returning to where her passion had begun while holding where it had taken her. The SAP-23 was safe.


The lights of the city soon faded into gray. The cabin was twenty miles or so below the North Carolina line. Mountains began filling the horizon. The air became thinner and crisper than over the city. No one spoke. Around twenty minutes later, the fuel light indicator rang out as it illuminated. Fortner checked the map and asked Adi, "Is there a place we can land near the cabin?"

"You should see a clearing beside the river marked on the map. Pick any spot you want. There's nothing up there to worry about," Adi said. She was right about nothing being near the cabin. Dean purchased the cabin during his first year as a game warden. It had remained unchanged for thirty years. There were rations in plastic tubs, well water for drinking, and an old wood-burning stove. Everything someone might need to ride it out for a long time.

"That field? The one by the Riverbend?" Fortner asked.

"Yes, that is all my father's land," Adi said.

The helicopter landed fifty yards from the cabin. Adi exited the craft running for the front door of one of her most beloved childhood places. She lit several candles and placed them throughout the structure.

*Candles are so calming*, Adi thought. Not far behind Adi, JJ came with the bags of SAP-23, and the team brought up the rear. Winters and Gunn's bodies remained on the helicopter.

Mabrey, Sims, and JJ met with Fortner on the front porch. "Look, we can't carry Gunn and Winters around any longer," Fortner said.

Both bodies were entering the early stages of decomposition. They needed to be buried. Adi stepped out onto the porch as she heard the conversation from inside.

"Go past the tree line. There are eighty acres here, so no one will ever find them," Adi said.

"Are you sure?" Fortner asked.

"Yes, I'm sure." Adi began tearing up again, seeing the outline of Barry's body.

Mabrey and Sims began digging Gunn's grave while JJ and Fortner started Barry's. Adi came to the mounds, and they all paid their respects and then retired to the cabin for the night. Adi's mind flashed back to her mother, who would soon merge herself. The others were all sitting around the fire catching up on much-needed nutrition, while Adi found an old microscope she used during high school in a closet. She pulled the three vials of the sister's blood from her pocket and prepared to work. Adi had a day to save her mother's life or inform her dad about what was to come, in order to save him.


## Houseguest

Jake crossed over into North Carolina, and to his surprise, was making good time toward Atlanta. Hersey had either lost interest in Meyers or something more urgent had come up, that had pulled the doctor's attention away. Luckily for Jake, his stunt to cause a scene proved very effective. For a brief time, 'The Refuge' had become a frat house full of inebriated men with too much time on their hands. Jake felt oddly confident in the enterprise of his escape compared to his last attempt to be the hero on the private jet.

Soon though, SAP-9 reentered his mind, the unknowns weighing heavily. Jake was burdened to the point of discomfort. It wasn't that SAP-9 was a terrible creation or that he was unsure of the breakthrough he had discovered at Hersey's lab. It was the uncertainties of what was happening on a cellular level inside the man's body that bothered him. After viewing news report footage of merged attackers, he was right to be concerned.

Jake continued looking through the rearview mirror, every few minutes expecting a posse of black SUVs gaining ground behind him. He thought about calling his most recent test subject again but decided against it, at least for now.

The urgency of putting as much distance as possible between him and Hersey remained top priority. Contacting the Roth's to get bearings on Adi was the second. He pressed redial from Private Robert's phone.

Dean picked up, "Dr. Meyers, it's kind of late you know."

"I know, sir, I'm so sorry, but I need your address."

"My address. For what?" Dean asked.

Jake thought, for a second, about what he should tell Adi's father and did the smart thing by electing to lie. "Sir, I spoke with Adi, and she felt it best if I stayed with you guys while she was gone."

"Yeah, it might be good to have another set of hands in case that Higgins guy comes back around."

*Higgins*, Jake thought. Anyone who experienced the 'privilege' of meeting Higgins would never forget the encounter. The fact that Jake spoke with Dean after such an encounter meant the Major's questions had been sufficiently answered, providing no need to eliminate the Roths. Meyer's subconscious took over driving duties. His mind began to wonder why Higgins would have gone to Adi's parent's house unless she was close by.

Jake responded, "Yes, that's exactly why she called me. I should be there in about four hours." There was so much more Jake wanted to ask Dean, but he resisted the urge to bombard Mr. Roth with a million questions over the phone.

## Shame of Defeat

Higgins gazed out at the blue-domed building from the wounded helicopter and braced for another disappointing call with his master. Twice now, the Major had failed to secure the target set by Hersey. Never had he experienced such defeat. However, Higgins previous successes would garner him no sympathy for his pain. Like his boss, it was his pride that was to blame for his current predicament.

Tom Higgins was a highly respected and decorated soldier. He endured many dangerous combat tours overseas in and around the same area as Captain Fortner. After America was attacked on 9/11, Higgins, like so many other young men and women, joined the military. He wasn't overly physically assuming. He was of average height. A little on the leaner side, but his muscles had become hardened after years of training and fighting, and he could fight. His mind was always alert, excelling in calculating endgame strategies. His greatest strength was observing points of weakness in any foe. Only during his time working under Hersey had the Major descended into deeper levels of power and ruthless behavior.

Higgins met Fortner, fresh out of Ranger school himself, in Afghanistan. The two even conducted joint missions together with other sects of special forces. Higgins, a captain at the time, was Fortner's senior commander during a raid of Taliban supply lines hidden by a network of caves deep within jagged mountains near Pakistan. The two men worked well together during the mission, but to say they were compatible as friends would have been a stretch.

Higgins wasn't concerned with loss of life or the brutality warranted to complete an order. If a mission proved successful, collateral damage would be justified and forgotten about. John Fortner believed in the chain of command and did as he was told. However, he had a moral code and followed it. Fortner saw men like Higgins as too eccentric and brash. Fortner would only serve under Higgins on one mission, and it would leave a good impression on him, for he was an excellent tactician and superb fighter.

Higgins would remember this later when needing someone to 'keep an eye on' Dr. Roth. However, what Higgins had not counted on was Fortner's unbreakable consciousness of right and wrong. John Fortner could not follow any order or obey any command he felt was immoral or founded on indecent grounds. Despite his many faults, a few being stubbornness, a lack of sympathy, and being overly pragmatic, Fortner was a better man than Tom Higgins would ever dream of becoming.

Now the men were locked into a deadly game of cat and mouse. Higgins would not stop coming after Adi. He was Fortner's antithesis, his Moriarty. Higgins snapped out of his brief mental trip down memory lane and stared down at his phone.

"How did it get this far out of hand so fast?" he asked himself.

What was supposed to be an easy recon mission at the CDC had turned into an all-out war. Nevertheless, Higgins was too deep into the pit to back out. His only course of action was to keep going after Adi and Fortner to appease Hersey. The phone dial tone began ringing as Higgins sighed and stepped out of the broken helicopter.

# 14. Pledge of Appeasement

**Pressing Matters**

"Major, I assume the lateness of your call equates to indicates you found and eliminated Ms. Roth, or perhaps, she eluded you yet again. I hope for your sake it's the first." Dr. Hersey was growing tired of failure from his top enforcer, and only because his many years of loyal service did he allow Higgins more than one chance to rectify his recent failure apprehending Roth.

"Sir, we engaged Fortner and Roth over the city of Atlanta. They had a helicopter and continued north," Higgins said.

"Don't you also have a helicopter, Major?"

"We encountered gunfire and took on damage. Our helicopter is inoperable at this point. We had to make an unplanned landing next to the Atlanta CDC." Higgins stood on the ledge of the building, looking into the windows of other buildings and across at the CDC. A few people in high-rise condos watched Higgins' men drag the dead body out of the aircraft but took no further action as it was normally best to mind your own business.

"Do you know where they were going?" Hersey asked.

"Sir, they could not have had much more fuel. My guess is no more than an hour or two away."

Hersey waited for what seemed like forever to respond. He had left his bed and returned to the balcony, watching his new security conduct perimeter checks. Secret Service members were precise with detail, which was very pleasing to Hersey, such a stark contrast to the man who had served him longest. "I want you to go and meet with the new CDC director in the morning. There is a more pressing matter I need your assistance with. Let the authorities hunt Ms. Roth for a while."

"Sir, what am I meeting the director about? What is the new mission?" Higgins asked.

The Major was relieved by the new assignment. Nothing could be worse than chasing Fortner and Roth all over Georgia at this point.

"In the morning, shipments of a newly approved medicine will be delivered to the CDC. I need you to make sure nothing happens to my medicine major. After the drug is expedited from the CDC, you may continue your hunt. Do I make myself clear Major?"

Higgins was not given any other details about what was being sent, but he had learned by this point not to ask questions he didn't want to know the truth.

Hersey's plan was to send out the new SAP-9 formula to the Atlanta CDC and use the location as ground zero for distribution. Other CDC offices around the country might have asked questions about the sudden arrival of an unknown treatment, but the new director was deep in Hersey's back pocket and would do as he was told.

In the morning, Hersey would hold a press conference along with the new Chief Medical Advisor, also a recommendation and puppet of Hersey, at the White House. The press conference would provide information about SAP-9 or AD2 as it would be known to Americans. Citizens who had received the AD1 injection could go to any pharmacy, health department, or hospital and receive AD2 injections free of charge.

"Sir, my team and I will stay here and wait for the new director's call in the morning. Thank you, sir," Higgins concluded the call and returned to his men. The new orders went over very well with the men as they were growing tired of watching their friends die chasing Dr. Roth.

## Lies of One

Hersey checked the time and opted to write his monologue for the upcoming press conference instead of sleeping. "I can sleep when I'm dead," he said, finding an old pen.

The pen had been a gift from William Hersey Sr. to his son upon graduating from Harvard and was one of the few possessions Hersey would never part with.

His new speech needed to connect on a deeper level this time. Hersey had learned from his last attempt to connect with the common man. The Patriot Party was also banking their future on his willingness to appear humble. Hersey remembered feeling out of touch after leaving the stage and speaking with his late friend Frank Richards. He hated being vulnerable more than anything, and he would remedy this weakness with more lies.

Hersey took a few minutes and gazed through his bedroom window out onto the fountain. The water rose high into the air, falling back into the pool only to be recycled again through the mechanical workings of the structure back into the air. The fountain's cycling of water mechanism was engineered to reuse itself infinitely.

This gave the doctor the idea, "I don't need to reinvent myself. I only need to sound like Frank." Hersey would convey his best Frank Richards portrayal and write a speech the American people could not help but agree with.

Hersey's speech read:

*I come to you today as an American broken and hurting inside by the recent loss of our leader Frank Richards. Before his death, we met and discussed a new life-changing medicine that would help all Americans.*

*I will never give* up on making America strong and safe for you, the *people. That is why with the cooperation of President Harding, a new breakthrough in medicine, AD2 is ready for distribution.*

*Any citizen who received the AD1 injection can receive their AD2 shots starting today at noon at local health institutions. All other citizens suffering, who or have family inflicted with infectious diseases, can join the waiting list to receive their inoculations.*

*Together, we can continue to make America the greatest nation on earth. And together, we can and will continue to overcome all threats foreign and domestic. As Vice-President, I intend to see that America does just that.*

*Thank You, and God Bless America.*

Dr. Hersey smiled and gently set the pen beside his elegantly written lie to the American people. *They really will believe anything if you tell them to*, he thought. Everything was in place now. SAP-9 would be spread throughout the United States to remedy the SAP-23 debacle. Higgins would provide oversight during CDC distribution. In the unfortunate event, the new director had a change of heart, Higgins could "re-direct" the situation. Either way, Hersey would become stronger and more popular with the American people.

Shortly after contriving his newest deception, the sun broke over the tree line brightening the landscape. Despite his ambitions and negative traits, Dr. Hersey was very good at spotting beautiful scenery. The first time he saw the land where 'The Refuge' was to be constructed, he knew there was unlikely a more beautiful stretch of land within five hundred miles. He was correct. The sunrises and sunsets were immaculate.

Henry knocked on the chamber door, "Sir, the Secret Service has indicated that your motorcade will be leaving for the White House in an hour."

"Thank you, Henry. I'll be down shortly." Hersey selected his best suit, a dark blue Armani. He grabbed the perfectly folded speech, written on thick cream-colored stock and left 'The Refuge'. His confidence had never been higher.


**For the Greater Good**

The same beautiful sunrise that started Hersey's day illuminated the gentle slopes of the mountains outside the Roth cabin. The silence and peaceful serenity of the location were almost enough for the sleeping bunch to forget about the last few days, almost.

Not for Adi though, she hadn't slept a minute. The slides containing blood droplets from the sisters littered the table. "It…it looks like the cells merged with the serum, and somehow they were coexisting together," she said, adjusting the microscope lens. She could not help but think about how the news had already referred to the inflicted people as the merged. *I guess the media is correct sometimes.*

The SAP-23 entered the infected cells of both sisters and destroyed all traces of the infections but was not dissolved or metabolized by the body. Instead, SAP-23 remained inside each infected cell mutating the organelles into regenerative factories for the SAP-23 serum.

Adi sat back from the table after reaching this conclusion which had eluded her since beginning human trials at the CDC. "It's regenerating the serum, and the serum is keeping the cell alive." What Adi had not figured out yet, was why SAP-23 caused the injected to become mindless beasts or how it was mutating the eyes of each serum recipient.

Adi was consumed in deep thought and hadn't noticed Fortner had come to sit beside her at the table.

"What's keeping what alive?" he asked, breaking for thoughts.

"I figured it out, Captain. I know how it's working."

"How is what working, Ms. Roth? And remember, I don't speak scientist."

Adi went into a long explanation of her recent findings, "SAP-23 is killing the infection because they pose a threat to its survival inside the host cell. Once the infection is out of the picture, it actually takes over the functions of the cell so it can regenerate itself."

"Okay," Fortner said. "Let me try this again. I do not understand anything that just came out of your mouth. Please try to explain this to me like someone that isn't married to science."

Adi began talking very slowly only to be interrupted by Fortner, "It's not how fast you're speaking, it's the words coming out of your mouth. Try again."

"Basically, once you get the shot, your body becomes a slave to the serum forever. That means once you Merge, you stay Merged, got it?" Adi had finally conveyed the message in a way the captain could understand.

"So how do we stop it?" Fortner immediately went into mission directive mode. It wasn't his fault. He couldn't help it. Years and years of getting intel and executing a plan to fulfill the mission had trained his mind into a single approach method for eliminating the opposition.

"The Merged? That is easy. You just cause severe trauma to the host so the serum cannot regenerate," Adi said.

"Figured that part out already," Fortner said alluding to the giant man that had pulled him from the storm chaser. "I mean the SAP-23 inside the people part."

Adi stood and walked away from the table thinking about her mother, "I don't know."

Voices from the other side of the cabin began calling for the captain, "Sir, you have to s see this."

Fortner and Adi entered the room noticing Hersey delivering his newly written speech. Just as reporters began asking follow up questions, JJ turned the TV off, "This is the guy hunting us, the Vice-President of the United States."

"What is AD2?" Mabrey asked Adi.

"I've never heard of it, it has been something Hersey had concocted to cover up AD1," Adi said.

"Well, whatever it is, people are going to start going in droves to get it and your ex-boss is now one of the most powerful men in the world," the Lt. said.

JJ turned to Adi and Fortner, "Do you think that Higgins guy is still looking for us, I mean I hate to be the bearer of bad news, but I think we are done for." Wilson had no funny quip or comeback from the speech this time. He was starting to feel hopeless and he wasn't the only one.

"Do you think the new stuff can stop it?" Fortner asked Adi.

"We'll find out, but from what I know about Hersey, it's not about helping people. He never says or does anything unless it benefits him first. My gut feeling is to be cautious."

Adi went over to JJ, "I need to borrow your phone again. It will only take a minute." She was preparing to make the most difficult call of her life. How she was going to explain to her father that his wife, her mother, would soon change into the merged and try to kill him, she didn't know. Knowing it was her fault was the worst part, and it was eating her alive from the inside out. Adi waited for the call to connect.

"Hey, Adi, long time no see. It's about time you called." Jake Meyers had made it to the Roth home. Never had a person been so surprised as Adilene Roth was at that moment.

"Jake, oh my god. You're okay."

"What are you doing at my parent's house?" she asked as it just registered from which phone he had answered.

"I escaped 'The Refuge' and figured your parents would know how to find you. Your dad told me about Higgins. I'm sorry they were brought into this," Jake apologized.

"Wait, you escaped 'The Refuge'? I thought you went there on purpose. What happened?" Adi stepped out onto the front porch of the cabin and noticed a large flock of flamingos in a field about fifty yards away. She began squinting her eyes at the pink figures.

"Yeah, I had no idea how far into this I would fall, Adi. Hersey has gone completely off the deep end. He had me give SAP-9 to people at Camelot and made me leave before I could find out what happened to them." Jake was talking a mile a minute, and Adi was doing her best to keep up with his comments.

"You gave SAP-9 to people? Did it work?" Adi said, more worried about the results than the patients.

"I think so. The new formula worked too. I injected it into an infected patient at 'The Refuge'. He recovered and is also the reason I made it out," Jake said.

"A new formula? Let me guess, AD2?" she asked.

"Bingo, and it looks like it's ready to roll out to the public. I don't what's going to happen, but if it makes more of these Merged terrorizing people, things everywhere are about to get much worse," Jake said.

Adi did not have time to continue the back-and-forth of SAP discussions and who did what. Ethel Roth had but a few hours until she Merged. Adi broke the news to Jake first, sparing her parents for now.

"Jake, my mom, she got the AD1 injection. She's going to merge unless we do something," Adi said.

"Merge? Your mom? I'm looking at your mom right now. We're having breakfast with your dad in the kitchen. Looks perfectly fine to me."

"I know she does, Jake. It happens fast, in a matter of seconds, and takes over every system in the body. You have to bring them here."

"Okay, but where's here?" Jake asked.

"Tell my dad we are at the cabin and that they are in danger. That's what I want you to tell him. Don't mention my mom."

Jake was silent for a few seconds before responding to Adi. What he was thinking was sure to upset her, "Let me take her to get the AD2 injection before we come. I know it's not what you want to hear right now, but it helped my test subject at 'The Refuge'. It cleared the SAP-23 from his system." Meyers wasn't sure what the new SAP-9 solution would do, as there was no way to know long-term effects, but it had bought the man time, so maybe it could do the same for Ethel Roth.

Adi had no choice but to go along with the new plan set by Jake. If anything, Adi and Jake, now back together, could finally figure out the SAP-23 mutation problem. "Okay, do it, then get everyone here. I don't know how much longer we can wait it out before Higgins finds us."

"We?" Jake asked.

"It's a long story, Jake. Take care of my parents and get here as soon as possible." Adi completed the call and began walking out to the flamingos. Flamingos were not, nor have ever been, native to Georgia, so to see an entire flock in a mountain pond was quite the scene.

JJ had also noticed the birds and sprinted past Adi toward them, laughing and shouting, "I know why you're here. It was the storm. You guys are lost, aren't ya?" JJ stopped a few yards from the birds as Adi caught up to him. "Do you see that? The EMP messed up their navigation," he said.

"How? They have to be close to 1000 miles from their home," Adi remarked.

Now, Adi was the one who needed to have the situation explained. She was the queen of her lab but had little knowledge of how the earth affected animals' migratory tendencies. JJ tried his best to explain how flamingos had made it to north Georgia, "Birds have little magnets in their brains that use the earth's electromagnetic field like GPS to navigate. The recent storms are messing with their minds. Kind of like your SAP stuff is messing with people's minds."

"Will they figure out they're lost or how to make it back home?" Adi asked.

"Oh, I'm sure they know this isn't where they belong. Maybe they don't want to try finding their homes yet, or maybe they're not ready. Who knows. I've done a lot of strange things before, but I can't speak to animals. We'd need a Dr. Dolittle for that," JJ said.

By this point, everyone inside the cabin came to view the pink birds flapping around in the pond. The storm had caused numerous species of animals, mainly birds, to behave sporadically. JJ informed the group of another storm system approaching that would impact the area in a few weeks. However, there was no way to tell if another solar event would take place. JJ knew he needed to talk to Dr. Julie Rieser soon. But for now, they all enjoyed watching the birds.

After a few minutes, Adi pulled Fortner aside and told him about Jake Meyers and her parents. She explained that her mother would get the new AD2 injection, and Adi would monitor her condition once they were at the cabin. "They'll be here in a few hours. We can't leave until I know my mother is okay," she said, looking at Fortner with regained confidence. The Adi of old was starting to come back around.

Fortner had only been around Adi for a few hours before the sky fell, crushing her world at the CDC. He was not accustomed to the strong confident Dr. Roth most knew her as. He liked this version of Adi much more.

*It suits her*, Fortner thought after their latest conversation.

Adi's last statement also drove home an important aspect of the captain's mission of getting everyone away from Higgins safely. He had no way to know if his commander had been persuaded by Hersey's man to turn them over. All of his eggs were placed in one basket. There was no plan B. Fortner needed closure, so he decided to call and find out.

"Hello, John," General Baskin answered.

"Sir, I know during our last talk, I was on my way to meet you, but that's impossible right now," Fortner said.

"About that Captain, my orders are to arrest you on sight. No questions, per the Pentagon. It seems you have made some powerful enemies, John."

"I understand, sir. Are you sending men for me?"

"I'm not, but Higgins was adamant that you either turn yourself in or the heat is going to pick up. I'll do what I can to keep them off your tail, but my hands are tied now."

"Understood, sir. I do have one favor, just one."

"What is it, son?" Baskin had long favored Fortner over any officer, or man for that matter, that had ever served under him.

"I need to know where I can get a plane," Fortner said.

"Lt. Mabrey still serving with you, Captain?" the General asked. "Yes, sir."

"I'll call his old commander in Pensacola. Tell him an old friend wants a joy ride in one of the cargo planes. That's the best I can do for you, John."

"Thank you. I'll make this right, sir. You'll see." Fortner concluded the call, unaware Adi had been listening to the phone call until she asked,

"So, no exoneration, I'm guessing?"

"Not as long as Higgins is chasing us and Hersey is calling the shots," Fortner said.


## For Whom the Bell Tolls

Dr. Hersey entered the Oval Office after exiting from the front lawn where he had given his morning speech. President Harding was pleased with the message Hersey delivered to the people and confessed his confidence in the new AD2 wonder treatment. Hersey was feeling incredibly self-assured, bordering invincible, with his latest deception.

"William, I'm glad the new CDC director is working out so well. I'm blown away by how fast they were able to find a solution to neutralize these new drug heads out there terrorizing our communities," Harding said.

"Thank you, sir. AD2 will render the new merge drug utterly useless. Americans infected by the drug's addictive properties should return to normal in a few days. We will reestablish law and order soon, sir."

"Well, if this works William, you better get your campaign team together real fast. I have a feeling you'll be taking Frank's old spot as the new nominee."

President Harding was indifferent to who would succeed him. Like he told his boss before, Harding was happy to retire to Montana and ride out his remaining days living a peaceful existence. For all he cared, Hersey could have the ivory tower and the headaches that came with it.

"Yes, that idea has indeed occurred to me as well, sir," Hersey said.

"Alright, report back to me when things start to get better out there. Who knows, I might need an AD2 shot myself."

"I certainly will, sir," Hersey said, leaving the Oval Office and returning to his space in the other wing of the building.

Hersey spent the next hour or so watching footage of more merged attacks on the news. He found that the most accurate coverage of events was on social media, those produced by thrill-seeking watchdogs hoping to score views and subscribers by finding and observing the merged.

Thousands of cases were popping up all over the internet. Some showed an attack on a busy train outside of New York, while others, more isolated cases of single victim attacks.

The infected all showed the same characteristics: black eyes of death, blood oozing from somewhere on their bodies, and relentless mindless rage. The merged moniker even made into the urban dictionary as someone who gets easily upset and throws rage-filled tantrums.

Memes of people merging were becoming synonymous with any situation or ordinary life circumstance that drove people insane.

One of the memes actually made Hersey laugh. A young woman posted a video of herself at the DMV waiting to get her driver's license picture renewed. In her frustration she said, "I swear y'all, I'm about to merge out up in this place if they don't hurry and take my picture."

Now the waiting game began.

Hersey needed AD2 to work. This was true not so much because he cared about curing the people, but more so he could pad his ego and further promote his reputation as these would only help him to achieve the ultimate prize of becoming president.

*How small-minded of me to think of enjoying being second fiddle*, he thought.

Everything that could go right was going right. He was on the cusp of the breakthrough of his life, and all Jekyll had to do was tie up the one remaining loose end, Adilene Roth.

Hersey once again phoned his lackey, who had assumed the title of acting Atlanta CDC distribution manager, "Major, how are the shipments coming along?"

"Fine, sir. All cases should be gone before nightfall." Higgins assured him that the trucks carrying AD2 were secure upon their departure from the CDC, and that the drivers understood their instructions for delivering the solution. The new director appointed by Hersey wasn't much for bossing people around and relinquished most of the logistics to Higgins. Hersey would have been better off making Major Higgins director. He would then, at the least, have a yes man with the fortitude and capacity needed to see an assignment through.

"Excellent, Major, nothing better than a small accomplishment to get back on the path to redemption," Hersey said with a demoralizingly sarcastic tone.

"If you say so, sir. I'm ready to continue the mission of apprehending Dr. Roth whenever you send me a new helicopter," Higgins said.

"Soon, Major, you just focus on getting my newest pride and joy out to the public, where it belongs."

Hersey ended the call, but continued dwelling on Adilene Roth. She was the only person left who he felt could rain on his parade. The only one to which Hersey lost sleep. She was much more than the troubling dreams of recent. She was becoming his living nightmare.

As hard as Hersey had tried to contain her genius and direct it toward his own goals and ambitions, she had found a way to create something that had changed the world. To make matters worse, Roth had disappeared before he could understand how she had done it, never mind the fact SAP-23 was producing adverse side effects. Hersey did not doubt that if given enough time, Roth would figure out a solution for counteracting the unwanted properties of her SAP-23 serum.

Jake Meyers had been really no more than a consolation prize, but had served his purpose. As Hersey spoke to himself inside his office, AD2 was being injected into countless bodies of Americans. Each more unaware than the other of the consequences soon to follow. How blindly arrogant Hersey was proving to be. How ignorant so many Americans remained.


**The Reunion**

The green F-250 crunched along the dirt road leading to the cabin. Sims messaged Fortner from the tree line, "Sir, a green pickup truck is approaching."

Adi overheard the transmission and went out to wait in front of the cabin. It had to be her father's old truck. It came around the bend of the last curve before reaching its destination, like finding an oasis in the desert. Adi's parents were safely back to her, and so was Jake.

Jake was the first to exit the truck, running toward Adi but looking over her should to stare at Fortner as he emerged from the cabin, "Jesus, that is one big… Hey Adi, miss me?"

Adi stuck her arms out and waited for Meyers. The action from Roth severely confused Jake. Adi had never hugged, fist-bumped, or so much as high-fived anyone their whole time together.

"What's this?" Jake asked.

"If there was ever a time a hug would be appropriate, I assume this would be it," Adi replied just as Jake had days before, when Moucious Clay had survived the initial SAP-23 injection.

"I see your memory is still as good as ever. Be honest Adi, you missed me didn't you."

"Maybe, but I still owe you an ass-kicking," Adi said.

Fortner watched the playful reunion between Adi and Jake and figured it was time to introduce himself. "Captain John Fortner, Army Ranger, nice to meet you, Dr. Meyers." Fortner's gesture felt disingenuous to Adi, but Jake was oblivious.

"Dr. Jacob Super Manly Meyers at your service, Captain. Allow me to comment on your increased physique. You must do a million pushups a day, huh?" Jake said.

Adi was sensing something more was going on here. Fortner had never made such an effort before to introduce himself. She remembered how he insisted at the weather center that he didn't want to leave the ambulance.

*He's jealous…too funny*, Adi thought, sporting a fiendish smirk.

"Where in the world did y'all get a helicopter from?" Dean asked, stepping onto the porch with Adi. Dean was waiting on Ethel to appear, but she had already begun making her way toward the flock of flamingos. JJ and Lt. Mabrey were coming back from the water and met her halfway to the pond. They returned to the porch together.

"What is going on here, Adi? Flamingos, helicopters? I don't even know what to think?" Ethel said.

Adi could say nothing to her mom. Ethel looked vibrant and healthy. Her skin looked great, her hair was perfect, and her eyes were the purest amber brown any person had ever seen. She turned to Jake in tears, "Thank you."

The gesture hit Meyers extremely hard. He decided to space himself from the others for a few minutes and went to check out the pink birds in person. He wasn't sure what to blame. Not sure whether it was the hope of SAP-9 curing Ethel Roth or how Adi had said thank you to him, but Jake had tears rolling down both cheeks. The emotional outburst, however, did not last long. The others heard Jake taunting the flamingos from the pond.

Dean went inside the cabin with Ethel to tidy up and begin supper. Anyone from the Deep South of the US understood when lunch was over, dinner preparation began. After a few minutes, Jake returned from the birds, and for the first time, the entire group, everyone left against Dr. Hersey, gathered together…and began preparations of their own.

Adi began the think tank session by asking Jake, "AD2? Anything we need to know about your new SAP-9 formula?" Her question drew suspicious looks from the other men. All they had learned about Adi and Jake's work was what they had seen after encountering the merged.

"I need to make contact with my patient," Jake said.

Adi continued, "Captain, we can't touch Hersey until we capture or eliminate Higgins. What do you think we should do first?"

Fortner once again was impressed with Roth. She was now taking charge and leading the group. He no longer viewed her as a weak-minded scientist. It was also the perfect time to relay his last conversation with General Baskin.

"We cannot return to Ft. Benning. Hersey has given Baskin orders to arrest all of us on sight. I was able to secure a plane in Pensacola. Lt. Mabrey should be able to get us onto the base and fly the plane, allowing for our extraction."

Mabrey and Sims confirmed the captain's words by nodding in agreement. Mabrey knew the old air base like the back of his hand. He would have no problem getting in and out quickly. "Let me guess? An old C-130 cargo plane? General Baskin was always a sucker for the classics," Mabrey said.

Fortner asked Adi, "What about your findings with SAP-23? What we talked about this morning?"

Adi looked in the direction of her mother. Ethel was opening all the curtains in the cabin to let in as much sunlight as possible. Adi refocused on the group and said, "SAP-23, in its current state, is 100% responsible for the merged. Without a proper lab, I cannot do anything to stop or reverse this. Anyone injected with AD1, as Hersey labeled it, will change, will merge within two days."

Jake returned to the group, "No answer. I tried the number like twenty times. Sorry, Adi, we might have to wait and see what happens here," Jake said. None were happy to hear this.

Jake was referring to Ethel, for now she was the guinea pig, the barometer of what miracles or horrors lay in store for anyone injected with SAP-23 and AD2 together.

The focus centered back on Higgins. "Why don't we go to him this time? We've been engaging him while always running. Why not make him fight us on our terms?" Fortner suggested. The comments drew a few loud yesses from Sims and Mabrey. "We need a place we can go and not worry about Hersey, only Higgins."

Adi looked at Jake as if they were thinking the same thing. "Camelot," they said in unison.

"Camelot, what is a Camelot?" JJ asked.

"It's the lab in which Jake and I worked, under Hersey. All of our research is there. Everything is there," Adi said.

Fortner asked Mabrey, "Can the C-130 get us from Florida to Alaska?" "Shoot! That baby can get you anywhere in the world on full tanks," Mabrey said.

"What about the Vice-President, Doctor Hershey Bar Gone Bad?" JJ asked. That was one of a dozen million-dollar questions going through everyone's minds at the moment.

"One thing at a time, JJ," Adi said.

"Excuse me, but who is this?" Jake asked.

"Jeremiah Wilson, National Weather Service."

"Wait. What? Let me get this straight, we've got a group of badass soldiers, a couple of genius scientists…and a weatherman!" Jake turned to the others, "Were you guys afraid you were going to have to negotiate with Mother Nature or something?"

"Did you not see the EMP that hit the country?" JJ asked.

"Sorry, I was locked up in a creep's million-dollar mansion for a few days," Jake said.

"JJ is with us. He is as much against Higgins as anyone here," Adi said, not mentioning Barry by name, but JJ understood what she meant and appreciated her saying so.

"So, the last question is how do we get Higgins back to Camelot?" Adi asked Fortner. If anyone was going to be able to get the Major to bite on a trap, it would be his oldest acquaintance in the group.

"You leave that up to me. Once we're in the air, I'll make the call," Fortner said.

During the last few days of their joint mission in the mountains of Afghanistan, Fortner had saved Higgins' life by taking on five Taliban alone. Their entire squad was killed by an ambush attack leaving just the two men alive. He killed all the enemy fighters, with just a knife and his bare hands, while protecting a severely wounded Higgins in the process and Higgins hated Fortner for it. He hated owing anyone anything. Fortner knew all had to do was dig a finger into that wound again, and Higgins would crawl the earth to get to him.

"Then it's settled. We wait until I feel good about my mother, then we take the helicopter to Pensacola, and fly to Camelot," Adi concluded.

The meeting adjourned. Jake, JJ, Mabrey, and Sims went inside to watch a movie and forget about their troubles for a while. Dean helped Ethel in the kitchen while Fortner and Adi remained on the porch.

Adi looked at the captain, smiling, "Admit it. You were jealous when you saw Jake."

"What? No, just assessing the situation," Fortner said.

"Really? Since when do you ever jump to introduce yourself using your full title?"

"All the time, Ms. Roth."

If not for his bullheaded stubbornness, Fortner could be cute. "You know you pull your shoulders back when you are nervous. Is that something they teach you in the army, or are you trying to block out the world with your pectoral muscles?" Adi said.

Fortner looked down at his chest and became very nervous, immediately pulling his shoulders back into their previous position, "I only get nervous when I don't know the situation. Right now, I am…I am…leaving," Fortner said, standing abruptly and returning inside to join the others.

Adi let out a girlish giggle. She enjoyed watching Fortner squirm. Even more so, she was very grateful for his leadership and steadfastness. John Fortner had kept her alive, and Adi was hoping he would continue to do so.

# 15. Apprehension

## Hurry & Wait

The next morning at the cabin began much the same as the last. Adi stayed up all night mulling over theories and working out hypotheses with the sister's blood samples. The difference is that she now had Jake. Everyone else in the cozy haven was getting much-needed rest. Soon there would be little chance for more.

JJ woke up and stared at his phone for a few minutes, thinking about Barry and Alice. He decided to tell Barry's wife in person rather than taking the coward's way out and phone the terrible news. The choice to do so would prove more beneficial for JJ than anyone else. He could hear Adi and Jake talking to each other from the kitchen.

Adi was becoming frustrated with Jake about the new SAP-9 formula, "Look, I know what you are trying to say, Jake, but I am not sure how you boosted mitochondrial efficiency without affecting the other functions of the cell."

Jake had every tool under the sun at his disposal at 'The Refuge', so he understood how Adi was getting upset sitting at a kitchen table looking through an underpowered second-rate microscope.

"Listen, once we get to Camelot, I'll show you, okay? Trust me. It works."

"What about your latest subject? Are you sure it worked?" Adi said.

Jake was trying his best to put out of his mind the possibility of SAP-9 having a similar outcome to the serum that created the merged. "I don't know, but I can try to find out again." Jake dialed the man's number. He hoped to hear either two things, the man answered and sounded fine or nothing, so he could continue to speculate that everything was fine. The call connected, causing Adi to freeze in the midst of her work and look up at Jake.

"Pain," the man said.

"This is Dr. Meyers from the lab. You were sick. Do you remember me?"

"Pain." The man's voice was becoming deeper and he was taking very labored breaths.

Jake looked at Adi and began shaking his head slowly to indicate no, not good. "Do you feel pain? Are you hurting?"

There was a long pause of silence, then a loud thud as the phone hit the floor. Jake was breathing heavily now himself. He was having a hard time focusing on the call with his heart pounding in his ears.

The man sounded off again in the background, "Pain…kill." His last gargled gibberish followed by the sound of breaking glass. Screams of his neighbors soon filled Jake's ear.

"Hey, Mikey…Mikey what are you…no, stop…"

Jake ended the call and looked ominously toward Adi, "He changed, merged."

"Who merged?" JJ asked.

Jake did not respond, opting instead to slam his phone on the table.

"We have to go now, Adi. Right now. If we don't leave right away, your mom is done for."

Fortner and Echo team made their way into the kitchen. "I agree with Meyers. It's time." Fortner though had no idea of the gravity of the situation. Ethel Roth had been given naught but an extra day of sanity by receiving the AD2 injection. With a deep breath, Jake's eyes met Adi. Words like millstones crossed his lips.

"You have to tell her, Adi."

Adi went to her parent's door and knocked hesitantly. Her mother was sitting at a small table by a large window, looking out toward the pond. Dean Roth was tying up his boots.

Ethel spoke to Adi, "The flamingos are gone. I guess they got homesick."

*Sick*, thought Adi. The word struck her insides like a jackhammer. "About being sick, Mom," Adi said, joining Ethel at the table. "How do you feel this morning?"

"Just wonderful, dear. Your father and I are about to go on a little hike to take in the morning air."

"That's great, Mom." Adi turned to her father, "Dad, can I talk to you in the kitchen for a minute?"

Dean stood without saying a word and went toward the kitchen. Everyone was still gathered around the table talking to Meyers about his most recent phone call but became deathly quiet as Dean entered the room with Adi.

Adi began, "Dad, Mom is going to get very sick at some point tonight or tomorrow. The shots she got are making people turn into the merged things like on the news. I'm the reason it's happening. I made the stuff that's inside Mom. I'm the one responsible for everyone killing and dying."

Dean was processing every word. He never blinked or even took a breath for what seemed like forever. Fortner was looking at his watch, this was taking too long, but even he understood that this could be the last time she had a chance to talk to her father.

"I'm not going to kill your mother. I don't care what she turns into," Dean said.

"No, Dad, you just need to tie her up or contain her until I can get back from my lab in Alaska," Adi said.

"Then what? You make something else that will turn your mother into what, back to normal or something worse?"

"I can fix her, Dad. You have to trust me. When she starts speaking funny, really slow and doesn't make sense, you tie her up and don't let her go. Not under any circumstances," Adi said.

Dean looked around at everyone else. They were all nodding in agreement with Adi. He slumped his shoulders, letting out a long sigh before speaking, "Okay, but what happens if she gets untied?"

"Then you run or defend yourself because she will try to kill you," Fortner said.

Adi left the room, and made for the front door. Ethel entered the kitchen, "You ready for our walk?"

"You go ahead and get a little head start. I'll catch up in a sec," Dean said.

He turned to Fortner, "You make sure my little girl gets to that lab and back to me safely. I can't lose both of them, you understand, not both." Dean extended his hand, and Fortner was shocked by the strength in Dean's grip. Fortner knew Dean Roth was a good husband and father. He held as much respect, as any man could, with the captain.

Fortner said, "You have my word, sir." He turned to everyone still inside the cabin, "We are leaving. Get whatever you need."

"Sir, we need fuel if we're going to make it to the air base. I'd say we got about twenty minutes of flight time left in the tank," Lt. Mabrey said.

"There's an old ranger station with a helipad just east of here. Adi knows how to get there. It's my old station headquarters. They'll have some fuel there. If anyone asks, tell 'em I sent you," Dean said.

Adi watched as her parents disappeared around the curved road near the pond. They held hands and were enjoying their time together, as they had for almost forty years.

The helicopter roared to life, and the group watched the cabin grow smaller and smaller in size until it was but a tiny blot from the sky.

"The outpost is that way," Adi pointed to Mabrey. The ranger outpost was one of the few left in the area containing an old fire lookout tower. The landmark made finding the location quick and easy. Mabrey put the helicopter down perfectly in the center of the helipad.

"I need ten, sir," Mabrey said.

Adi and Fortner went inside the station cabin to speak with the ranger on duty. They heard banging and noises coming from upstairs. Fortner took Adi back to the helicopter and returned with Sims.

"Upstairs, be ready," Fortner said as they re-approached the station.

Fortner reached for the door handle while Sims had his rifle at the ready. The loud clanging continued from inside the room. They flung the door violently, and Sims entered with Fortner pointing his hand cannon directly at the commotion.

The room went silent, "See anything?" Fortner asked.

"No, sir…" A large raccoon jumped from behind a desk, scaring the men.

"What the…" Sims screamed and began looking frantically for the animal.

The raccoon ran down the stairs and out the front door. Fortner and Sims exited the cabin as laughter erupted from the helicopter.

"Wow, you have to watch out for those merged raccoons," JJ said.

The laughter was interrupted by a loud scream from Sims. The park ranger had appeared form nowhere, grabbed the sergeant, and was began biting his neck and face. Mabrey dropped the fueling hose attached to the helicopter and ran to assist Fortner.

The ranger had received his AD1 injection after being bitten by that same raccoon near the outpost. He opted to get the new medicine in tandem with his rabies shots to help prevent an infection forming in the nasty bite wound on his hand. A day earlier, while patrolling the area around the cabin, the ranger merged.

Sims let out toe-curling screams as blood poured from his face and neck. Fortner placed two shots into the ranger's left side, causing him to release the Sims.

"Bad," the ranger said and charged Fortner.

Mabrey and Fortner unloaded every almost round they had into the ranger, but he kept coming. Jake, Adi, and JJ ran to assist, picking up whatever they could find around the cabin. Roth plunged a machete into the ranger's leg while Jake and JJ began thwacking away with shovels, buying Fortner and Mabrey time to reload their weapons.

The ranger turned toward Adi and grabbed her by the throat, lifting her almost a foot off the ground. Fortner slammed into the merged creature freeing Adi from its grip. The captain mustered all his strength and lifted the man over his head, throwing him against the wall. The ranger regained his balance, and before he could attack, his head disappeared from its body.

Smoke from the captain's revolver rose into the air. The merged ranger's eyes remained black as they peered out as if watching the group from the dead.

"Sims. Can you hear me?" Mabrey asked.

The sergeant was not dead but severely wounded. He had deep lacerations on his face and neck.

"Let's get him back inside the helicopter," Fortner said.

Mabrey finished refueling, and they were off toward Pensacola. Adi and Meyers used every tool inside the first aid kit to patch Sims up. He was in severe pain but was now no longer bleeding.

Fortner said, to Sims, "You're one tough hombre. Hang in there, Sergeant."

The crew was now about 400 miles from their destination, desperately hoping for no more surprises for the rest of the day.


## Chance for Redemption

Higgins watched as the last shipment of SAP-9 left the grounds of the Atlanta CDC when a large SUV approached the Major from inside the docking garage. Six, large, heavily armed men exited the vehicle and approached Higgins. He wasn't sure if they were assassins there to execute him, as Hersey had finally had enough of his failure, or they were the FBI looking for leads on Roth. To Higgins' surprise, neither was the case.

"Gentlemen," Higgins said.

"Major, we were sent by Vice-President Hersey to assist you in any way you see fit in apprehending Dr. Adilene Roth." The men were from the Secret Service and were ready to serve their new master just as Higgins had for so many years. "We have transport waiting at Dobbins AFB. Please come with us."

"And just where are we going?" Higgins asked.

"Sir, the helicopter you chased was reported stolen to the FAA from a weather station in west Georgia. They have picked up movement as of this morning. They are currently heading south," one of the agents said.

Higgins boarded the SUV, and headed toward the AFB. Higgins was thoroughly surprised when they pulled up beside a hangar housing a new state-of-the-art V-22 Osprey airplane. The aircraft offered unrivaled fighting capabilities with the benefit of it being a VTOL. VTOL is short for vertical take-off and landing, meaning the large plane could land and take off like a helicopter but fly like a fixed-wing plane allowing for better combat applications.

Higgins' phone rang as he stepped into the plane. "Major, I have given you a new team with new toys. Don't make me regret giving you another chance. Happy hunting," Dr. Hersey said.

"Sir, we are ready to lift off. Is there anything else you need before we go?" one agent asked.

"No, take her up."

The Osprey looked foreign compared to the more traditional aircraft of the base. The propellers rotated from the upright position until they were parallel with the rear rail of the plane, then sped off into the blue sky. Higgins was hours behind the group and their weather helicopter but would have the advantage speed now.

"Sir, is there anything we need to know about Dr. Roth before we engage?" another agent said.

"She is with a team of Army Rangers led by Captain John Fortner," Higgins said.

"What do you want us to do with them?"

"Everyone dies. Understand?" Higgins said.

"Neutralize all threats. Understood, sir."

## Civil Unrest

Hersey ended the call and prepared for more briefings from his senior staff. The merged continued causing more civil unrest as attacks and public paranoia grew. Conspiracy cover-ups began circulating in the news and media. Many talk shows around the country started covering the merged not as a drug induced condition but as a disease targeting people at random, released for population control.

The Rundown, a popular panel talk show, had requested Dr. Hersey soon after his being confirmed as Vice-Presidential running mate for Frank Richards. Hersey's team was preparing him for his big television break into the mainstream media.

"Okay, sir, remain relaxed and use your knowledge of the situation to your advantage." Hersey's chief advisor said.

*My dear if only you knew the knowledge that I possess about the current situation*, he thought. After today, Hersey was sure that Roth and everything associated with her would be behind him. He planned to reorganize and reestablish Camelot as a national research center to find a cure for the merged and in doing so likely ensure him the presidency. He would once again be the savior the country so sorely needed.

Adilene Roth would go down in history as the archetype for meddling in genetics, playing god to bolster her own ego, a modern Dr. Frankenstein with the merged as her own horrible creation. Her tainted legacy on humanity solidified. She would be forever known as the matriarch of the merged.

Hersey's plan as Vice-President was to go all in, using Roth as the scapegoat for everything he had been responsible for. Adi would transition from being a localized terrorist to becoming the focal point of a full-scale national manhunt. Jake Meyers would also fall into the mix with Roth as her love-crazed partner in creating the American epidemic. All Hersey had to do was convince the public to believe him.

"Too easy. This story writes itself," he mumbled.

"Sir, do you have any other questions before you go on?" the chief of staff asked. The car ride from the White House to the talk show studio seemed like a blur. Hersey pondered his diabolical scheme with such intensity that he was oblivious to everyone else. The woman's question finally registered with Hersey's brain after a few seconds.

Hersey said. "No, I am quite aware of what needs to be done." He entered the studio and waited in a small green room.

One of the talk show attendants entered the room, "Good morning, Mr. Vice-President. It's an honor to have you with us today. Mrs. Nance and the other Rundown crew will be ready and waiting once you enter the stage. Good luck, sir."

After the attendant left the green room, Hersey checked his appearance in a floor-length mirror. His suit was perfect. No wrinkle would have dared appear on such a superb creation of fabric. He checked his hair and smiled a toothy grin into the mirror. His teeth were white as the fluorescent lights that hummed above him. Most important of all, his mind was sharp today. Jekyll was in top form this day. He would need to be.

Hersey began to hear cheers from the audience as his name was announced. The attendant knocked on the green room door again, "Sir, they are ready for you."

He entered the stage to thunderous applause. Every member of The Rundown stood and clapped until he reached his seat. The cameras glared from the balcony. It was show time, and millions of Americans were watching. The Patriot Party was watching as well.

The Rundown was a longtime renowned talk show that ran on the precipice of government secrets and Hollywood scandals. There were seven members of the panel, three men and four women. Patsy Nance was the official orator and creator of the show. She called the shots and was one of the few people Hersey could share a stage with that was more famous than he had ever been.

"Mr. Vice-President Dr. William Hersey, welcome to The Rundown," Nance said to start the show. That was Nance's signature entrance statement for all guests. She stated their name or title, followed by a long pause, then the welcoming part making sure to emphasize the name of her show.

"Tell us. Just what are you planning to do about this government cover-up? You can't possibly expect the American people to believe that drugs are to blame for these recent attacks in countless communities around the country?" Nance asked Hersey.

Hersey once again began to channel his inner Frank Richards. "First, I want to thank The Rundown for its continued commitment to truth for Americans." Hersey waited for the applause to die down before continuing. "Next, I want to inform you all that the White House has confirmed that Dr. Adilene Roth and Dr. Jacob Meyers are to blame for the creation of the drug that is infecting so many American lives right now."

Patsy Nance asked, "It's funny that you brought up Adilene Roth, Mr. Vice-President. We have obtained records from your time as CDC director that indicate you hired Dr. Roth to work directly under you. Would you care to explain this?"

Hersey was feeling the pressure now. His attempt to steal the show and control the narrative was not unfolding as he had planned. Frank Richards himself would have had a hard time lying his way out of this question. Fortunately, Hersey was a much better liar than Richards.

"Ms. Roth, indeed, was hired by myself at the Atlanta CDC many months ago. I saw the potential as she was a leading scientist, helping to create solutions for burned victims. However, never would I have thought her to be creating drugs for the black-market using CDC resources," Hersey said.

"So, you just left her alone in one of the most dangerous labs in the world to do what she pleased?" Nance asked.

Hersey tried to end the interrogation with one final attempt of shock value, "Like I said, Mrs. Nance, Dr. Roth is a fugitive from justice of the American Government. We will hunt her down and make her pay for what she has done to the American people."

The response drew more applause from the panel and the crowd. Patsy Nance looked at her manager behind the stage and received the 'thumbs up' signal that a commercial break was needed.

"We'll be right back with the Vice-President in a few minutes. We are America, and this is The Rundown." Patsy Nance turned toward Hersey, "You're good, Mr. Vice-President. I can see how you've remained squeaky clean from this mess."

Nance went back to talking with her panel. Hersey wasn't sure if she was playing with him or if she actually knew more than anyone else he had spoken with thus far about Adilene Roth. He had to assume that she was trying to get under his skin for a boost in ratings. His assumptions were correct.

The show resumed for another segment. Hersey continued deflecting more questions about Roth and Meyers until there nothing was left to dodge. Nance thanked him, along with her panel, and the crowd cheered as Hersey left the stage. The show proved to be a success. Dr. Hersey was now an American household name.

The car ride back to The White House was a celebratory one for Hersey and his staff. His staff were all bragging about how stately Hersey had looked and how callers were bombarding his office with support for capturing Roth and Meyers. Hersey entered his office as the phone was ringing.

Hersey answered, "Yes, this is Dr. Hersey. Ah, Mr. Reynolds, yes, good to hear from you. I would love to meet with the Patriot Party this week. Thank you, I'll transfer you to my chief of staff, and she will set everything up. Goodbye."

The call Hersey was waiting for had come. The chair of the Patriot Party wanted to meet Hersey about presidential campaign possibilities. Everything was going better than expected. Hundreds of miles from Washington D.C., Roth intended to do her best to ruin those plans.


## North to Alaska

Mabrey put the helicopter down in an empty construction site about a mile from the base. The plan was to let Mabrey enter the Naval Air Station Pensacola and secure the C-130. Fortner, along with the rest of the crew, would board the plane and leave for Camelot. For any of this to work, they were relying on General Baskin to have held his promise and contacted the AFB commander ahead of time.

Mabrey went to the entrance of the base. The tension was fever pitch as Mabrey spoke with the guard. After a few minutes, the Lt. entered as everyone else waited. He reappeared and gave the crew a hand motion to come over.

Fortner looked at Adi, "I guess my commander came through."

"You guess? What would have happened if he hadn't come through?" Adi asked.

"Then we go to jail where would most likely be shot or hanged."

JJ said, "I swear, I need to find new friends. I'm tired of dodging tornadoes, worrying about getting eaten by monsters or shot."

Fortner entered the facility and went straight to the base Commander's office, an old friend of General Baskin. "Gerald called and used his one-time no questions asked favor yesterday, Captain. You have five minutes to get off my base, or I'll have no choice but arrest you all."

The group was escorted outside to the airstrip, where they all saw the hulking craft towering over other objects on the runway. The old C-130 was recently returned and decommissioned from the recent Iraqi War. Mabrey entered the cockpit and began completing preflight checklists. Everyone else settled in, and the behemoth of a plane took off north to Alaska.

Mabrey informed everyone, "Okay, people, we got about ten hours until touch down at Elmendorf. You are now flying Mabrey budget flights. Please keep your butts in your seats. Your inflight entertainment will be provided by Janice Fortner." Fortner threw an MRE at the head of Mabrey after hearing the Lt.'s last comments.

JJ asked, "Janice Fortner? Do you have a sister or something?"

Sims began laughing so hard he almost fell out of his seat. Jake and Adi were now intrigued by what Mabrey's comments were about as well. Fortner was in no mood.

Mabrey chimed in from the cockpit again, "Our fearless leader once had to impersonate a woman to get into a village near Kabul for an intel-gathering mission. He had to wear two burkas to cover his fathead."

Adi looked at Fortner, trying to picture the massive man as a woman and finally commented, "You do have nice cheekbones."

Jake and JJ began laughing too. Their joy was short lived, stolen by a stern look from Fortner. Fortner was not going to be embarrassed much longer. He was still reeling from the last conversation he had with Adi one on one.

Fortner said, "I saved a battalion of men with that intel, so it was worth it."

"Yeah, and you stole one of the local village leader's hearts in the process," Mabrey said.

"Enough, Lt., or I'll call your mom," Fortner said, holding up his phone.

Mabrey became stone-cold and deathly quiet. Fortner was one of the few people Mabrey's mom loved as much as her own son and would defend him as such.

Adi turned her attention to Jake, "How many people did you say were left at Camelot before you left?"

"There were four male test subjects, four nurses, and the usual amount of guards, so I'd say around fifteen people in total," Jake said, using his fingers to count the number of people. "Why?"

Fortner interrupted, "Because either everyone is dead, or the place is crawling with Merged."

"Can I get a gun?" JJ asked Fortner.

"Do you have weapons training?" Fortner replied.

"Not like you, but I used to shoot beavers at my uncle's farm."

Jake replied to Fortner and JJ, "Well, the merged are kinda like huge beavers, except they're eating your face instead of trees."

Fortner wasn't thrilled with arming civilians but felt everyone should have the opportunity to defend themselves in case of a merged attack. He grabbed a bag from a locker near the back of the plane and gave JJ, Jake, and Adi each a pistol with one magazine of ammunition.

"Only use it if you feel your life is in danger, and never point it at anything you don't plan on killing," Fortner said.

JJ looked at his new gun as if it was the key to a magical castle. He would later view his newfound power as a lifesaver and a burden.

Jake and Adi placed their weapons into their packs and continued about Camelot. The most powerful weapon for combatting the merged remained inside Camelot, their lab equipment.

Adi said, "You know we won't be able to stay there very long. Hersey will send people for us as soon as we land in Alaska."

"I know, but there is no way he expects us to go all the way out there to get away from Higgins. He probably thinks we're hiding in a building somewhere in Atlanta waiting to be captured. My best guess is we have a few hours to get what we need and figure out where to go next."

Adi became fixated on Jake's last word next. She hadn't thought that far ahead yet. Adi began asking herself, "What happens next?" The idea of life after eluding Higgins and Hersey hadn't entered her mind. There was nowhere to go as long as the newly appointed vice president continued to hunt them down as fugitives. Adi couldn't concern herself with those thoughts right now. Her mother was still priority number one. Ethel Roth had been awarded only one more day of sanity with her recent AD2 injection. Many Americans would share her same situation.

What had started with a few hundred injections of SAP-23 or AD1 was soon to be dwarfed in scope. AD2 was a nationwide program. Anyone in threat of infection would have access to the shot free of charge. Everyone who had received AD1 had already merged. Soon, AD2 recipients would either be dead or causing death.

The effects of SAP-9 or AD2 were unknown. Jake's first participant of his new serum had merged but into what? Did they share the same effects and characteristics of the SAP-23 Merged, or were there differences? Nobody knew yet but would not have to wait long to find out. The SAP-23 and AD2 combined merged were unlike anything Adi or Jake could have prepared for. They had changed into something new.

# 16. Ground Zero

## Setting the Trap

The plane flew closer to its final destination as Fortner concocted his scheme. The plan was for Fortner to contact Higgins and poke the bear once on the ground at Elmendorf AFB. Higgins would, without a doubt, come for Adi and Fortner.

"How much longer?" he asked Lt. Mabrey.

"Forty-five minutes, sir. Have you thought about how the base is going to respond yet?"

Mabrey was landing the C-130 regardless of the reception from Elmendorf. There was no turning back now. Fortner was banking on his ability to defuse the situation once on the runway or fight through to Camelot if negotiations fell through.

"You just focus on landing the plane Lt. I'll handle the rest," Fortner said.

Fortner turned to everyone else, "Listen up. We should arrive at the airbase in a few minutes. Be prepared to fight. I don't know what kind of welcome awaits us once we've landed."

JJ asked, "What about the merged? Do you think any of those things made it out this far?"

Wilson was right to be concerned. After Jake had finished developing the new SAP-9 formula, or AD2, Hersey sent it to many people under his sphere of influence. Everyone at Camelot had received the serum. That is except for Private Jones. Jones refused to take the injection and was wise to do so. Hersey contacted the four nurses while they were helping with the human test subjects at Camelot. Their orders were to stay at the air base until all available AD2 doses were distributed. All contact from Elmendorf AFB and Camelot ceased two days ago.

Adi looked at Jake, "Your patients, you left them at Camelot?"

"As far as I know, they are still there, but who knows what's going on at that place now?" Jake said.

"So, we don't know. That's what you're saying. We could land and get eaten up by those monsters or shot as terrorists. Great, just great," JJ said.

Mabrey interrupted everyone, "There's the runway. Prepare for landing." The C-130 smoked every wheel as it touched down. For it to be the middle of the day, there wasn't a soul-stirring on the base. No trucks or personnel came out to meet the plane, and there was no radio traffic.

Fortner grabbed his phone and made the most dangerous call of his life, "You want me? Come get me." Fortner paused, "Does Camelot mean anything to you? Good, I'll be here waiting with bells on."

The captain threw his phone back into a pack. He dangled the meat in front of the tiger. The trap was set. Higgins was coming, but Fortner did not know how soon Higgins would arrive. The Osprey plane Higgins was traveling in was much faster than the old cargo plane they had used. Higgins would see his old friend very soon.

"Did it work? Is he coming?" Adi asked.

Fortner pressed the rear door release, and the large door creaked and moaned as it began lowering. Once the door had opened, he turned to everyone. "Higgins will be here soon. We need to get to Camelot and prepare for the engagement."

JJ asked Fortner as they walked down the runway, "With bells on? Who says that?"

Fortner did not respond to JJ but did squeeze out a smile and walked over to Sims. "Can you fight, Sgt.?" Fortner asked.

Sims was still on the mend from the attack at the ranger station, but he would survive and do his best to complete the mission, "I can fight, sir. I'll be ready."

The entire group walked down the runway of the AFB like a posse of cowboys entering a ghost town before a long-awaited scrape with their rival gang. The base was still showing no signs of life. Not one person showed their face.

Jake asked Mabrey, "You used to work on an air base, right? Is it supposed to be this quiet?"

Mabrey gave Fortner an ominous look, and they each prepared their rifles. Everyone else also readied their weapons and prepared for the worst. They were right to do so as merged began pouring out from a nearby hangar. The main terminal and headquarters of the base also gave up the Merge from within it.

"Everybody, run! Now." Fortner made for the main offices, "There, through that door." Mabrey and Sims stayed back and began picking off the merged that were closing in.

The mutated men and women were surprisingly fast but were not running like normal humans. They ran with stiffened legs as if their knees wouldn't bend. Nevertheless, they were moving fast enough to cause serious concern.

More merged appeared from inside the building. Fortner began shooting the monsters and noticed that apart from having the same black eyes as the large man that had attacked him before, these merged were more aggressive.

Adi, Jake, and JJ began shooting at the merged as well. The excitement of JJ getting his first taste of combat was a blur. The adrenaline surged through his body. He was moving faster than his mind could comprehend.

Fortner saw the main exit of the base and instructed everyone to keep moving, "There's the door. Everyone out."

Mabrey and Sims were about fifty yards behind the others when they were ambushed by a large group of Merged, cutting them off. Sims and Mabrey went back to back, shooting in all directions. Their movements were perfect, shots precise, reloading fast, but even the two highly trained and effective Army Rangers would need a miracle if they were to make it out alive.

"It's been an honor, Lieutenant," Sims said, reaching for another magazine.

"Likewise, Sergeant," Mabrey echoed.

The Merged were almost in arms reach when Fortner plowed a luggage carrier into a few of the monsters. A few of the merged began howling out, "Kill. Man."

Fortner yelled to his men, "This way. On me." The luggage carrier had cleared enough space for the men to escape through. Echo Team ran for their lives as there were too many merged to engage, and each man was low on ammo.

Jake found a military Humvee parked outside the main entrance and raced back to the front door for Fortner and his team. A few merged crashed through the entrance windows and made for Adi, JJ, and Jake.

JJ and Adi used the rest of the ammo on the approaching Merged. One of the creatures, a woman wearing an Air Force uniform, jumped onto the hood of the Humvee. She began clawing and punching at the front windshield.

Jake screamed at JJ and Adi, "Shoot it! Shoot it!"

"No more bullets," JJ said.

"I'm out too," Adi shouted.

The windshield glass began to crack, and no one inside knew what to do. Jake braced for the worst and then saw blood explode all over the front of the vehicle. Fortner had drawn his revolver and made quick work of the last Merged standing in their way of leaving the AFB. The head of the Merged woman containing the black eyes of death rolled off the hood and into the road, as the Humvee sped away.

"Well, the good news is maybe those things will kill Higgins before he can get to us," Jake said.

Adi turned to Fortner, "The entire base was injected. It had to be one of Hersey's sick experiments or something."

JJ paused, "Unless."

"Unless what?" Mabrey and Sims asked.

"Unless they are spreading the disease. Haven't you guys ever seen 'Night of the Living Dead?' If a zombie bites or scratches you, you turn soon after."

"You have seen my face, right?" Sims said, pointing to his lacerated face, "I'm still here."

"I don't know, Sims, you are starting to get pretty damn ugly," Mabrey said.

Adi interrupted the men, "No, Sims is right. It doesn't work like that. You need to be injected with the serum to become merged. It has to infiltrate your cells in a pure, unadulterated form. Once SAP is inside your cells, it changes and becomes something different."

"And how do you know this?" JJ asked.

Roth held up a vial of one of the infected sister's blood from the CDC, "Because I made the serum, and I made the merged." Adi had discovered this revelation on the kitchen table of the cabin. The disease could not be spread from person to person. DNA inside the cells was specific to each individual, making transmission incompatible with other merged.

The genetic anomaly was also thwarting Adi's ability to contrive a universal solution for curing the inflicted.

Currently, she would have to create an antibody to neutralize the serum for each separate merged individual, making it nearly impossible to fix. Adi sighed and returned her gaze to the exhausted and bewildered faces of her comrades, "It can't spread. At least, not yet."

"What do you mean, not yet? See, I don't like the way you said that," Mabrey replied.

"Bacteria and other diseases are always adapting and evolving for survival." Adi was right to be concerned about the long-term effects of SAP-23 and 9. Once the infected cells began dying, they would have no choice but to figure out a new way to survive or die. The transmission was the next most likely step for existence.

"And this is why you don't play God," JJ said.

Everyone agreed with JJ's last statement, Adi included. She was sorry SAP had ever been created. It started as a journey and calling to help people, but all SAP had accomplished was destroying life. Adi thought about her mother again. "I have to call my dad tonight."


## Close Call

Hersey entered his office and began writing down campaign slogans while screening news stories, a few featuring his latest publicity stunt on The Rundown. His television time was soon interrupted by a loud commotion from the room across the hall. At first, Hersey paid the noises little mind, but he soon realized something more was happening with his staff.

Two secret service agents burst into Hersey's office and advised him to get under his desk, "Sir, we have reports of an attack."

"Attack? What do you mean an attack?" Hersey asked.

Hersey's chief of staff had received her AD1 injection while on a recent trip with her girlfriends. She had cut a deep gash into her calf on Virginia Beach. The cut and swelling healed within minutes of her injection. The Merging began to take hold of her after leaving the talk show and fully manifested once she was back in her office.

Screams filled the hallway, "Elizabeth, what are you doing? Stop. No!"

Elizabeth Derner killed her intern, tearing away at her former friend's face and neck as secret service agents opened fire. She turned violently and charged the two men, killing them both. Her gunshot wounds were instantly healing. More agents arrived and engaged, her merged form absorbing the trauma as she continued her bloodlust rampage.

One of Hersey's agents commanded, "Sir, we are going to make for the door at the end of the hallway and get you into the safety bunker." The White House had bunkers under most of the structure. The short distance would feel like a mile to Hersey.

"What is out there?" Hersey asked.

"We don't know, sir. One of your staff is attacking everyone. That is all we know."

"One person?" Hersey deduced the threat after hearing the last statement from the agent, "My God, it has to be one of those."

"Stay between us, sir, and don't stop no matter what happens."

The door flung open to a horrific scene. Blood was splattered all over the walls. Agents screamed in agony with an assortment of gashes and broken bones. The merged Derner had an agent off the ground with one hand choking, breaking his neck. Turning toward Hersey, and saying, "Doctor," she came at the three men. The black eyes were almost hypnotizing. Blood dripped from her hands.

"Take the Vice-President. I got this," one of the agents said. He turned and faced the merged woman, shooting her several times. She stumbled but did not go down. Hersey's last sight before the elevator door closed was Derner's hand engulfed in the agent's chest. He struggled for a few seconds and then went lifeless. Derner killed six people in a matter of minutes, and Hersey would have been another if he hadn't made it to the bunker.

After a few minutes below ground, Hersey got the message, "Sir, the threat has been confirmed dead at this time. Please remain here until we have the all-clear."

The Vice President sat in a chair, and the gravity of the situation finally hit him. *That could've been my corpse strung up by that monster. Dr. Roth almost had me do her a favor,* he thought. The attack by the merged served as a wake-up call for Jekyll, "We need to get this under control," he told the agents in the bunker.

Hersey returned to the ground floor of The White House and was immediately taken to meet President Harding, "Are you okay, William? These things, what are they?"

Hersey walked with The President on the front lawn, "Sir, these things are the product of Dr. Adilene Roth and the biological weapon she created at the CDC. She has to be captured or eliminated."

"Do you know where she is?" the President said.

"No, but I have the best men on the job looking for her as we speak."

"What about this new drug, AD2?"

"Sir, Dr. Roth has nothing to do with it. AD2 is completely safe," Hersey said.

"Alright, William, find Dr. Roth and bring her to justice."

Hersey returned to 'The Refuge' and phoned Higgins, "Major, tell me you have a lead on these misfits."

"Sir, they are at Camelot. I'm in pursuit and should arrive in an hour."

"No excuses this time, Major. Either succeed, or you can stay in Alaska."

Higgins replied, "They won't get away this time. There's nowhere else to go."

The recent events at The White House weighed heavy on Hersey's mind. Dr. Roth had but to leak any detail of Hersey's involvement with Higgins or SAP-23, and he would be a co-conspirator of terrorism. The merged had killed hundreds of people at this point. Hersey had miscalculated the degree of danger he had levied with SAP-23 and 9 in order to gain power and influence. *What good is gaining everything if you die in the process?* he thought.


**House of Pain**

Adi saw the gates rising against the mountain horizon, "There it is, in all its horrible glory." Camelot stood tall in the distance. The once beacon of scientific progression and hope was about to become a fortress against its creator.

"How many men are normally present? Is there an armory?" Fortner asked. The recent gun battle with the merged at Elmendorf had severely diminished Echo Team's ability to fight Higgins. Without an armory, even the best plan would fail.

Jake said as he reached the main gate, "There's an armory on the first floor in the west wing beside the barracks. Normally, I'd say there are around ten men on duty at any given time."

"Interesting," Adi said. The front gates to Camelot were wide open. The only time she had ever seen the gates open, someone was entering or leaving the compound. "These gates should not be open."

"Merged?" JJ asked.

Adi shrugged her shoulders, "Who knows."

The group exited the truck and entered the atrium. The compound wasn't known for being a lively place, but it was too quiet, even for Camelot.

Jake cried out, "Where is everybody? Roger! Roger Jones!"

Adi joined Jake, "Private Jones?"

They entered the security barracks sector and found the armory. Any weapon a soldier could ask for was housed at Camelot. More firepower than a scientific research lab should need.

"Captain, RPGs, frag grenades, what the hell!" Mabrey exclaimed.

He asked Adi and Jake, "Why does your lab contain enough weapons to start a war?"

"If we make it out of here, you can ask Dr. Hersey," Adi said.

"Gear up, and we make for the top floor," Fortner said.

Sergeant Sims returned to the atrium where he encountered Private Jones, "Sir, are you okay?" Jones collapsed into Sims' arms. The others ran to help. Adi and Jake began talking to Jones, but he was out cold.

JJ asked, "Is he one of them?"

"No, but he's severely dehydrated and is bruised up pretty badly," Jake said.

Private Jones was the last man standing. Jake's first SAP-9 merged patients remained on the second floor. Soon after Jake had whisked off to 'The Refuge', Camelot's security detail approached the medical wing of the lab, and the merged attacked. Jones' men fought bravely but were overrun by the men. All but Roger Jones died on that floor.

Jones came around long enough to warn everyone, "Second floor, don't…still up there."

Adi looked at Jake, "Your subjects?"

"SAP-9," he said.

"Let's take him to my office on the third floor. We can figure out the merged problem next," Adi said.

Private Jones was placed on Adi's office couch. The rest of the men surveyed her office. Adi grabbed her favorite picture off her desk when she noticed the guitar was missing, "Meyers, where is my guitar? I swear if you lost it…"

Jake's mind flashed back to the jet ride and the honey-blond guitar placed in the chair next to him, "No, I know exactly where it is."

"And that is?" Adi asked.

"Well, I kinda left it on Hersey's private jet."

Mabrey passed by Jake, "Sucks to be you right now buddy."

Adi did not have time to respond to Jake as they were interrupted by a loud whirring sound. Higgins had finally caught up with Roth and Fortner and opted to forgo landing at Elmendorf for a more direct approach attack. The V-22 Osprey looked like an alien invader ready to besiege a foreign planet as it lowered itself down and into the compound.

"Sir, they have a VTOL," Mabrey said.

"I see that Lt., get into position. We will engage from the third floor, make him come to us," Fortner said.

Sims and Mabrey ran to the main hallway and set up near the windows in front of the elevator. Adi, Jake, and JJ stayed with Fortner inside Adi's office with Jones. The three civilians received some last-minute training from the captain, then Fortner left for the hallway directly outside the office.

JJ said, "I never thought I'd go from chasing tornadoes and solar flares to fighting a war in Alaska. If this is it, I can at least fight for Barry."

Jake also had a few final words for Adi, "I'm sorry about all of this, you are the best scientist…person I've ever met. If we make it through this, I hope you will still call me a friend."

"I'm sorry too. I'll make this right. I have to," Adi said.

Thousands of miles away in Georgia, Adi's mother merged. Dean had done as instructed and tied Ethel to a chair using a thick rope. Adi's father was heartbroken by the sight of his wife. Ethel's only hope now, if she ever had a chance to become normal again, was soon to be fighting for her life too.

Sims called out to Fortner, "Sir, five men, body armor."

"Do you have eyes on Higgins yet?" Fortner asked.

A loud voice boomed from Osprey's loudspeakers rang out, "Dr. Roth, Captain Fortner, come out, and we will let everyone else go. You have my word."

Fortner replied through a window, "Come and get me. I'll be waiting for you on the second floor."

"We can't go to the second floor. Are you crazy?" Jake said.

Adi said, "No, the captain is right. The second floor is perfect."

As soon as Fortner had heard Jones' earlier comments, he hatched the idea. Higgins would have to make it through Camelot's fun house of horror before making it to the group. For once, Fortner hoped the merged would serve as a much-needed ally.

Higgins sounded off one more time from the plane, "Your funeral." The Major approached the five secret service agents before exiting the plane, "I don't know what he has planned, but do not underestimate that man. And remember, they don't leave this compound alive."

Higgins was right to worry about Fortner and Echo Team, but neither he nor his agents were prepared for what lay in store on the second level. The merged would play their part in this fight.

The scene for the showdown was now set. Fortner and Higgins would finish what they had started many years ago inside a cave in Afghanistan. Adi and Jake would finally have a chance to get Hersey's enforcer off their backs, and Hersey could end the only incriminating threat left. The person who could reveal his involvement in creating the merged.

# 17. Death Becomes Us

## Final Showdown

Higgins entered the main entrance of Camelot. The large atrium was silent. The Major made a few hand gestures, and the five agents headed up the stairs. "No elevators. They could be rigged to go down," Higgins said.

The men climbed the two flights of stairs with weapons drawn. They were ready for Fortner and his crew. However, it was not Fortner that lurked behind the next door. Higgins' men opened the door and entered the lab hallway. Two men went left into the first door and two right. Higgins and the remaining agent slowly began to make their way down the center of the hallway. Large glass windows looked out onto the Osprey plane outside.

"Sir, last doors ahead," an agent said.

The final doors went into the lab where Jake had injected the four men earlier in the week. The agents were within arms-length of the doors when they swung open, knocking two men down. The four, merged rushed Higgins and his men. The agent closest to the door was mauled by all four merged. He died instantly due to blunt force trauma to the head.

*What the...*, Higgins thought and began walking backward back to the stairs.

One of the agents began screaming, "It's eating me. It's eating me." One of the merged men had the agent by his leg, biting large holes into his hamstrings and calves. The agent fired his weapon into the merged several times. The other three agents opened fire, killing the creature.

Fortner heard the gunshots coming from downstairs and sent Mabrey and Sims down to flank Higgins from behind, "Mabrey, you and Sims, go around and down the other stairs. That should put you behind Higgins."

"Sir." The men began down the stairs opposite Higgins and the remaining agents.

"You're sending them down there? Those things are down there. You're sending them to their deaths," Adi said.

Fortner knew his men could take care of themselves, "I know what I'm doing. You stay in this office."

JJ and Jake were becoming frustrated as well. If they were going to die, they at least wanted the chance to fight on their terms. Fortner planned to draw Higgins, and the merged closer to their location.

"Let us go with them," JJ said.

Fortner replied, "Negative."

"No, he's right. It's at least eight to one against your team Captain. Let us help. I *have* to help. I'm the reason those things are down there," Jake said.

"Nobody leaves the room. Do you understand?" Fortner said.

Down below on the second floor another agent was killed by the merged. He was thrown through one of the lab windows, cutting a large crevice into the top of his abdomen. The liver of the agent was sliced in half, and dark blood ran out from under the rib cage guarding the organ. Two of the merged began eating the man's flesh. He was still alive, and his screams were enough to cause one of the merged to pause and let out a scream of his own, "Blood."

The body armor the men adorned protected the top of the head, chest, and back, but the merged proved too vicious. Against well-placed gunshots, the armor was quite effective. Against mindless beasts, it was trivial.

Higgins fought his way back to the stairs, and he began ascending to the third floor. Mabrey and Sims came around behind the remaining agents and merged. Everyone in the lab area was still fighting to the death. Three agents and three merged remained in the room, and the battle was not faring well for the secret service agents.

Mabrey and Sims saw the men and beasts fighting as they approached. One of the merged noticed them and charged. Sims opened fire, striking the monster numerous times, staggering it. Mabrey joined the fight with at least twenty rounds into the merged man. The beast grabbed Sims, throwing him into the wall. The sergeant let out a scream. The pain in his already bruised and battered body was immense.

Upstairs, JJ and Jake had heard enough. They burst through the office door, running toward the stairs. Fortner could do little to stop them as he could not leave Adi alone.

"Be smart, men. If everyone is already dead when you get down there, make for the Humvee and get out of here," Fortner said.

Fortner entered the office with Adi and said, "Get behind the desk."

Adi did not say a word and acknowledged Fortner by nodding her head. She held the pistol he had given her on the plane ride from Pensacola and prepared to fight anything that came through the office door. Private Jones remained unconscious on the couch. His fighting days were over, for now.

Mabrey took one of the frag grenades from the armory and stuffed it into the pants of the merged man attacking Sims. The Lt. then pushed the creature with all his might through the nearest window leading outside. The merged tried grabbing the ledge to the window but exploded into large pieces before he could climb back into the building. The mangled body fell to the ground below.

The remaining agents fought the monsters ferociously. They knew it was kill or be killed. JJ and Jake caught up to Mabrey and Sims. There was blood everywhere. The sounds coming from that area of the building were incomprehensible.

"What do we do now? Where's Higgins?" Jake asked.

"He must be in there somewhere. Let's see what happens here first. We can clean up what's left," Mabrey said.

They were going to let the agents and merged fight it out. No need to put themselves in danger unless necessary. For all they knew, Higgins was already dead in one of the pools of mangled bodies.


## Paid in Full

Higgins rounded the final flight of stairs to the third floor. He stopped when saw John Fortner coming out of Adi's office. The two men locked eyes and stared. For a few seconds, their faces remained locked onto each other. Higgins remained standing on the threshold of the stairwell door while Fortner turned back to Roth.

"Don't open this door for anyone except me. Everything's going to be alright, Adi," Fortner said.

Adi looked at Fortner differently this time. She needed him to return to her alive. The man who all she wanted to do when they first me was get away from, was now who she worried about never seeing again.

"He said my name," Adi whispered.

Fortner shut the door and raised his arms in front of Higgins with his rifle in one hand and revolver in the other. Higgins knew this was now a close and personal fight. Fortner wanted to punish Higgins with his bare hands. Higgins welcomed the gesture and laid his guns aside as well.

"I'm going to enjoy killing you, then I might feed your girlfriend to those monsters below," Higgins said.

Fortner walked toward Higgins, "You have to get to her first."

Higgins threw the first punch connecting across the right jaw of Fortner. The strength of the smaller Higgins surprised Fortner. This fight would prove to be a worthy challenge. Fortner countered with a crushing blow to the stomach sending Higgins back a few feet.

The Major regained his breath quickly and continued, "I can see you haven't forgotten how to take a punch." Higgins landed a swift kick to the side of Fortner's head, sending him to his knees. Higgins went for the final blow when Fortner caught his punch and twisted his left arm, breaking it in half as he rose back to his feet. Higgins let out a loud yell heard downstairs.

The Major was also down to his last agent as the rest had been killed by the merged. The final agent landed a killing blow to one of the merged men as he drove his knife deep into the temple of the beast. Before the agent could rise from his knees, the final merged ripped the throat out of the agent, killing him. The it turned toward Echo Team, Jake, and JJ. The men opened fire, filling the infected monster with over a hundred shots cutting it in half near the waist.

All secret service and the four merged patients of Meyers lay dead. The second floor of Camelot was a kill box. The amount of blood and death contained there would have been enough to haunt any demon of hell.

"Look for Higgins," Mabrey said.

"No sign of him," Sims said, as they all heard the scream from above them, "Upstairs, the captain."

Jake turned to JJ, "Oh, no, Adi."

Higgins regained his balance and pulled out a long, serrated knife, "I can't let you win. You can't beat me."

"Coward," Fortner said.

Higgins charged, slashing away violently in every direction. Fortner was cut on his right shoulder, causing him to wince in pain. Fortner countered again with a blow to the face.

Mabrey stopped everyone at the hallway entrance when he saw Fortner and Higgins fighting, "Let the captain settle this. It's his fight now."

"I'm going to cut your heart out," Higgins said. The Major lunged for the killing strike.

Fortner dodged, caught his hand, and broke his other arm causing Higgins to drop the knife. "I'm going to find out if you ever had one," Fortner said, picking up the knife and driving it through the heart and out the back of Higgins.

Higgins let out a final breath and collapsed. Fortner watched the eyes of the Major remain locked with his own as he fell. The fear and turmoil of Higgins were sweet retribution for Fortner. Never again would Adi, Jake, or anyone else have to worry about Hersey's lap dog again.

Fortner knocked on the door, "It's me, Ms. Roth."

JJ stepped up to the Major's body and let out a deep breath thinking of Barry.

Adi opened the door and gave Fortner the biggest hug of her life. Fortner hesitated but hugged her and said, "You're safe now. It's over."

The others came to check on Fortner and Adi.

"Hell of a fight, sir, but why are you bleeding?" Mabrey asked. "Sometimes you have to bleed a little to show you care," Fortner said.

JJ asked, "Wait, was that a joke? Did you just make a joke?"

Fortner turned to Jake and JJ, "You guys would have been excellent Rangers, well done."


## Clean Up Crew

Fortner reached down, taking Higgins' phone from his lifeless body, and called Dr. Hersey, "This is Captain John Fortner, and your man is dead at my feet. Everyone you sent is dead, and you're next." The look on everyone's faces was priceless.

Jake said, to Adi, "I would give anything to see Hersey's face right now, anything."

Fortner turned on the speaker function so everyone could hear Hersey's response, "Congratulations, Captain, it seems you have allowed Dr. Roth and Dr. Meyers extended time alive just so they can suffer more. There is no scenario where you can win, Captain."

"And there's no scenario where we stop coming until you pay for what you've done," Adi said.

"Good luck and hang tight, dear. I'll send for you," Hersey said.

Fortner ended the call abruptly, "We have to go now. There's no telling who he sends for us now."

"Where are we supposed to go now?" Jake asked.

"I think I may have a place we can go from here," JJ said. Wilson phoned his boss Jack Crowder again, "Jack, I need you to call the NOAA center in Vancouver, Canada." Crowder was yelling obscenities on the other line.

JJ continued, "Look, I'm not asking. Call Vancouver, or I swear I'll tell everyone about you and Linda. I'm sure your wife would love to know her husband is having an affair with the new weather girl, so you get on the phone right now and tell them I am coming with a film crew to conduct a documentary in Vancouver."

JJ turned to the group, "We can go to the NOAA center in Vancouver. I don't know how long I can keep the scam going, but it's something."

Fortner asked Adi, "How much time do you need to get everything from the lab to find a cure?"

"Not long, half an hour, tops," Adi said. "Let's go, Jake." The group only had less than an hour before Hersey would have men from other military installations in Alaska pouring into Camelot.

Higgins surprised Fortner by landing the VTOL directly onto Camelot grounds bypassing the merged, still running free, at Elmendorf. Fortner was not keen on driving back into the AFB, killing his way back to the C-130. He walked over to the window and looked at the Osprey, "Mabrey, can you fly that?"

"I thought you'd never ask, sir. It's got wings and propellers. I was born to fly that baby."

"Sir, what about the mess downstairs? People are gonna start asking questions when they see all those dead secret service agents," Sims said.

"How much ordinance is left in the armory? I know the perfect send-off for this place," Fortner asked.

Fortner, Mabrey, Sims, and JJ took Private Jones to the plane and returned to the armory on the first floor. The men took every grenade, container of gunpowder, and all the fuel they could find to the second floor. The smell of death was fresh in the air. There were mounds of flesh strewn throughout the lab. There wasn't any part of the floor not covered with blood or guts.

"My goodness. I don't know where the men start and the monsters end," JJ said.

Fortner's first experience viewing the carnage that ensued during his fight with Higgins shook him to the core. "Just terrible. No man should have to die this way." The captain was through seeing death for the day, and he knew that every minute they lingered at Camelot was a minute closer to joining Higgins and the merged.

Sims and Mabrey placed the explosives in the four corners of the wing and laid down a trail of gunpowder out through the front atrium to the Osprey.

"The explosion should take care of any trace that we were ever here," Mabrey said. The men remained out front and waited on the scientists inside.


## No Tears

Jake smiled as he and Adi entered their old lab, "Would you look at that." Moucious Clay had survived all this time and was looking healthy as ever. The mouse showed none of the symptoms the merged exhibited after SAP-23 or 9 injections.

"How is that possible, Jake? It looks completely normal," Adi asked.

"Told you he was a fighter."

"He comes too. There has to be a reason the serum did not interact the way it did with people," Adi said.

Adi and Jake grabbed everything they could and placed it on top of a large rolling table. All of Adi's hard drives and notes were still in her office, "Okay, take the cart down to Fortner. I need to grab my data."

Jake rolled the table into the elevator, and with help from the others, loaded everything into the Osprey. Roth returned to her office, and found her data. Before leaving the room, she stopped and took the photo of her parents off the desk and placed it into a bag. Her most prized possession hit differently now, seeing her mother so vibrant and happy. There was nothing left for her at Camelot. "I should have never come to this place."

Adi made it down to the Osprey with everyone standing at the bottom of the front steps leading into the main entrance. Fortner smiled and handed her a burning red flare, "You can do the honors. If anyone deserves to destroy this place, it's you."

Mabrey started the plane, and everyone went aboard as Adi turned and took one final look at the building that was once her greatest hope. Now it stood for everything she had come to hate. It was Hersey incarnate, an abomination.

"Camelot, how unoriginal," Adi said, tossing the flare down and disappearing into the plane.

Everyone from inside the plane watched the trail of fire snake up the stairs and into the building. The Osprey rose and hovered at five thousand feet, waiting for the fireworks.

A few seconds passed, and JJ asked, "I'm not going back down there if that place doesn't…" JJ did not have to worry about returning to Camelot because the entire right wing of the building was vaporized by the explosion. The shock wave was felt through the plane as a massive plume of fire and smoke rose high into the Alaskan sky. Higgins, his men, and the merged were gone for good.

"Beautiful," Adi said.

A few minutes later, Jake pointed to a small wooden structure outside the compound, "Hey, isn't that your cabin, Adi?"

"Does everyone in your family own a cabin in the woods?" JJ asked Adi.

"It was a great little place, best views ever," Adi said.

"Was great? It's still yours, right?" Jake said.

"Speaking of great, where's my Jeep, Meyers? What part of don't touch my stuff did you forget about?"

"How dare you accuse me. Maybe the merged took it. The last place I saw it was Elmendorf, after all," Jake said.

"If those things learn how to drive, I'm on the first rocket off this planet," Mabrey said from the cockpit.

Adi could get another Jeep, but what bothered her was that she knew that most of the places she loved would now be off-limits. Her parents' secret cabin in the Georgia Mountains being the exception. Hersey would not sleep until Adi never spent another restful night anywhere as long as he hunted her.

Adi sat down beside Fortner, "Thank you for what you did back there."

"Sorry you have to deal with all this. I know it must be hard," Fortner said.

"Every minute of worry we cause Hersey, is one more smile on my face."

Adi saw the cut on Fortner's shoulder and paused for a moment, "You know you said my name. I was starting to think you didn't even know I had a first name."

"Well, I…"

"It's okay. You can call me Adi from now on."

Fortner sat quietly, but his mind raced through a million scenarios. Adilene Roth was unlike any woman he had ever met. She was smart and tenacious, and when he looked into her eyes before turning to fight Higgins, John Fortner knew that he would never let anyone hurt her.

As for Adi, she feared the worst for her mother but also for Dean Roth. "Jake, give me your phone," Adi said. She dialed the number for her father and was relieved when he answered.

"Adi, are you alright? I was worried sick," Dean said.

"I'm fine. How's Mom?"

"What you said happened soon after our last walk. Her eyes are just…I can't talk about it." His grief was almost unbearable. Ethel tried with all her might to free herself from the thick bindings. The rope and leather could only hold her for so long.

"Look, Dad, you'll have to leave her there until I can figure this out. Lock the door to the cabin and go somewhere safe."

"I'm not leaving her here alone. I'm staying," Dean said.

"You'll die. Mom is different now. She will try to kill you. You have to trust me."

Dean was becoming angry, "You listen to me. I don't blame you for what happened. I know you didn't let that stuff loose on the public on purpose, but you let me figure this out because I'm not leaving your mother."

Adi mentioned the idea no more. If there was anyone more stubborn than her, it was Dean Roth. She didn't give her father enough credit though. Years of being a game warden and thousands of instances of tracking and caging animals made him an expert on staying away from danger. Ethel would be his craziest hunt and contain yet.

"I'll be back there soon. Just stay safe. I love you." Adi ended the call and began sobbing.

"We'll get this sorted out, I promise," Jake said.

The elation felt at the great victory at Camelot was sobered by the fact that so much had been lost during the last few days. They had escaped their most immediate threat, but Hersey remained and he was already making his next move.

# 18. The Rich Get Richer

## As the World Turns

Hersey sat at his desk and stared through a window, pondering variables for and against him going forward. The prospects of him remaining unscathed by recent events looked good. Cleaning up Camelot wouldn't be a matter difficult to conceal as only a handful of people knew the secret lab existed in the first place. By Roth destroying the facility, she had unknowingly done him a favor. Of course, even if Adi knew Camelot could be used to vilify Hersey, she still would have gone through with the destruction. Camelot had no business ever being operational again.

Higgins and his men had not accomplished their goal of capturing or killing Roth and Meyers, so Hersey saw their deaths as deserved, "All you had to do was kill them, and you'd still be here, Major." Also, eliminating Higgins rendered the video footage from the Atlanta CDC useless. Being an acquaintance of Adilene Roth or William Hersey was proving a detriment to one's health.

America as a whole was experiencing a wave of unification after the death of Frank Richards. There were national public outcries against drug abuse, the merged, and biological weapons. All of which Hersey had direct control over. Current President Harding was in no mood to take on such headaches. Hersey would continue his distribution of AD2 until the supply ran out, *"I need a way to make them want me. What better than a national emergency to bring the people together."*

The media touted Dr. Hersey a smart leader who had great ideas in helping America through the recent struggles. He had also begun a publicity stunt advocating against global warming. He blamed the recent solar events, exacerbated by the rising temperatures of earth due to the overuse of depleting natural resources. The effects of the most recent CME left many local power grids and infrastructures in shambles.

Hersey's greatest threats remained Adilene Roth and Jake Meyers, now under the protection of John Fortner. Secretly, Jekyll wished that the two scientists would come to their senses and help him find a way to control the merged, "They have so much potential. The beasts only need to have the reins tightened." However, Dr. Hersey knew this was a farce of a dream as Adi would never join him.

Hersey continued his smear campaign on the scientists, blaming the outbreak of infections on Adi and Jake. Most news outlets and internet blogs presented the two as heretics and traitors to America. Even shows like The Rundown began covering the scientists on the run, condemning them.

The news coverage also produced an unintended effect of causing some people to sensationalize them as activists on the run from big government. Adi's fan club began calling themselves *The Merge Mancers*. They believed the merged were a result of secret government lab experiments for population control. Of course, the ideas were condemned as conspiracy theories and outlandish paranoia by Hersey and the mainstream media. Hersey read one of the headlines from the founder of *The Merge Mancers*.

"The government wants to merge you, so they can control you."

The merged themselves were not deemed inherently evil, just angry they had been tricked into experiments by government lies. How crazy to think this was the closest to the truth of any information the government allowed the public to receive.

"These fools will do a better job discrediting Roth better than I ever could," Hersey said.

A knock came on Hersey's office door, "Sir, the chair of the Patriot Party is waiting outside for you."

The Patriot Party had become very interested in Dr. Hersey as the election drew nearer. In a few months, a new presidential election would be held. The newly elected president would also inherit the current crisis affecting the country. Hersey had gone from an unknown, untested politician to the front-runner for replacing Frank Richards. Lance Stephens was Frank Richards' campaign manager and head of the party.

"Mr. Stephens, always a pleasure," Hersey said.

"Mr. Vice-President, please allow me to be frank. The Patriot Party would like to nominate you for president," Lance said.

Hersey held back every impulse to bring to light the uncouthness of Lance's last comment, yet he could not help but see the irony of how relevant the words were. *I hope to do just that, be Frank*, Hersey thought.

Lance offered Hersey a drink and continued, "The Patriot Party was founded on principles that represent the little guy, the underdog. We can think of none better than a non-career politician, the doctor that has dedicated his life to helping people."

The motorcade driving the two men arrived at the campaign headquarters, where only a few days ago, Hersey stood alongside Richards as 'the rookie'.

"And what do I need to do in return for your endorsement, Mr. Stephens?" Hersey asked.

"Just remember the kindness of those involved in putting you into The White House, Mr. President."

Hersey saw potential in Lance, another man enticed by power and influence, a new piece on his chess board, "I can see why the people within your party look to you for answers. You are both doer and a thinker, like me."

The men entered the large stage overlooking thousands of empty seats. The next big rally was set for a few days from now. Lance wanted to unveil the party's nomination for the entire country to see. Hersey would have another opportunity to prove his worth as a leader.

"They need you. America needs you," Lance said.

"I accept your nomination, Mr. Lance."

"And my competition? Any threats I should know about?" Hersey asked.

"Natalie Owens, Maggie Renner's niece, is showing strong capabilities for the LibMo Party," Lance said.

Maggie Renner's niece, Governor of New Jersey, had also catapulted to notoriety after Air Force One went down. Natalie Owens was a younger, more ruthless version of the late Secretary of State. She started several investigations into the cause of her aunt's death and was recently named the nominee by The Liberationist Movement or LibMo Party as it was known.

New Jersey also was the only state that refused to administer AD1 or AD2. Her state exhibited extremely low cases of the beasts while showing an overall increase in drug abuse. Thus proving, that the merged were not substance abuse addicts raging war on America.

"When I become President, I will make sure that whoever was responsible for this attack on our nation will be brought to justice. They will pay for their crimes against humanity. I will not allow this country to be poisoned any longer."

"Can I beat her?" Hersey asked.

"Sir, you are the Vice-President of the United States, and President Harding has already given you his endorsement. The only way you lose this election is if you were to merge on live TV."

Until Lance's last statement, the thought of merging himself had never entered his min.

*Imagine the implications if someone put SAP-23 or 9 inside of me? What if I became one of those things?*

Hersey entered his motorcade and returned to The White House. He would make his grand entrance as the Presidential nominee for the Patriot Party at the convention later that week. First, he wanted to announce his plans on cable news on the front lawn of The White House.

Natalie Owens would soon begin a smear campaign, harping on Hersey's lack of experience and close previous relationship with Dr. Roth as a detriment to America. Hersey would have to prepare for a two-front war between Owens and Roth. History had provided several examples of this approach being a failure, but like the dictators and egomaniacs of the past, Dr. Hersey believed his fight would end differently. He would be the first to achieve victory. William Joseph Hersey would etch his place in history. For what his story would tell was yet to be seen.


## The Ruse

"Okay, you guys are now part of my film crew working on a documentary about the effects of global warming on sea lions," JJ said.

"You have got to be kidding me," Jake said.

The Osprey was an hour away from landing at the National Oceanic Atmospheric Administration office in Vancouver, Canada. The NOAA was responsible for National Weather Service centers across America and had collaboration agreements with other countries like Canada. Crowder did as JJ asked and called in a huge favor to the head of the Vancouver office. Crowder asked if JJ and his 'film crew' could observe sea lions. He also wanted access to research facilities for data analyzation.

Wilson's scheme was Roth's and Jake's best chance to gain access to equipment and space they could use to begin finding a cure for the merged.

Fortner remained opposed to going into hiding, but Adi was safe, and he felt his calling was now keeping her that way, "Your mother?"

"Yes, merged," Adi said.

"Father?" Fortner asked.

Adi held the picture of her parents, "Don't worry about him. He's a survivor." Her words a bluff. It hollowed out her insides to think of the situation her father was facing.

Jake was showing mouse 628 to Sims and JJ, "You are looking at the first creature to ever receive the SAP-23 injection."

"SAP-23, injection, get that thing away from me," JJ said.

"Every person on earth will have this little guy to thank once we've found a cure."

Sims put his face close to the cage to get a good look at the mouse, "I don't know, he looks pretty sketchy to me. Jake scared the life out of Sims by letting out a roar."

"There it is," Mabrey said.

The osprey landed beside the office, and the group went over the plan before entering. JJ would be himself. Mabrey, Sims, and Jones were currently the only members of the crew not being hunted by the American Government who would be the film team. Fortner, Adi, and Jake would round out the group as the research and data analysis technicians.

Jones awoke from knowing nothing of the recent events at Camelot, "What? Dr. Roth. Dr. Meyers. What's going on?"

"Here put this on," JJ said, giving Jones a weather service t-shirt.

JJ entered the main office and spoke with the director.

"Mr. Wilson, a pleasure to have you in Vancouver." The director noticed the Osprey in the parking lot, "You guys in the States get new reconnaissance craft?"

"You know, increased budgets and stuff," JJ said.

"We've heard about the monsters killing and eating people, crazy stuff." The director and JJ glanced at Roth and Meyers. Photos of the fugitives had not yet been distributed internationally.

"Yes, horrible, just horrible. Do you have a space for us?" JJ asked.

"Right this way, you can have this entire area. There is plenty of monitoring and video equipment for creating your film. Crowder also told me about your work with solar flares and geomagnetic storms. I assume you saw the latest event."

"I was in the thick of it for sure," JJ said.

The group entered a large room with many screens forecasting the next storm system JJ had noticed in LaGrange days before. It was shaping up to be twice the size of the last system. JJ wanted to contact Dr. Reiser at NASA just as soon as he had the time.

"Thank you, sir. We are grateful for your hospitality," JJ said as the director left the room.

"Okay, like I said before, I don't know how long we can keep this going, but you should be able to start working on a cure. If you need extra supplies, I'm sure we can get them somewhere in town. I'm going to try and get Dr. Reiser here. She might be able to help us too." JJ was turning into quite the mastermind. His plan was solid.

Mabrey called the group to a screen covering international news stories, "Yo, this guy never stops. Unbelievable."

A red banner caption ran across the bottom of the screen:

*"Vice-President, William Hersey, to receive the Patriot Party nomination."*

"He's going to be President?" Jake asked everyone.

"Not if I can help it. We have work to do," Adi said.

The lab equipment was unpacked, and Adi was relieved to have a modern, more powerful microscope to further her analysis of the sister's blood. Jake began drawing samples from mouse 628.

Adi called out to Jake, "First, we find a way to cure the merged, then we go after Hersey."

"Whatever it takes," Jake said. The plan was full steam ahead.

Fortner approached and asked Adi, "What can I do?"

"You've done more than enough, Captain. It's my turn to make everyone safe now."

Mabrey turned the news conference volume up after seeing the pictures appear on the screen, "I'm afraid out time her may have reached an end."

"What do you mean? We just got here," JJ said.

Mabrey pointed at the pictures of Adilene Roth and John Fortner. The burning, smoking rubble of Camelot played behind their faces. The reporter continued the story:

*"Terrorists and wanted murderers, Adilene Roth and Johnathan Fortner, continue their wave of destruction at a cancer research center in Alaska. The*

"We leave tonight," Fortner said, turning to Adi, "I'm sorry, we can't stay here."

The entire world would soon be after Roth and those associated with her. There were no more ideas, no places to go now. It would be dark in a few hours, then back into oblivion. The group was no better than the merged. They belonged nowhere.

As night fell, the Osprey was loaded and lifted off for an unknown destination. Fortner took out Higgins' phone for the last time and handed it to Adi, "I'll give you the honors this time."

"You can't imagine the feeling of getting a call from a dead man," Hersey said.

"No more of your idiot charms, Hersey. As long as I have breath inside my body, I'll make your life a living hell," Adi said. "You can't kill me. I've already died inside a long time ago. I'm not afraid of you anymore, and if I have to, I'll use the merged to get to you. I'll create something far worse to make you pay."

Every eye on the plane was like saucers. Adi's outburst was unexpected but inspirational. She became possessed with rage.

Hersey had no cute quip, no calculated comeback this time. He ended the call, quickly looking down to see the withered hand from the dream. Adilene Roth could cause more destruction than he ever could. She was beginning to come to terms with the prospect of mutual annihilation. They could die together, the one variable he never prepared for. Jekyll would never sacrifice himself to accomplish his goals, but now, Adi would.

"What was that?" Jake asked Adi.

"Scorched Earth," Fortner said. "Ms. Roth just played the one hand Hersey never expected. They both die, so nobody wins."

Jake turned to Adi, "You can't be serious? Are you crazy?"

"Anyone that wants off this plane can go anytime," Fortner said.

Adi threw Higgins's phone out of the plane as it sped away from Vancouver. She had become mad enough to do something stupid again. But unlike the lab with the sisters, she was smart enough to wait for the right place and time.

Adi turned to Fortner, "What have I done?"

"You made him fear you, that's what," Fortner said.

# 19. Something Worse

## Eye of the Storm

Hersey returned to 'The Refuge' but hardly felt safe that night. Roth could be anywhere. He dismissed Henry early and stared through the humid air and out into the darkness from the balcony. There was little to say at this point. Having the presidency, power, and the ability to manipulate people was for nothing as long as Roth remained free. That night, Hersey had the most severe nightmare of his life.

*Hersey was on a platform just large enough for him to stand. Surrounding him in all directions was a vast darkness. A voice came from the distance, but he could not tell from which direction or who the voice belonged to. It sounded like a woman, but it was different. He wanted to flee with all his might. There was nowhere to go. The voice became louder and closer. Hersey saw nothing in the distance. He began yelling at the unknown voice to show itself.*

*A cloud appeared again. The same cloud from the last dream, but this time there was no veil of water, no other hand coming toward Hersey. This time the cloud burned white hot. The heat was so intense he thought about leaping into the unknown below. The pain became excruciating. He had no choice but to jump. As he fell, a hand reached from the cloud and grabbed hold of Hersey. The hand dripped with blood, but it also caused the heat from the cloud to cease.*

*He was amazed, thankful, yet still frightened. The hand held him in place as the voice grew nearer, "Hersey." The voice sounded eerily familiar.*
*Hersey cried out to the mysterious voice, "I am he."*

*A head began slowly emerging from within the cloud, "You are weak." The face became clear to Hersey, and for the first time, he felt the horror of looking* at a merged Adilene Roth in the eyes. The black soulless gaze. The all-knowing glare stared right through him. It was unbearable.

Hersey swatted and screamed for the hand to let go. The hand-held firm and the eyes never stopped watching. The voice stopped. Only the screams from Dr. Hersey continued to be heard. He wished for death, but it never came.

Hersey's commotions from the dream were enough to awaken and alarm Henry on the floor below. "Sir, wake up. Wake up, sir."

Hersey jolted from his dream, pushing Henry away from the bed. Never had Hersey been seen this way. The pain in his friend's eyes began to frighten Henry as well, "Sir, are you ill?"

Hersey ran to turn the lights on in the room. Hersey turned and looked into Henry's eyes, "You're normal. I'm here."

"Sir, I'm going right away to call a doctor for you."

Hersey went onto the balcony to view the fountain, then turned to Henry, "No, the lights, turn them all on. Every light on this property, I want them all on now."

"Are you sure, sir?" Henry said.

"Every light must be turned on right away."

Hersey dismissed Henry and watched as all exterior and interior lights displaced the darkness of night. Hersey would never sleep in darkness again. Adilene Roth had become something much worse to him. She was the manifestation of fear in his mind now. The merged was her tool, her infection injected into Hersey's consciousness. He had no diagnosable symptoms, but Dr. Hersey would never be totally well again. The hopeful future leader of the free world was now a slave to fear. Adilene Roth was driving him insane.


## Destination Unknown

Only Mabrey, Adi, and Fortner remained awake on the plane as it flew to an undisclosed location. Mabrey was instructed by Fortner to fly north as far as the osprey could go, then land near the closest man-made structure. Even Fortner had no clue where they would all end up. However, it didn't matter. Everything and everyone important was riding beside him.

Adi had calmed from her explosion of fire and brimstone directed at Dr. Hersey. She looked out into the same darkness that Hersey was now terrified of. Adi, however, had help now. Everyone on that plane was fully committed to seeing her through this storm.

The merged continued growing in number. People were dying in every major US city. Fear was increasing among the public. Everybody looked for someone to rescue them from the horror of these new creatures. Marshall law had even been enacted in a few locations as more merged were running free.

*We'll see who needs the merged gone the most,* Adi thought.

This battle was far from over. Adi's mind went back long ago to the woman's missing arm from the Appalachian Trail. A little blue lizard in her hand provided the catalyst for a lifelong endeavor of using science to create for the betterment of humankind.

Adi now needed to create again, not for others, but for herself. All other possible variables remained unknown. The little mouse, currently held by Jake, would play its part in this war. It had all started with a single cell. Now the key to ending the merged, Hersey and Adi's suffering remained locked away within Synthetic Antimicrobial Proliferation variants 23 and 9.

Adi turned to Fortner as they sat together, "What do we do now, John?"

Fortner took her hand, "We endure, then we take the fight to him."